Love-Challenged Life

by

Judy Sharer

A Plains Life, Book Four

Love-Challenged Life

Cover Art by *Diana Carlile*

The Wild Rose Press, Inc.
PO Box 708
Adams Basin, NY 14410-0708
Visit us at www.thewildrosepress.com

Publishing History
First Edition, 2022
Trade Paperback ISBN 978-1-5092-4559-8
Digital ISBN 978-1-5092-4560-4

A Plains Life, Book Four
Published in the United States of America

A gun shot rang out. Lydia grabbed Steven as he was about to jump from the wagon.

"Let me go," Steven shouted. "Billy might need me."

"No! He told us to wait here." Lydia clasped his hands in hers and said a quick prayer.

More shots were fired.

Lydia clutched the pistol and scanned the road for Billy's return. In the distance a young black boy appeared running toward them. She raised the pistol.

As Oat approached, he saw the gun. "Don't shoot." He raised his hands. "Don't shoot! Mister Billy sent me. Hurry!"

Lydia shoved the pistol in her pocket. The young boy jumped in the wagon, and Lydia slapped the reins. The horses galloped toward the house.

"Hurry, he's shot and bleedin' awful," the boy said.

As Lydia and Steven approached the farm, a body lay face down in the dirt by the well, and another body by the corral.

Lydia screamed, "Where's Billy?"

"Inside," Oat said.

Lydia rushed to Billy's side and examined his shoulder wound. "I need to get that bullet out."

Billy nodded. "Steven, fetch Lucky and unhitch the team. I'll be fine."

With pain-filled eyes, Billy whispered, "Don't let Otis leave. I'll explain later. I trust you, Lydia." He grasped Lydia's hand before slipping into unconsciousness.

Previous Books in the series

A Plains Life

Settler's Life – Book One
Available in Paperback, E-Book and Audio Book
***
Second Chance Life – Book Two
Available in Paperback and E-Book
***
Civil War Life – Book Three
Available in Paperback and E-Book
***
Purchase through online retailers
wherever books are sold
Published by The Wild Rose Press, Inc.
Cactus Rose Division

Dedication

Dedicated to Johanna, Jo Ellen, Kathy, Mary, and my beta readers for all their time and assistance, input, feedback, long phone calls, and emails that keep me on track.
Also, to my husband who never complains about the time I spend working on manuscripts, allowing me to fulfill my dream of being an author.

Chapter One

Kansas—beginning of April 1866
A year after the War Between the States

Lydia Clark, with her adopted brothers, Billy and Steven Henry, were headed to Billy's place after spending the long winter at the Hewitt's farm. Riding along the turn-off road, Billy caught whiffs of wood smoke in the chilly spring air. His was the only homestead in the area. As they made the final turn out of a patch of trees and brush, Billy stopped the wagon abruptly and pointed to the sky. Smoke was coming from the direction of the farm.

"It looks like someone's made themselves at home. It could be innocent enough, but I'm not taking any chances. Lydia, you and Steven stay here. I'll check things out and come back for you once I'm sure it's safe."

He untied his horse from the back of the wagon, pulled his rifle from the holster behind the seat, and gave Lydia one of the pistols he had picked up on the battlefield at Westport, Missouri. "The gun is loaded. You have one shot. Don't hesitate if needed. I'm hoping for the best, but you never know. Pull the wagon off the road and wait for me here."

"Be careful, Billy," nine-year-old Steven said, hugging his brother tightly.

Lydia ruffled Steven's hair. "We'll be fine. Don't take any chances, and come for us as soon as you can."

Mounting his horse Lucky, Billy instructed Lydia. "Do not come to the farm, Lydia, no matter what!" When the farmhouse came into sight, Billy saw three horses tied at the corral filled with unfamiliar cattle. The curtains were closed, and he couldn't see inside the house.

Tying Lucky to a bush, Billy cautiously crept to the lean-to for cover. His heart and mind raced. Perhaps whoever was inside was only spending the night. He knew after coming home from the war, fighting for the Union North, that some men were homeless and felt helpless. They drifted from town to town and did what they could to survive. Billy took a few minutes to think his plans through. *I must get the intruders outside and persuade them to leave peacefully. Short of burning down the place to get them out, I'm not sure what to…unless…*

Crawling to the corral, Billy untied the horses and noted different brands on the cows, but none he could identify. Sliding the bottom rails of the corral fence off the beams, he loosened two more and then scuttled back to the shelter of the lean-to. He hurled a few stones at the horses and cattle to rile them. The cattle began stirring and mooing. A few broke through the rails, causing a ruckus. As Billy wiped the sweat trickling down his face, the farmhouse door suddenly swung open.

A man yelled, "Grab your guns. The horses and cattle are getting away."

Two men ran out, an older man and a black teenage boy. Billy waited to see what they'd do. When they arrived at the corral, Billy stood and called out, "This is my farm. You're trespassing. Get your horses and leave. Now."

The potbellied older man wheeled around to run back to the house. Billy shot the ground in front of the man's feet, and dirt kicked up as the man dove behind the well for cover and began firing in Billy's direction.

The teenage black boy was still at the corral hiding behind the cows that quickly jumped over the downed rails. Soon his only cover would be the corral posts, and a post wasn't enough to cover his entire body.

Billy shouted again, "Leave now, and I won't shoot. I don't want to hurt you. I want you off my property. The horses haven't gone far. You can still catch them and be on your way. So what's your answer?"

A curtain moved enough for someone to peer out. While distracted, a shot from the teenaged boy behind the corral hit the edge of the barrel where Billy squatted. Another shot from the man behind the well winged by. Billy's mind flashed to the Union battlefield with bullets and cannons exploding around him. He didn't want bloodshed if he could help it. He called once again, "This can end right now. Throw out your guns, and I'll let you go. You can all leave before someone gets hurt. I'll hold my fire."

The person in the house threw a rifle through the open door. The gun landed on the dry ground kicking up a haze of dust.

"All right, who's next?" Billy called out.

The man behind the well shot in Billy's direction and yelled, "Do you take us for fools? If I throw out my gun, you'll shoot us all. Don't do it, Davey. Don't believe his lies. We outnumber him. We can wait him out. Find cover."

But there wasn't any cover for Davey. Soon he would be exposed. Only a few cows remained in the corral. Davey made his way around the back side of the corral and yelled, "Don't shoot, Mister. I'm giving up. I'm throwing out my gun."

A pistol skidded across the hard-packed soil of the corral, but the young boy remained crouched behind a post.

"Give up, Roy," Davey called to the older man. "We can leave. Throw out your gun while we can still catch our horses."

"You fool! He won't let us leave. He's probably after the reward. You and your little brother have been nothing but trouble ever since I let you join up with me. I'm not giving up." With those words, Roy let off a shot in Davey's direction to keep him from stepping out from the corral. "You listen to me, Davey. There's one of him and three of us. I say we wait him out."

"No. I'm leaving alive and taking Oat with me. You're on your own, Roy," Davey said and raised his hands as he clambered to his feet.

Roy let off another round that found its mark, and Davey dropped. Billy stood looking in Davey's direction, and Roy fired again, catching Billy in the shoulder and knocking him to the ground. He advanced on him, raising his gun, but Billy shot first. Roy fell face down in the dirt.

The person in the house shouted, "I'm coming out!"

Seeing a young boy emerge, Billy yelled back, "Go check on your brother."

Ripping off his shirttail, Billy winced as he shoved the rag into his bleeding wound. He didn't see Roy's chest moving and called out to the young boy, "How's your brother?"

"Not so good," the boy yelled back.

Walking toward the brothers, Billy listened as Davey gasped for air. "This weren't your fault, Oat. Get away. Get a job. Make somethin' of ya. Make Mama proud." With those words, Davey went limp.

Cradling his brother in his arms, the young boy sobbed through his tears. "I will, Davey. I will make Mama proud."

Billy wanted to comfort the boy, who appeared to be about fourteen years old, and tell him everything would be all right. His brother looked seventeen or eighteen, too young to see fighting in the War Between the States. Billy was sure there was a story behind why these brothers would be with a man like Roy.

Reaching with his good arm, Billy pulled the young boy to his feet. "Come along now. I'll help you bury him when I can. Don't be afraid. I won't hurt you. I would have kept my word and let you all leave, but Roy wouldn't give up. When your brother threw down his gun, the old man shot him, then at me."

"I know. I saw from the window," the boy said.

"Good. You can tell the sheriff the truth and clear all this up when we go to town."

"But you said we could leave. I want to leave, but I gotta bury my brother first. If you take me to the sheriff, they'll hang me for cattle rustling. I can't hang. I gotta make Mama proud. I ain't gonna talk to no sheriff."

Just then, Billy stumbled and almost fell. "Do you think you can get me to the house?" he asked.

"Yeah, I'll get ya to the house, Mister, then I gotta bury my brother," the boy insisted.

"I'm Billy, Billy Henry, and this is my farm. What's

your name?"

"I'm Otis Daily, but everyone calls me Oat." Oat got Billy to the bed and turned to leave.

"Oat, I need you to do something else for me. Lydia and my little brother are down the road in a wagon. I need her to get this bullet out, and she's going to need help. I trust you, and you can trust us."

Oat nodded. "I'll go get 'em, Mister Billy, and I'll help get the bullet out, then I gotta go. I don't want no trouble and I ain't gonna hang for what Roy made us do." Oat wiped his nose on his shirt sleeve.

"Follow the road, and you'll find them. And throw another log on that fire, would you? We'll need hot water. Thanks for your help. Now hurry!"

Oat replenished the fire and then ran down the road to find the wagon.

****

A gunshot rang out. Lydia grabbed Steven as he was about to jump from the wagon.

"Let me go," Steven shouted. "Billy might need me."

"No! He told us to wait here." Lydia clasped his hands in hers and said a quick prayer.

More shots were fired.

Lydia clutched the pistol and scanned the road for Billy's return. In the distance, a young black boy appeared running toward them. She raised the pistol.

As Oat approached, he saw the gun. "Don't shoot." He raised his hands. "Don't shoot! Mister Billy sent me. Hurry!"

Lydia shoved the pistol in her pocket. The young boy jumped in the wagon, and Lydia slapped the reins. The horses galloped toward the house.

"Hurry, he's shot and bleedin' awful," the boy said.

As Lydia and Steven approached the farm, a body lay face down in the dirt by the well and another body by the corral.

Lydia screamed, "Where's Billy?"

"Inside," Oat said.

Lydia rushed to Billy's side and examined his shoulder wound. "I need to get that bullet out."

Billy nodded. "Steven, fetch Lucky and unhitch the team. I'll be fine."

With pain-filled eyes, Billy whispered, "Don't let Otis leave. I'll explain later. I trust you, Lydia." He grasped Lydia's hand before slipping into unconsciousness.

"Otis," Lydia called out. "Please fetch some water and warm it in the hearth."

"I took bullets out before. I'll help, Miss Lydia." Oat grabbed a bucket and ran for water.

Lydia remembered the knife Billy always carried, the knife Mark gave him for his first birthday after Billy joined their family. She located the knife in a sheath on his hip and brushed the blade with her thumb. The razor sharpness would work well to dig out the bullet. Lydia loosened Billy's belt to make him comfortable before cutting off his shirt and ripping it into bandages.

The water on the hearth was boiling. Lydia placed Billy's knife on a fork and submerged it for several minutes in the boiling water, then dried it with a towel. She asked Oat, "How many bullets have you taken out of people?"

"I helped Ma take out a few. Don't worry, I'll hold him, Miss Lydia." Oat took hold of Billy's shoulders. "He's out now, but when you go diggin', he's gonna move. Work fast and don't stop. Get the bullet out, heat a spoon and burn the skin, then wrap with bandages. Wounds heal inside out. That's what Ma did."

Steven walked in and asked, "What can I do to help?"

Oat said, "Sit on his legs. You gotta keep him still, so she can dig out the bullet."

The boys held Billy tightly while Lydia steadied her nerves and cut into his shoulder. Working quickly, the tip of the knife soon revealed the shiny, blood-soaked bullet. The bullet wasn't deep and probing carefully, she was able to dislodge the offender and remove it.

Lydia looked at Oat and Steven and whispered in relief, "We did it!" She heated the spoon in the fire. What she had to do next would cause Billy pain but would help the wound heal. Billy jerked and moaned some, but the boys held him. Mercifully, he was passed out, and the bleeding subsided before she wrapped his shoulder with bandages.

"Thank you for all your help, boys. I couldn't have done this without you. I'm sure Billy will be all right. He needs rest. We should get blankets from the wagon and keep him warm. Steven, would you and Oat fetch them and the food basket, please? Afterward, could you set a snare for a rabbit and then help Oat choose a place where he can bury his brother? Billy will need to eat when he wakes up, and fresh meat always tastes best. I packed food that we can eat for our noon meal. Afterward, Oat, Steven and I will help you dig a grave for your brother."

The boys made several trips carrying in necessities, and while Lydia prepared the food, the boys ran to the woods and found a good resting place to bury Davey.

Lydia rang the supper bell. The boys returned, and

the three of them sat at the table to eat. "Oat, Billy knows you and your brother didn't do anything wrong, and he wants to help you. Do you have any family you can live with?"

"Nope. Ma died two years ago. I only had Davey. Pa never come home from war. Our master in Arkansas sent all men to fight. Only some come back. Pa died and broke Ma's heart. She took ill with fever. She never got better. Davey and me made a break one night. The master didn't catch us. Now I guess we'd be free. We heard Mr. Lincoln, that President, signed those papers."

"Yes, Oat, you are free. Nobody owns you now or can ever take claim to you," Lydia said.

Steven added, "But now you're by yourself."

"Davey and I was gonna be farmers when we got money to git us a farm. I can work a field. We both could. But now Davey's dead." Oat hung his head and stared at the floor. "I took Roy's money. It's mine now, 'til I find work."

Steven put his hand on the sad boy's shoulder. "Oat, you can stay with us for now. When Billy gets better, he'll know what to do."

"Yes, Oat, promise us you'll stay." Lydia began clearing the table. "We can use your help until Billy is strong enough to get back on his feet."

Oat nodded. "All right, but only 'til Mister Billy is feeling better. Now I gotta bury my brother."

"I'll help," Steven said. "You already picked the spot. I know where the shovels and picks are."

Lydia helped the boys wrap Davey and Roy's bodies in blankets and lifted them into the back of the wagon. "I'll be out to help after I check on Billy. Did you put out the rabbit snare?"

"We already set it," Steven called back as the boys headed toward the woods in the wagon.

Chapter Two

That evening, after sending the boys up the ladder with clean sheets and blankets, Lydia made a steaming pot of tea and settled into the chair beside Billy's bed. She decided to stay with him all night in case he woke and needed something.

What a day, she thought, looking back on all the events that took place since arriving.

Billy attempted to turn onto his side and in pain called out Lydia's name. She lay beside him and held him gently until he quieted. With a new awareness, she realized she was reluctant to release him. She liked the warmth their bodies made together, and she liked holding him in her arms. Kissing his forehead softly, Lydia quietly returned to the chair beside the bed. He may have been brought into the family as a member, but tonight she recognized a different connection.

A bit later, Billy became restless and called out, "Lydia. Where are you? Lydia?" Once again, she held him in her arms, pressing her cheek to his to check for fever. Instead of returning to the chair, she crawled under the covers beside him and tenderly wrapped her arm around him. A fitful night unfolded.

In the gray pre-dawn light, Billy was conscious enough to ask, "Did you get the bullet out? Is Oat still here?"

"Yes, Billy, the bullet is out. And yes, Oat is here.

We buried his brother and said prayers together yesterday. He said he'd stay until you're back on your feet," Lydia responded.

Billy, seemingly satisfied, lapsed back into sleep.

With two hungry boys who would awaken soon, Lydia started breakfast. She was setting the table when she heard Billy calling her name. She discovered him trying to sit up.

"Let me help." She slipped her arms around his chest, and as she pulled, he assisted. She straightened the pillows behind him. "There, that's better. How are you feeling?"

Billy reached for his shoulder and winced. "It hurts something awful. I need something for this pain."

"I'll brew you extra strong ginger tea, and you should try to eat something," Lydia said. Placing another pillow behind his back, she helped him lean against the headboard. "I'll be right back. Try not to move too much." At the stove, she poured boiling water into a mug and added dried ginger root, three times as much as usual.

****

Just then, Steven came down from the loft. Running to his brother's side, he said, "Lydia got the bullet out. I helped by holding your feet. Oat said you'd have to rest for a while. I bet you're hurting, aren't you, Billy?"

"The wound hurts, little brother, but I'll heal. How are you and Oat getting along? Billy winced whenever he moved.

"We get along fine." Steven grinned. "It's nice having someone to do things with."

"Well, you'll have to fetch wood and help Lydia keep the fire going. Make sure to feed the horses. Did you catch any of the horses or cows?" Billy held his hand to his shoulder, wishing the throbbing would stop.

"They didn't go far. We tied up the horses and gave them grain and water, but we left the cows in the clover pasture. Oat said they needed to eat whatever they could find." Steven crawled up to sit beside Billy as Oat came down the loft ladder two steps at a time and heard them talking. He poked his head in the door.

Lydia arrived with the tea and made Billy drink half the mug. "I'm sorry I don't have anything stronger to give you for the pain, but ginger root is all there is."

"Ginger is good, but let me fetch some plants to help." Oat insisted.

"Breakfast is about ready, boys. But you better check your rabbit snare before you eat." Before she finished the sentence, the youngsters rushed out. "I had Steven set a snare to catch some fresh meat. Fingers crossed he caught one. You rest. Your food is coming in a little while. You need to keep your strength up."

Before Lydia had the oatmeal on the table, the boys came back with a rabbit, cleaned and ready for the pan.

"Oat taught me how to skin and dress a rabbit, and he didn't even need a knife. I'll teach Billy when he's better." Steven put the animal in the dry sink. The boys washed their hands and attacked the bowls of porridge.

Lydia brought Billy a bowl and helped him lay against the headboard to rest.

"Thanks for staying, Oat. I'm thankful for your help," Lydia said. "And Steven, would you two please finish unloading the wagon and fetch firewood while I mix up bread and get the stew on the stove?

Chapter Three

The boys helped Lydia pack the wagon and hitch up the horses. They made a special spot with blankets behind the seat for Lydia and Billy, so he wouldn't be jostled around.

Billy looked at the brand on the horses...all the same. "Are the horses stolen, too, Oat?"

"Nope, Roy bought them from a man. The sale bill is in his saddlebag."

"That's good," Billy sighed and looked at Lydia before crawling into the back of the wagon. "And oh, we better take the horses with us. The cows will be fine in the pasture where there's food and water for a few days."

Steven and Oat tied the horses to the back of the wagon, managed the reins, and talked the entire three-hour trip. Billy and Lydia talked too. Billy shared his thoughts for the farm this year but was equally interested in Lydia's plans.

"It was my dream for some time to buy a sewing machine. I saved my money and finally bought one last fall, but I'm still learning all the features. I'll still work for Jack, but my thoughts are I could design my own dresses and sell them in town. At least that's my plan for now."

During a lull in the conversation, Billy got his nerve up and properly thanked Lydia for all her help over the past weeks while he mended.

"You did a real good job of getting that bullet out of my shoulder. I woke up a few times during the night and realized you lying beside me," Billy said. "I was surprised, but I didn't mind at all."

"Well, you'd wake up and call my name and try to move." Lydia blushed a little. "After the second time, I slept on the bed in case you needed me."

"You don't have to explain. I liked having you close to me. I've always felt that way about you, ever since I came to stay with your family. You always took time to listen."

"We do seem to understand what the other is feeling, Billy. I remember the day you learned that the little dog you and Jack came upon on the way to the Frazer's place had died. I wanted to hold you in my arms and make your sadness go away. But I didn't feel I should."

"Lydia, you're the only one I trusted to tell about the necklaces Elizabeth's lover Quinn gave her before her death. If I couldn't have shared that with you, I would have exploded. You've always been there for me. How about letting me be there for you now, too?"

"What do you mean, Billy? You are always there for me, like Jack."

Billy took Lydia's hand in his. "Do you think you could ever look at me as more than just a brother?" Billy wanted to explain, but before he could, the wagon came to a halt in the yard.

Steven took off running to his father Mark and little sister Johanna as they came out to greet them.

Hugging Johanna, Steven began introductions. "Pa, this is my new friend. His name is Otis, but he likes being called Oat." Steven explained.

Oat took off his hat and looked to the ground.

Mark shook the boy's hand. "It's nice to meet you, Oat." Looking around, he asked, "Where are Billy and Lydia?"

"They're in the back of the wagon, but Billy might need help getting out. He'll tell you about it."

Mark pulled open the canvas flap to find Billy struggling to get to his feet. "What happened to you, Son?"

Billy winced as Mark helped him from the wagon.

"Let's get you to the house first," Mark insisted.

Once inside, Sarah checked the wound and when satisfied Billy was all right, everyone sat around Sarah's table laden with hearty food and sumptuous desserts."

While they enjoyed the repast, Billy recounted the events with Steven and Lydia adding bits and pieces, making Oat a hero.

"How about a second piece of pie for our hero?" Grandma Hewitt asked.

Oat nodded and smiled.

"Guess what? Oat's going to come live with Billy and me." Steven blurted out.

"Hold on, Steven. Oat hasn't given us his final answer yet. He'd be part of our family and my responsibility." Billy looked at Mark and asked, "Pa, I need to get those stolen cattle off my property and to the sheriff soon. I'm afraid someone will come around and think I took them. Would you mind making a trip into town with me?"

"Billy, you're in no condition to ride a horse right now." Sarah insisted.

"I guess that leaves Oat and me," Mark said.

"What about me, Pa? I can help too." Steven puffed out his chest. "I'm old enough to ride a horse to town and help keep those cows in line."

Mark looked at Billy, who started to say, "You might be…."

Mark cut him off and said, "You might be a big help, Steven. You can go along if you want, but you'll be in a saddle all day, and you must stay close and heed my words."

"I will, Pa. I'll stay real close." Steven walked over to Mark and gave him a hug.

Oat spoke up, "But Billy, you said you'd tell the sheriff Roy made Davey and me help. And you said fer sure the sheriff won't hang me."

"Don't worry, Son," Mark said. "I'll explain everything to Sheriff Sloan, and there'll be no hanging. You mustn't worry about that. I'll be right there, and I won't let anything happen to you. We won't stay in town. We'll return as far as my other son, Jack's house to check on him and his wife. And we'll come right home."

"You're going to like Jack," Steven said. "He and his wife Abby are going to make me an uncle pretty soon. I'll be a good uncle." Again, Steven puffed out his chest.

Clearing the dishes, Sarah said, "We'll see what the weather is like in the morning and you can get an early start. Steven, why don't you and Johanna show Oat around the farm? I'll check and see if Jack left some of his clothes that might fit you, Oat."

"I hope you'll agree to join our family, young man," Grandma Hewitt offered.

"See, Oat," Steven grinned. "I told you my family would like you. "Come on, wait until I show you my horse, Cloud."

****

The next morning as Mark and the boys rode to

Billy's farm, Steven got Oat to open up a little about his family and life on the plantation. "Did your ma teach you and Davey how to read or write?"

"No. She and my pa didn't know how." Oat hung his head, and his shoulder slouched.

"Well, if you want to learn, I can teach you." Steven offered.

The corner of Oat's mouth turned up. "Yeah, I want to learn. If you read and write, you get respect. I want respect."

Steven added, "I better teach you how to do arithmetic too."

Oat's grin grew, and he said, "Yes, arithmetic too."

"Billy went to a real school and is teaching me," Steven said. "He can teach both of us, but I can help you get caught up. Grandma Hewitt is a good teacher too."

"What about chores? Did you have chores to do on the plantation? I help around the farm with the horses, cows, and chickens, and Ma makes me do indoor chores too, like setting the table or washing or drying the dishes." Steven rolled his eyes.

"My chores started early. Sometimes before light. Men watched me to see iffin' I worked right. Too slow, I'd get a whippin'. I weren't slow too much. At dark, we went home. Ma cooked supper. We ate and slep' on the floor. Got up and done it again.

"Every day? Even on Sundays?" Steven's eyes grew wide.

"No. Sundays, we stayed with family. We helped Ma at the shack, cut wood, worked the garden, carried the wash basket and heavy things.

When the threesome arrived at the farm, Mark counted sixteen head of cattle in the clover pasture. After a quick midday meal of biscuits and jerky Sarah sent along, they rounded up the cattle and continued their journey. Mark and Oat took the sides, and Steven brought up the rear, calling out when a cow lagged behind. The cattle plodded along the road with only a few mishaps of them straying, but when they did, Oat and Mark were quick to hustle them back to the group. Moving slow to keep the cows together made for a longer trip than Mark had figured.

The lit oil lamps on the street showed the way as the threesome crossed the bridge into Dead Flats. Piano music, some off-key singing, and other loud voices came from the saloon. Main Street was quiet as they drove the cows to the sale barn and corrals. The person-in-charge was confused with cattle arriving so late at night until Mark told about the dead rustlers. Pointing out the different brands, the man knew right away who the cattle belonged to.

"Can you please hold them and see that they're returned to their owners? Assure them the people who stole them are dead. I'm on my way to talk to Sheriff Sloan right now." Mark shook the man's hand, and he and the boys headed to the sheriff's office.

Luckily, Sheriff Sloan hadn't left for supper, and Mark recounted everything, as Billy had explained.

"Well, young man." Sloan looked at Oat, "I'll take Mark's word for it. You're in the clear."

"You mean I ain't gonna hang? I can go stay with Billy if I want?"

"That's what I'm saying, young man, and staying with Billy Henry sounds like a real smart idea. Mark, I'll follow through on the cattle and make sure the owners get them back." Sheriff Sloan patted Oat on the shoulder.

"Thanks, sheriff. I'll stop by the next time we're in town when we can talk longer." Mark grinned.

"Come on, Mr. Hewitt, I'm free now. I don't want to come back to this place again." Oat put on his hat and headed for the door.

Mark and the boys arrived at Jack's farm well after dark, but lamplight streamed through a window, and he was sure Jack and Abby would be happy to put them up for the night. After introductions, Mark explained what happened to Billy and about Oat's brother. Sitting around the table eating a hearty meal, Mark thanked Oat and Steven for their help. "You did a great job keeping up with the strays today, Oat. And Steven, I can't wait to tell Billy how well you did riding in the saddle all day and never once complaining." The weary lads headed off to welcome sleep while the adults talked around the table, catching up after a long winter.

Mark gave Abby the baby clothes Sarah located when she was looking for clothes for Oat. He inquired about Abby's folks, Jack's leather business and then asked the question Sarah wanted him to ask; would they be coming for a visit before the baby was born?

"Abby's mother has taken ill. Doc is treating her, and the medicine seems to be working. The leather business is doing fine. Tell Lydia we now have a few of our leather goods in a store in Clay City, but coming to visit might be a different story," Jack said. "Abby hasn't been feeling well the past few weeks, and if she doesn't perk up in a few days, we're going to make a trip to town to see Doc Glasgow."

"I'm sorry to hear you're not well, Abby. Would you like Sarah to come along with Billy when he goes to have Doc Glasgow check on his shoulder? She could help care for you when you need off your feet. You know she wouldn't mind, and she'd love to see you."

"I'd like that. If Mother can get away, I'd love to see her. Tell her that she and Billy are welcome to stay as long as they'd like," Abby said and then excused herself to retire.

"Jack," Mark said, "Billy wanted me to ask how you'd feel accepting Oat as your brother. Billy wants to take the boy in and let Oat live with him and Steven on their farm. Steven has taken to Oat. I think they'll be good for each other. Your mother and I feel blessed having one more child added to our family. Oat doesn't have any relatives and is all alone. He's only fourteen, the same age Billy was when he came to live with us."

"Tell Billy I'd be honored to call Oat my brother. He wouldn't have asked if this boy didn't mean a lot to him. Sure, Oat is colored, but you raised us to treat all people as equals. If Billy gives this boy a new start, I will too."

"I knew you would, Son, and I'm proud you said yes. I'll let Billy know. Now I better get some shut-eye. We're going the whole way home tomorrow, so your ma doesn't worry. She's always been a worrier. That will never change." Mark stretched out on the floor in front of the fire with a pillow and blanket beside the boys.

"See you in the morning, Pa." Jack blew out the lamp.

****

The next morning, Jack sent along leatherwork for Lydia to sew, figuring she could send it back to him with Billy.

As the threesome rode toward home, Oat asked Mark, "When you talked to the sheriff, you said I was an unwilling partici…"

"Unwilling participant," Mark finished the word for Oat.

"What does that mean? Unwilling participant sounds important."

Mark grinned. "It is important, Oat. Unwilling means you didn't do it of your own free will. Roy forced you to steal those cows. Participant means you helped. You were there when it happened. Do you understand now what the words means?"

"You mean because Roy forced Davey and me to help him take those cows, and we was there, but we don't want to steal, we was unwilling participants?" Oat took a big breath.

"Yes, because you didn't want to steal, but Roy forced you to help him take the cows, you and Davey were unwilling participants," Mark stressed

Oat smiled. "I learned something today. I won't be an unwilling participant again. I won't do anything wrong again."

Mark grinned. "And if you ever have a question about something you don't understand, please ask. I'll always explain what things mean to you."

****

Back home at the farm, Mark shared the news from the visit with Abby and Jack. "Lydia, Jack has expanded the business and is now selling leather goods in Clay City on a trial basis. And Abby said to thank you, Sarah, for the baby clothes. She isn't feeling well, so Jack will take her to Dead Flats to see the doctor this week if she isn't better. Perhaps you might accompany Billy when he has Doc Glasgow check on his shoulder? I suggested that you would stop at Jack's and stay and help Abby if she needed anything. I know they would both be happy to see you."

"Of course, I'll go," Sarah said. "This being Abby's first child birthing, I'm sure she's bound to have questions. Lydia and Grandma Hewitt can take care of things around here. I wish Abby's parents could be there, but Abby's mother, Betsy, is in poor health. And her father, Harold, has to stay home to care for her. I'm sure she'd be with her daughter if she could and must be sad she's not there now."

Chapter Four

Sarah attended faithfully to Billy's gunshot wound, changing bandages every day and rebuilding his strength with nourishing broths. But Billy began running a fever that Sarah couldn't break even with herbal teas. She was concerned and worried about the wound and wanted Doc Glasgow to take a look. They would leave for town tomorrow, pick up the seed order for themselves and the Frasers, and on the way home, stop by Jack and Abby's place to see how Abby felt. She would ask Oat to come along and drive the wagon. The time together would give Sarah a chance to get better acquainted with the newest member of her family. As Sarah packed for the trip, she remembered the births of each of her children.

When Jack and Lydia were born, my first husband, Samuel, was so attentive. He wouldn't leave the room even when the doctor ordered him out. He couldn't stand to see me in pain, but on each occasion, he watched over the doctor's shoulder as the baby arrived. He died so young, and I miss him terribly. Then Mark came into my life. We married eight years ago and had Johanna. What an adventure Johanna's birth was. With Mark by my side, we brought Johanna into the world in the back of the wagon before Doc could get to us.

After packing, Sarah sat down and wrote a letter back home.

April 19, 1866

Riley County, Kansas
Dearest Mother,

I am not sure where to start, so much has happened.

We had a wonderful Christmas, but missed having Jack and Abby with us this year. They are settled into their new home and Abby is expecting. Mark visited with them and related that she was not feeling well. Keep them in your prayers and I will keep you informed as best I can.

Billy ran into trouble last month when he returned to his farm after wintering with us. Lydia and Steven were with him when they came upon rustlers using his place to hide out with a herd of stolen cattle. He settled the issue, but not before taking a bullet in the shoulder which Lydia had to dig out. He is here now, and we are heading to town tomorrow to get the wound looked at by the doctor.

One of the three rustlers was a fourteen-year-old, freed slave who had been drawn into the rustling because of family circumstances. Billy took a shining to him and asked him to stay and live with him and Steven on his farm. It looks like Otis will agree. Mark and I are proud of Billy for extending a helping hand but worry that certain people clinging to old beliefs might make it difficult for the family.

Having Mark's mother Ruth with us has made a real difference for everyone, but especially Johanna and Steven. She spends time with them and helps them with their schooling every day. She is definitely happy she came west when she did. She said the other day that she did not think she could have made the trip if she waited until now. We are so glad to have her with us. I know Mark takes comfort in having her here also.

How I would love to have you and Pa with us too, but I know that family back home needs you with them, and they take good care of you both as well. Just wishful thinking.

Tell Matthew he needs to find a girl and settle down. We are so pleased he is back at his old job at the newspaper and still enjoying the work.

I am hoping when I pick up your letters in town that there is news of Matilda and Robert expecting a child, or maybe even Emma and Abel expecting a second.

I pray you and Pa are in good health, and the family is doing well. We send our love to everyone back east, and I promise to write about Abby and the baby as soon as I can.

Your loving daughter,
Sarah

"Ruth," she called, sealing the envelope. "Do you have any letters to mail?

Ruth fetched a letter and gave her three cents for postage. "I still write to one friend from time to time to let her know I'm still alive. Do you remember Edith Whitmore? We grew up together right there in Tidioute. So many fine memories, and now I'm making new ones with my grandchildren. Thank you again, Sarah, for making room for me in your home. I miss the old homestead, but I certainly don't miss all the work that went along with the upkeep. The family who bought the place loved the large yard and garden plot and were sure they'd spend lots of time on the front porch. I was lucky to sell the property so quickly."

"We're all glad to have you with us, Ruth. I know I've said it before, but Mark is pleased you joined us, and you have brought so much joy to the children's lives. I worried the trip might have been too much for you to handle, but you proved me wrong. If there is ever anything you need, please don't hesitate to ask."

"Sweet Sarah, being here is all I could ever want or need. I never thought I would live to see my son's family. I can see you and the children make him happy, and that makes me happy." Ruth walked to the sitting room, picked up her Bible, and settled in reading her favorite passage, "Faith, hope, and love abide, but the greatest of these is love. First Corinthians 13:13"

****

Oat, Sarah, and Billy left before dawn and made good time on the trip to town. The roads were better now with not as many ruts and holes, the children were older, and the threat of war was no longer an issue. They arrived in Dead Flats late in the afternoon.

As they passed the bank Quinn Harris and an associate of his with the same mindset against blacks stepped out and saw a young black boy driving Billy Henry's wagon as it stopped in front of the Doctor's office.

Quinn watched as the boy helped Billy off the wagon. Billy's arm was in a sling. Quinn noted that his mother hurried down the street toward the postal office.

"I haven't seen Billy Henry or his family in quite some time. I wonder what that black boy is doing with them. If Billy were alone, I'd give him a piece of my mind. You know he stole Elizabeth Parker from me when I was away at war."

"Yes, yes, you've said that several times since Elizabeth's death. Come on, Quinn, we're probably already late. I'm sure the men have already dealt the first hand of poker and I'm feeling lucky tonight. Let's get to the saloon."

"All right, let's go," Quinn said, casting a second look over his shoulder.

****

All eyes in the doctor's office turned to Oat when he and Billy walked in together. After the last patient left, Billy said, "Doc, this is Otis. He is living with us now and brought Ma and me to town. I took a bullet and can't break this fever. Could you look at my shoulder? Ma says it's healing but might need stitches to close it up. I got shot about four weeks ago."

Doc checked the shoulder. "There's only a little redness. I won't ask how this happened. Best I don't know. There's no festering. Looks like it's healing all right. Did your mother remove the bullet?"

"No, Lydia did, and Oat helped."

"Well, they did a good job. Hold still now. I'll put a couple of stitches in to close it, and you'll be fine. How long have you had this fever?"

"Three or four days now. I don't seem to have any strength."

When Doc finished stitching, he mixed some powders, gave Billy a tablespoon full and a glass of water to wash down the medicine, and then put the rest of the mixture in an envelope. "Take this twice a day. This should help you come around."

Billy reached in his pocket. "Thanks, Doc. What do I owe you?"

"This one's on me, Son. You fought in the war, and for that I'm thankful. Next time I see you, I hope it's under better circumstances. How's the rest of the family doing?"

"Everyone's doing well. I'll tell them you asked."

"It's nice to meet you, Otis. Get Billy home and keep him warm."

"I sure will, Sir." Oat said.

Billy shook Doc's hand.

Otis extended his hand as well.

Billy and Oat met Sarah back at the wagon. "Doc stitched me up, gave me medicine for the fever, and said I'd be fine. All we need to do is pick up the seed orders and we'll start for Jacks." Billy drew the blanket around him tight.

While the seed for the Hewitt, Henry, and Frazer families was loaded into the back of the wagon, Sarah selected her garden seed and got double so Billy would have plenty for his garden too. After paying the clerk and checking on Billy in the back of the wagon, she climbed up onto the seat next to Oat. He raised the reins, and an hour later, the threesome pulled up in front of Jack's place.

"Thank God you're here, Ma! Jack shouted as he ran to greet them. When we visited Doc last week, he said Abby could have the babies any day now."

"Babies?" Did I hear you right? Abby is having twins?" Sarah asked.

"Yes. Doc said he thinks there are two of them." Jack ushered Sarah into the bedroom, where Abby extended her arms for a hug.

"Mother Hewitt, I'm so glad you're here. I prayed you'd come. Jack and I both feel better having you here to help with the births."

Oat brought in Sarah's bag and then helped Billy down from the wagon and into the house.

Sarah stayed and chatted with Abby until she fell asleep.

"We're glad to have you join our family, Oat," Jack said. "And thanks for helping with Billy. Steven has taken a liking to you too. If you ever need anything or want to talk, you can always come to me. We're brothers now, and I'll always be here for you."

Oat grinned and extended his hand.

Jack shook it firmly and patted him on the back.

Under Abby's instructions, Jack had fixed a beef roast, potatoes, and baked pumpkin. There was plenty of food for everyone.

Billy said, "Oat will take me home tomorrow, and I'll send someone to come help. Maybe Grandma Hewitt or Lydia. I know Pa will want to get started on the fields, but I won't be much help for a while. Don't worry. We'll work it out. Hey, Oat, we better get some shut-eye. We've got to leave at first light in the morning.

****

Steven was the first out the door when he heard the wagon arrived at the Hewitt homestead. "What did the doc say? Are you better now? How is Abby? Did she have the baby yet? I sure missed you while you were gone. Lydia made pie for dessert. Hurry up. Get in the house. You don't look so good, Billy."

"Whoa! You didn't give me a chance to answer any of your questions. Help Oat with the supplies, and when we're inside, I'll tell everyone about our trip." As Billy got down from the wagon seat, Lydia and Johanna came out to greet them.

"Where's Pa?" Billy asked, accepting Lydia's assistance to the house.

"He's out turning soil. He said with you unable to help, he'd better get started," Lydia said as she slipped her arm under his shoulder to help him up the steps.

Johanna held the door open, and Grandma Hewitt walked him to the rocking chair and tucked a quilt around him.

"Supper's almost ready. Pa will be in soon," Lydia said. "Steven, why don't you and Oat start the evening chores and help Pa with the horses when he gets in? Billy needs to rest. We can catch up during supper. And Johanna, would you please set the table?" Lydia brought order to the chaos.

Over dinner, Billy and Oat recalled the visit to town, the doctor's office, and Jack's news about twins and how they could be coming any day.

"Ma asked me to please send someone to Jack's to help out," Billy said.

"Yeah, two babies are a handful," Oat added.

A smile creased Grandma Hewitt's cheeks. "I never thought I'd meet my grandchildren, let alone my great-grandchildren. Let me go help."

"Well," Billy said, "If one of the women goes to stay with Abby, Jack could come and help us get the crops planted."

"We may have to take him up on his offer," Mark admitted. "With your shoulder, not a hundred percent yet, we're going to need Jack's help."

"I'm strong. I can work a plow," Oat said.

"Don't worry, Oat. We won't leave you out. With the two farms and Jack's crops there's plenty of acres to plant."

"I can help," Lydia offered.

Mark said, "You might have to, sweetheart. I know it's hard work, but we didn't get this far without everyone pitching in and working together."

'Many hands make light work.' You taught us that,

Mark." Billy chuckled.

"Yes, and I taught him that when he was a young boy," Grandma Hewitt said. "I guess you were listening to me all those years ago."

"Ma, I always listened to you," Mark said as everyone joined in with laughter.

Chapter Five

Early the next day, Oat and Lydia took Grandma Hewitt and Steven to Jack and Abby's. Grandma would help Sarah care for Abby, and Steven would help Jack with the chores and plow the fields. After unloading the wagon at Jack and Abby's, everyone had a chance to visit while enjoying Sarah's hearty supper.

The next day after breakfast, Lydia said from the seat of the wagon, "I wish we could stay too," then blew a kiss and waved as she and Oat pulled away.

Sarah and Grandma Hewitt tended to Abby while Jack and Steven hitched the team and started on the fields.

A day later, Abby began experiencing random cramping.

"I'll go for the doctor and get him right away," Jack said when Abby first complained of discomfort.

"No, not yet, Jack. It's too soon." Sarah said. "Abby could have these mild pains for quite some time. Let's wait and see how long between them. That will give us a better idea of when we'll need Doc Glasgow.

"All right Ma, you know best." Jack peeked into the bedroom, "I love you, Abby. Don't worry. Steven and I will be in the fields. If you need us, ring the dinner bell and I'll hurry back."

Grandma Hewitt sat with Abby. "I saw you started crocheting a baby blanket, sweetheart. Would you like me to finish it for you? Working on the blanket will give me something to do while you rest. If you can get some sleep, dear, I'd suggest you do so. With two babies on the way, you're going to need your strength."

"That's lovely of you to offer, Grandma. I've been trying to finish that blanket for weeks."

Abby nodded off and slept until cramping suddenly woke her. "Would you like to take a walk?" Sarah asked. "Maybe walking will help. Let me help you to your feet, dear. How much time has passed since your last pain?"

"About an hour or so as far as I can figure," Abby replied.

Dinner, supper, and evening chores came and went. Abby was experiencing mild discomfort once or twice an hour. Come bedtime, Sarah suggested, "Jack, why don't you sleep in the loft with Steven tonight? I'll be close by if Abby should need anything. I'll wake you if need be, but tonight might be the last night in a while that you'll have a full night's sleep."

Before dawn, Abby awoke. As she got out of bed, a light, watery flow ran down her leg. She called to Sarah for help.

"Don't worry, dear. You're fine," Sarah reassured her. "There may be more of this before the babies arrive. That's how we'll know you're close to birthing. I'll take care of this, and you walk around the kitchen to settle yourself. Rubbing your belly might help you feel better. I'll be with you shortly."

Sarah put on water for tea. Grandma joined them at the table, and they talked softly until Abby was ready to crawl back into bed. Sarah thought it best to let the mother-to-be rest while she could. She sensed this would be the day she'd deliver her grandbabies into the world.

She prayed that she, Ruth, and Doc Glasgow, guided by the hand of God, could save Abby and both babies. The odds were against them. So much could go wrong.

****

The cramping became contractions that lasted longer and came more frequently. After the noon meal, Sarah decided the time had come. "Jack, you need to ride to Dead Flats and get Doc Glasgow as quick as you can. Don't worry. We'll take good care of Abby." Sarah put another pillow under Abby's shoulders. "You'll be fine, dear. Everything is going perfectly."

Before leaving, Jack caressed his wife's cheeks tenderly. "I love you, Abby," he said and brushed his lips over hers and gave her a good-bye kiss.

As the door slammed behind Jack, Sarah reached for a towel and wiped Abby's forehead, and called to Steven in the other room, "Fetch some water, dear, and set it on the stove. You can best help by keeping the fire going."

"This being your first time, Abby, the babies could take a while. Or they could decide to come all at once. But either way, I'll be right here. If you need to cry out, do so. The pains will get closer, and you'll know when it's time to push. Jack will be back as soon as he can. I pray he's here when the babies are born, but regardless, Grandma Hewitt and I will help you. I know you picked the names Annabelle and Benjamin, but what if it's two girls or two boys?" Sarah asked.

Abby caressed her belly. "We didn't get that far. We thought we'd have time to decide." Abby gasped, her voice reflecting the intensity of the labor pain that consumed her whole body and attention.

****

Riding hard, Jack reached town in under an hour.

Doc Glasgow was still in his office. "Can you come with me now, Doc? Abby is having the babies. Ma and Grandma are with her, but she's in lots of pain. Ma said to hurry."

"My horse is at the stable, Son, and I'll meet you out front."

Jack wasted no time fetching Doc's horse. Then he panicked, "What if she can't hold off until we get there, Doc?"

"Your ma's with her, Jack. Abby is young and strong. She'll do fine." They took off, galloping, and didn't stop until they reached Jack's place.

Meanwhile, Abby's contractions had become closer together and more intense. Three generations were in the room. Grandma Hewitt held Abby's hands and wiped her rosy cheeks and forehead while Sarah gave orders on when to breathe, bear down, and push.

"I can't bear the pain," Abby cried out.

"It will be over soon, dear. I see the baby's head. You must breathe and bear down as you keep pushing. Almost there," Sarah encouraged.

Abby let out another cry of pain.

"One more time, breathe and push," Sarah said. "One or two big pushes, Abby, and you can see your baby."

"I'm sorry, I'm trying. My back really hurts. I'm so tired." Abby panted, took a breath, and bore down hard, not stopping until she heard Sarah say, "You did it, Abby. It's a girl."

Sarah smiled as the baby let out a cry. Swaddling her in a soft cloth, she gave the baby to Ruth who placed Anabelle on Abby's chest and watched tears in her eyes as the new mother reached for her firstborn.

"Congratulations, sweetheart," Grandma Hewitt said, taking the baby as Abby's body was seized by a strong contraction. "You did just fine. I'm so proud of you."

Through twinges of pain, her body told her the next baby was ready for birth. Abby said, "Thank God. She is perfect. I so wish Jack were here.

In the yard, with a whoop and a holler, Steven shouted, "Get in there, Doc! I heard a baby crying a few moments ago, but Ma told me to wait out here." Steven jumped up and took the horses as Jack and Doc hurried to assist.

Sarah met them at the bedroom door and handed Jack the baby. "Congratulations, Son. You have a daughter! She has all the right number of fingers and toes and is perfect, just perfect." Sarah beamed as Jack got his first look at his beautiful baby girl. 'The child arrived head first, and we had no difficulties with the delivery. Grandma held on to Abby while Abby did all the work. Sarah gladly moved aside to let the doctor take her place. "You take Annabelle, Son, and wait with Steven. It won't be long now."

Grandma sponged Abby's face with cool water as the doctor greeted her.

"I'm so tired, Doctor," Abby said as a fierce contraction enveloped her body. "I'm not sure I have the strength to do this again."

"You'll find the strength, Abby. Look how beautifully you had the first baby. Congratulations to you and Jack." Doc shrugged off his coat and washed his hands in a basin of sudsy water.

As Grandma Hewitt held out a towel for the doctor, their gazes met and held for a long moment, neither wanting to look away until Abby moaned as another contraction engulfed her.

Ruth offered her hands for Abby to hold as yet another intense contraction gripped her body.

Doc said, "Push with all you've got, Abby."

Abby called out, "I don't think I can, Doctor Glasgow. I'm so tired. And my back hurts terribly."

"You don't have a choice," Doc whispered. "Abby, you need to push so this baby can be born. Now take a deep breath, bear down, and push."

A moment later, Doc Glasgow knew something was wrong. "Stop, Abby! Breathe, but don't push. Pant, short breaths will help. The baby is breech. I must turn it."

"It hurts, Doctor. Hurts a lot." Abby cried out.

"I know, dear, but I have to locate the feet and legs and turn them so the head presents first. Don't push right now. Breathe slowly, and don't bear down until I say to do so."

"Hurry, Doc!" I gotta push. It hurts. I want it out. He or she needs out now," Abby pleaded. "Hurry! Hurry! It hurts!"

"Focus, Abby! Listen to me. I'm rotating the baby now. Hold on. Aha, got it! Now, take a deep, deep breath and push real slow and steady. Don't stop. Good, Abby, keep pushing. That's it. You're doing fine. Now, take another deep breath and bear down. Push as though this baby's life depends upon it because it does."

After a few deep breaths and focused pushes, Abby's body lay back in exhaustion. The second baby was born. "I don't hear the baby crying," she said. What's happening? "What's wrong? Something's wrong. Why isn't it crying?"

"Abby, your little boy looks fine," Sarah said. "One

girl and one boy. Just as you thought."

"I don't know, Sarah," Doc whispered. "Let me dry him off. He's not breathing. He needs to take a breath." Doc rubbed the infant with a soft towel, lifted him by his feet, and patted him on the back. He opened the baby's mouth with his finger to clear the mucous and rubbed his belly to stimulate him.

"I don't hear him crying," Abby called out. "You said he looked fine."

Doc held the infant high enough for Abby to see and began massaging his feet, his arms, and his chest. Nothing. The baby was failing to thrive.

Willing her grandson to live, Sarah took the lifeless little form from the doctor, held him to her bosom, rubbed his little back and body briskly with a soft cloth, all the while imploring God to guide her. The tiny mewing noise that ensued was music to everyone's ears. Benjamin's little body turned a healthy, glowing pink and his arms and legs moved vigorously as he looked around. He was alive and fine despite a shaky start. Sarah swaddled him and handed him to his exhausted mother.

"Congratulations, Abby," Doc said, "You have one of each."

Gleaming with sweat and crying happy tears, Abby held her little boy. "Can Jack come in now? A girl and a boy," she said, "I can't believe it. We have a son and a daughter."

Sarah called, "Jack, bring Annabelle and come to the bedroom."

"We got our wish, Jack," Abby said. "We have two healthy babies, a girl and a boy. I prayed you'd get back in time. Thank God they're both alive and well. We have everything we could ever hope for."

"I'll thank God for this day for the rest of my life," Jack said. "I'm so proud of you, Abby. I prayed the whole time I wouldn't lose you and the babies. We'll have our hands full raising them, but I can't wait. We're a family now for sure."

After counting fingers and toes again and holding them a few minutes longer, Doc took the babies one at a time, and made sure their hearts were strong and that everything else was in good working order.

Sarah said, "I wish your father were alive to see his first grandchildren. He'd be so proud of you, Jack Clark. Take all the time you want to get acquainted with your new family. I'm going to make a pot of tea for us, then fix supper. We'll be in the kitchen if you need us. Enjoy your babies, your two healthy babies."

"I'll be out when I finish up here, Sarah. That cup of tea sounds like a mighty fine idea," Doc said.

In the kitchen, an excited Steven said to Sarah, "One of each! And I'll be the first uncle to hold them."

"Yes, you'll be the first, all right," Sarah said. "So how do you feel, Uncle Steven?"

"It feels great! But how about you, Ma," Steven said, "How do you feel being a grandma?"

"Older than yesterday," Sarah said and smiled.

And Grandma Hewitt, you're a grandma again, too, right?" Steven looked puzzled.

"No, Steven, this makes me a great-grandma, something I never thought I would live to see. And to have been involved with the births is beyond my dreams."

"How about a couple of biscuits to celebrate?" Steven suggested.

"Why I think that's a fine idea," Grandma responded

and plated thick raisin studded molasses treats she had baked.

Sarah poured tea for everyone and then took a tray to the bedroom for Abby and Jack.

Doc Glasgow said, "Rest now, Abby. The babies are fine, and so are you. I'll join you and the others for that tea now, Sarah. And my, those molasses biscuits look good."

"I'll have supper ready soon," Sarah said, exiting the room with the doctor.

At the table, Sarah made introductions. "I'm sorry, Doctor Glasgow. In the excitement, I neglected to introduce Ruth, Mark's mother."

Doc moved closer to the table. "Pleasure to meet you, Ruth. When did you arrive?"

"Last year, Doctor Glasgow, I came west from Pennsylvania by way of wagon train."

"You're a brave woman, Ruth, if I may address you as Ruth. That trip couldn't have been easy." Doc turned his chair in her direction.

Sarah could see a connection forming from their attention to each other. She began supper preparations while they chatted and soon said, "Doc, I'd like to write a quick note to my parents if you would be kind enough to mail it for me in town. It will only take me a few minutes. Oh, where are my manners? May I set a place for you at the table before you head back?"

"I'll be glad to mail your letter, Sarah. And thank you, but no. Supper isn't necessary. I have a standing reservation at the hotel restaurant, and tonight is poker night. I'll head back as soon as you get your letter written, but no need to hurry."

"Thank you. I'll get writing immediately."

Sarah knocked on the bedroom door. Peeking inside, the happy family snuggled on the bed, a contented baby in each parent's arms. "Jack, why don't you take the babies out and let Steven hold them while I help Abby freshen up." After washing and changing Abby into a clean nightgown, Sarah wrote her letter sharing the good news with family back east.

Slipping out so as not to wake the new mother, Sarah gave the letter and a half dime to Doc for postage.

"How much do I owe you for coming all this way to help us, Doc?" Jack reached for the money jar in the cupboard.

"I'll tell you what, Jack. In a couple of months, those babies will need to come see me. Have Abby bring me a pie or some sweet dessert. After all, I only arrived in time to deliver one, so I can only take half the credit," Doc Glasgow chuckled.

Jack shook the doctor's hand and asked, "Would you mind stopping by Abby's parent's place to let the Proctors know the happy news?"

"I'd be glad to, Jack," Doc said, patting him on the back.

Sarah smiled and said, "I know you have a sweet tooth, Doc. I'll bring you a dessert when I come to town next time too. I'm so thankful you were here. These are the first twins in our family."

"If I have time, I'll try to come out next week and check on everyone," Doc said. "Nice to meet you, Mrs. Hewitt, uh Ruth. Maybe when you come to town the next time, we can have dinner together?"

"I'd like that," Ruth said, smiling.

With that, Doc mounted his horse and headed for town.

Chapter Six

The following week, Doc Glasgow showed up unexpectedly at Jack's place. Smiling broadly when Ruth came out to greet him, he grabbed a basket from behind the seat of the buggy and said, "I thought I'd check on Abby and the twins and ask if you'd consider going on a picnic with me. The girls at the restaurant put some things together, but I know there is fried chicken and deep-fried apple pies." He lifted the basket higher, cocked his head quizzically, and waited for an answer.

"I'd be delighted to join you, Doctor Glasgow."

"Please, call me James. Doctor Glasgow is much too formal."

"All right, James. Now, come see my great-grandbabies. They have grown so in such a short while." Ruth escorted the doctor into the house. "Look who's come," she said in a delighted voice.

Expecting to see one of the family, Sarah was taken aback. "So good of you to come by, Doc," Sarah saw the basket over his arm and smiled. Abby is in the bedroom. Mother and I took care of the household chores, so she could enjoy being off her feet and spend time with the babies. Abby has caught on to nursing, and we've even taught Jack some fatherly chores to help with the twins. The happy couple is doing well, but then, I'll let you be the judge for yourself. Ruth and I will be staying on for a while. Jack is almost done planting his fields, and

Mother and I hope to put in the kitchen garden soon. When he's finished here, Jack will help plant our crops and then go on to Billy's to lend a hand. We might be here for another five to six weeks."

Doc smiled, held up the basket, and said, "Well then, that means I might get to enjoy a few more picnics with Ruth. Now let me check on those babies." Doc knocked on the bedroom door and announced himself. "Abby, do you have time for a quick check-up? I want to make sure you're healing and that the little ones are doing well."

"Yes, Doctor, please, come right in. We're doing fine for now, but I sure will miss Mother Hewitt and Grandma when they have to leave."

"You'll do fine, Abby. Get into a routine and stick to it. That way, the babies know what to expect, and so will you. How are you feeling?"

"I'm still a little sore, but each day there is less pain. The babies are eating well, and Jack is helping me with them."

Doc checked Abby and each newborn. "I pronounce you all fit," he said, patting her on the shoulder, and quietly backed his way out of the room as Abby began rocking the two swaddled forms to sleep.

Sarah handed Ruth a quilt and gave her a quick hug. "You two enjoy your picnic," she said, sending them on their way.

****

Since the twins were born, there hadn't been much opportunity for Jack to work on his leather business. He was too busy with basic chores, working the fields, and helping with the children. He and Steven worked for three solid weeks to get his crops in and were now turning the garden soil, readying the ground for planting.

"Steven, you've been such a big help. Are you all right handling the chores while I go back and help Father? I'm sure Pa would like to have us both there, but if you go with me, that leaves Ma and Grandma to do all the chores and help with the babies."

Steven's long face gave Jack his answer.

"I'll tell you what, Steven. I'll have Pa leave the pumpkin field for you to plow and plant. How about that?" Jack patted him on the shoulder.

Steven nodded, then asked, "How long you figure you'll be away?"

"I'm sure they've been working every day like we have. They probably have half the crops in by now. Billy should be healed up, and with my help, the planting should go faster. It might take two, maybe three weeks, and then they'll head over to your farm. By that time, I'm sure Ma and Grandma will be itching to get home. I'll leave tomorrow so I can get back as soon as possible. The rifle in the corner of the kitchen is loaded in case a fox comes around the chickens. That's the only reason I can think of that a gun would be needed. So don't remove it without asking Mother first."

"Don't worry, Jack. We'll get the garden planted while you're gone, and I'll do all the chores. We'll be fine but hurry back. And tell everyone I miss them."

****

With Sarah and Grandma away, Lydia assumed the household responsibilities and took care of Johanna. Each morning she made breakfast, packed a noon meal for the men, and once they left, she and Johanna did the dishes and began the baking and chores for the day. When she could, she took Johanna to the fields, and they helped alongside the men and brought back whatever firewood they could gather since the winter wood was depleted.

The spring days were getting warmer, and the flowers were in bloom. On the way to the fields one day, Lydia stopped and picked a handful of daisies and buttercups, but by the time they returned home that evening, over half were too wilted to put in the vase.

The next day, on Billy's way home, he jumped off the back of the wagon at a good picking spot and gathered a small bouquet of flowers to surprise Lydia. Once home, Billy's heart raced. As he handed Lydia the flowers, her face brightened.

"Thank you, Billy. They're beautiful," Lydia said. "That was so thoughtful of you."

"Well then, maybe we can take a ride sometime, and I'll show you where they grow." Billy smiled as he watched her put his offering in the vase on the table.

****

Jack arrived near supper time the next day and was about to join the men in the fields, but Johanna wanted his attention, and Lydia started in with questions. "Tell me, Jack. How is Abby? And what about the twins? Boys or girls, and what did you name them?"

"Abby is fine, and the twins are healthy and doing great. Ma and Grandma are life savers, and that's it." He set Johanna in her chair, took a paper and a pencil, drew a cat to one side, and said, "You finish the picture for me, Johanna." Turning his attention to Lydia, he said, "We have business to discuss. If I'm honest, I haven't worked any leather since the twins arrived and didn't bring any items for you to sew. Steven and I put the crops in, and I finished building a wide cradle to hold both babies after I learned Abby was having twins."

"I'm disappointed," Lydia said. "I have the leather pieces you sent with Billy and Oat all done. Do you have material enough to make more items?"

"I have supplies, but with everything that's going on, I didn't get items done. I will, though, I promise. I said I'd help Pa with his fields, and although mine are done, Billy still needs help. There just isn't time for leatherwork right now."

"What if I went along to help with Billy's crops," Lydia offered. "That way, you could stay home and get items made. Now that I have my sewing machine, all my money will go toward buying material. Mother says to make a good showing, I should have at least five or six different styles for a woman to choose from. I'm hoping to start my business this year. I'm so close."

"Well, that might work," Jack said.

"Then concentrate on making a few belts that are good sellers, the ladies' coin pouches, and a couple other items that sell well. If we don't have anything on the shelves, they could find someone else to fill our space."

"You're right, Lydia, but do you think Billy will understand?"

"He'll understand. I'll try to take your place. At least they'll eat better if I'm there. Billy attempted to cook a few dishes while he was laid up, but he didn't do so well." Lydia chuckled, and the conversation came to a halt when they heard the wagon pull up out front.

****

Sitting around the supper table, Jack recounted the day of the twins' birth. "I've never prayed so hard in my whole life. I prayed Abby, and both babies would live. I witnessed a blessing, a real blessing to see our little Annabelle and Benjamin in their mother's arms.

Annabelle was born first, and then Benjamin."

"Well, Oat," Billy said. "Since you're part of our family now, that means you're an uncle now too. You and I won the bet. We both said a boy and a girl. What would you like to do with your early day off?"

"Let's take the fishing poles and go fishing." Oat smiled and finished his glass of milk. "That way, everyone wins when we bring fresh fish home for supper."

"Great idea," Mark agreed. "Everyone wins. Congratulations, Son. How is Grandma holding up?"

"She's doing well, and so is Ma, but I want to get back in a couple weeks. Do you think we'll be done by then?" Jack put down his fork and pushed his plate back.

Mark swallowed his last bite. "Yes. Finishing might not even take that long with all of us working together, and then Billy wants to get started on his farm."

"Pa…Jack and I were talking about that before you got here. If you think you can manage with Johanna, I'll help Billy and Oat get started with their fields. You and Johanna can pick up Ma, Grandma, and Steven, see Abby and the babies, and drop Steven at Billy's on the way home. Jack needs time to get leather goods made plus be with his family. I'll stay at Billy's until we're done, and Jack brings me some items to sew. Afterward, the boys can bring me home. How does that sound?"

"Sounds like a good idea to me," Billy agreed.

"I guess that will work," Mark said. "Don't forget to make the garden bigger this year and use every seed. We have additional mouths to feed, and we must be prepared for whatever happens." Mark stood and took his plate to the dry sink.

Jack got up with his plate. "Ma and Steven were

going to plant our garden this week. I bet they'll start tomorrow."

"Billy, we'll need to plant the garden first and then start on the crops," Lydia said. "The three of us planted Ma's garden in two days. Steven will be there to help too, so I'm sure we'll get done and be enjoying fresh produce soon."

Chapter Seven

The next day Billy and Oat cashed in on their half-day of work and went fishing. They brought home nine good-sized fish for supper. Billy knew how to cook them but not how to make the accompanying dishes. "Lydia," he asked. "Could you teach me how to make a few meals for when I have to cook for Steven and Oat? Maybe you could share a few simple dishes that I could write down?

"Sure, Billy. This meal with the lovely fish you supplied is a great place to start. We'll have fish, fried potatoes, pickles, and herb muffins. How's that sound?" Lydia asked as she reached for the frying pan.

"Sounds good to me," Billy said, putting on his mother's apron. "What can I do?"

"Start by fetching water and heating it in the big kettle. We'll need a jar of pickles, enough potatoes for all of us, and a good-sized onion from the root cellar. And we'll need five eggs and a pitcher of milk," Lydia said as though born for the job.

"Five eggs? What on earth for?" Billy hunched his shoulders.

"You'll see. Now hurry. I'll get the muffins measured out." Lydia reached for the big mixing bowl.

Billy returned with everything on Lydia's list and offered, "I can start peeling the potatoes."

Billy followed Lydia's instructions, then began cutting the onion. His eyes started to water, and he rubbed them, making them sting even more. "Is there a better way to cut onions, so I don't go blind?"

"Nope, that's part of cooking," Lydia explained as she started slicing the potatoes. They both reached for potatoes at the same time, and their hands touched. A wave of warmth came over them as they momentarily gazed into each other's eyes.

Taking the last crispy-skinned fish from the pan and putting it on the platter piled high with the rest of the catch, Billy called out, "Time to eat."

Placing the feast on the table, he sat beside Lydia and taking her hand under the table, he said, "With a lot of help from Lydia, I was able to make most of this meal, but I've still got a long ways to go before I can cook well."

"Ma would be proud of you, Billy," Jack said.

Billy grinned, squeezed Lydia's hand, and then let go. "I'm going to help with supper from now on. I'll be cooking for Oat and Steven by myself, so I guess I have a lot to learn if we don't want to starve." Billy shoved a muffin into his mouth.

After supper, Billy finally got a moment to talk to Lydia in private. "Thanks for the help tonight, Lydia. If Oat and Steven get their way, I'm sure we'll be eating a lot of fish. What should we make for supper tomorrow night?"

"How about beef stew with potatoes, corn, and carrots in gravy? We can cook two pumpkins, make one into pudding and use the other for pie the following day." Lydia suggested.

"Beef stew with pumpkin pudding. I can't wait."

The cooking lessons went on while work in the fields continued. After a day of hard labor, Billy was always eager to work beside Lydia. He became confident he could cook well enough to keep Steven and Oat healthy.

****

With the fields planted, Jack wanted to head home. He gave Lydia a hug, smiled, and said, "Be sure to pack your sewing supplies. When I get some leatherwork done, I'll bring it to you at Billy's. I've packed all the items that you finished so far, and I'll get them to town as soon as everything is done."

"Don't worry. Getting them finished will be my first priority," Lydia said. "We can't lose our shelf space. I'll have Billy bring us when I finish the sewing, and we'll get to meet Annabelle and Benjamin." Lydia gave Jack a kiss on the cheek.

Jack picked up Johanna and twirled her around, kissed her, and said, "I'll see you soon, and you'll get to meet your new niece and nephew.

"Annabelle and Benjamin," Johanna said. "I want to hold them." She smiled.

Chapter Eight

After Jack left, Mark mused aloud, "I'm surprised Seth Frazer hasn't come for the seed that we picked up in town. Perhaps I'll take a trip to visit before heading out to pick up Sarah and Grandma. I may stay and help him for a few days. Little Ethan and Johanna get along so well together that I'm sure Emily won't mind watching her when I ride back and forth to care for the livestock here."

"I've been wondering about Seth too," Billy said. "I think Oat, Lydia, and I will leave for my place today, and we'll see you when we see you. Lydia's baking this morning, so we'll wait and go after the noon meal."

Mark nodded. "Then I'll leave for the Frazer's place after morning chores tomorrow."

****

As Lydia packed food and supplies, Billy and Oat hitched up the team, gathered some chickens, tied the milk cow on the back, and loaded the wagon.

"Come on, Lydia, we're waiting on you," Billy called.

Hurrying from the house, Lydia stopped to give her sister and father a kiss before climbing into the wagon. "Johanna, you take good care of Father, and we'll see you soon." Lydia waved as they pulled away.

Oat drove the wagon, and Billy rode his horse Lucky. "We'll trade places halfway, so we each get a break," Billy said and nudged Lucky to take the lead.

For most of the trip, Oat shared a story about living in Arkansas on the plantation. "Davey and me worked in the fields with my folks. Ma said when she birthed me, we both almost died. She didn't want no more babies. We lived in a small shack with 'nother family with a Ma and Pa, two boys and two girls. Sam, he was my age. The others was younger. Davey and I shared the end of the shack with Ma and Pa. We was lucky. We had a fireplace. Davey and I had to chop wood and keep the fire goin' in the winter. Mostly cooking was done outside. I sure like Billy's inside stove. First I seen. It works good."

"So your Ma cooked outside all year round?" Lydia inquired.

"Yup, all the mothers cooked outside. Each shack had a fire pit. We all had gardens too. We ate good during the harvest, but then we ate whatever Ma could dry, salt, or pickle. Davey and I set rabbit snares, and sometimes other critters got caught, and we ate them too.

"Did you have any chickens for eggs?" The wagon hit a large stone in the road and bounced Lydia on the seat.

"The owners had a chicken coop, and the task masters got eggs each week. But iffen you was jes a worker, you don't get no eggs."

"You *didn't* get *any* eggs." Lydia corrected him.

"Yes, any eggs," Oat repeated. "I sure do appreciate you helping me with words. I'm trying to learn."

"You're catching on, Oat. As you listen to how we talk, you'll pick up words. And remember, if we say a word you don't understand, ask, and we'll make it clear for you."

At the halfway point, Oat pulled off the road to change places. Billy dismounted and hurried to help Lydia down from the wagon.

Oat stretched the knot out of his back and said, "I'll ride ahead and get a fire goin' in the stove and heat water. That way, the house will be warm and everything ready for Lydia to cook supper."

"Thanks, Oat. I'll give the horses and the milk cow a little rest. Go slow on Lucky. We'll be behind you soon."

When Oat was out of earshot, Billy leaned in and said, "Hey Lydia, I couldn't wait to trade places with Oat. I must say, I enjoy having your time and attention all to myself. What do you say to a short walk to stretch our legs?"

Several yards from the wagon, wildflowers were in bloom. Billy veered off the road to pick a few for Lydia. Handing them to her, he said, "We have a lot of work ahead of us. Getting the garden and the fields planted will take a while. Are you sure you want to stay that long?"

"I don't mind helping. You must get the crops in, and I certainly can pick stones and plant seed. I've never handled the horses and plow, but I'd try if you need me to."

"No, Oat and I can handle the plowing. If you and Steven can manage the planting, we will have the fields finished in no time." Billy grinned and motioned to the wagon. "We better get going, or Oat will wonder what happened to us." Helping Lydia up onto the wagon seat, he noticed how small her hand was in his. He'd treat her with special care and couldn't imagine not being her husband someday, although ultimately, the final decision would be Lydia's. He would do everything in his power to persuade her to give him a chance to make her happy, but he'd be patient and wait for the right time to talk about his thoughts and a life-altering consideration.

****

After breakfast the following morning, Billy said, "I'm gonna hitch the plow to the team and prepare the garden plot. Mother bought seed enough to expand the garden to feed another mouth in the family," Billy looked at Oat and smiled.

"I'll come out to help after I get the dishes done," Lydia offered. "Oat, can you grab the bags of seed and put them on the table, please? And Billy, if you can find your plot chart from last year's garden, we'll know what order to plant this year."

"Plot chart?" I've never made a plot chart." Billy hunched his shoulders.

"Well, Ma taught me how to layout a garden. We'll use the same plan we did on the family farm. With a chart, everyone knows where different plants go, how deep to plant, the expected spread, and when the harvest is expected. Let's get to it."

Once the ground was tilled, Oat raked, and Lydia followed, laying out the garden in rows. Billy came next and dug the furrows for seed. Teamwork made the process go smoothly, and a variety of root and hearty vegetables and leafy greens would soon abound.

By evening, they were half way, and by supper the following day, they had completed the entire job. "You might think the garden took a long time to plant, but it'll pay off when the produce starts coming in. Now all we need is rain," Lydia said, wiping her brow.

That evening, Mother Nature must have heard her

request, for a storm passed over, thoroughly saturating the ground. The warmth of the sunny days made for perfect seed germination conditions.

The following day they started on the fields. "Pa and I talked, Billy said as he hitched the team to the plow. "He suggested we get the corn in first, followed by the oats, and then the wheat, rye, and barley. He also suggested turning additional soil on part of the pasture and seeding more clover. We have our work cut out for us, and I'm not sure when Steven will arrive to help."

"Well then, we better get started," Oat said as he loaded the shovel and rake into the wagon. Lydia climbed on, and they headed for the fields.

****

Johanna and Mark set out after the morning chores and were halfway to the Frazer's farm when they saw the Frazer's wagon coming their way. "Hey, neighbors, we wondered where you were. We have your seed in the back. Our fields are already planted, so if you're just starting, I can give you a hand if you'd like." Mark offered. A grin overcame him as he looked at Emily, and he blurted out. "Congratulations! We didn't know you were expecting. Sarah sure will be surprised."

"Emily smiled, patting her belly. " It's due sometime around the beginning to middle of July, we think."

"I'm happy for you. We wondered if you'd have another." Mark grinned and tipped his hat to Seth.

"Where is Sarah, and why do you have Johanna with you?" Emily inquired.

"Sarah, my mother, and Steven are with Jack and Abby. Abby had twins, Annabelle and Benjamin."

"Oh my, twins. How wonderful. And everyone is

fine, I hope?" Emily shooed a fly from about her face.

"Yes, and Jack sure is a proud father. He gave us the good news when he came to help with the planting. Jack went home, and Billy, Lydia, and Oat left to plant Billy's fields. So that leaves Johanna and me to go pick up the rest of the family at Jack's. Oh, I just remembered, you haven't met Oat yet. Otis is his true name. I'll explain, but first, is everything all right with you folks? I was a bit concerned since you hadn't come for the seed for your fields."

"We're fine," Seth said. The kitchen garden is planted, and the fields are plowed and ready. I appreciate your offer to help, but I'd rather you fetch Sarah and your mother, so they're around in case the baby comes early. We managed the birth of Ethan all right, but I'd feel better if Sarah and your mother were here. You know what I mean."

"Yeah, I know. Let's give the children time to play. There are a few things I have to catch you up on." Mark pulled close to the Frazer's wagon so they could easily transfer the seed. Seth helped Emily and Johanna down as Ethan scuttled out of the wagon himself.

"Stay where I can see you," Emily clamored, and the children ran off to catch bugs.

"I need to tell you about our latest adopted son," Mark said. "Billy took him in, and he will live with Billy and Steven, but the whole family adopted him. He is the nicest boy. He's fourteen, the same age Billy was when he came to stay with us. Well, I guess I better start at the beginning." As Mark recounted the story of how Otis came to live with the Hewitt family, the children played, delighted with each other's company. "The fact that Oat is black doesn't bother you, I hope?" Mark asked.

Emily answered first. "Not at all. And I don't mind having Ethan and the new baby around him either."

"No problem at all, Mark," Seth said. "Lincoln freed the slaves for a reason. Oat is free to live his life the way he wants, and so are you. Others may not see it this way, but we certainly do."

"Sarah and I knew you'd be all right with Oat." Mark nodded his head. "She'll be glad when I tell her we talked. Now I guess we better get going and let you get back to work. I'll leave early tomorrow to pick up Sarah and be back late tomorrow night. Makes for a long day, but it's doable. Once you get your fields planted, plan a day and come visit. I'm sure you gals will have plenty to talk about. We'll come to visit for a day as well."

"I'd like that," Emily said and then called for the children.

After the men moved the seed to Seth's wagon, Mark shook Seth and Ethan's hands and gave Emily a kiss on the cheek. Ethan gave Johanna a kiss on the cheek too.

Chapter Nine

Mark and Johanna got an early start and arrived at Jack and Abby's farm mid-afternoon. Steven was the first to greet them.

"Boy, am I glad to see you." Steven ran toward the wagon. "If you hurry, you can see the twins before Abby puts them down for a nap. They sleep a lot, but Ma says that's good for them so they can grow strong bones. I sure have missed you, Johanna. Come on, Abby will let you hold the babies if you ask." The children ran inside.

Sarah came to the doorway and then moved gratefully into Mark's arms. "It's so good to see you," she whispered in his ear as she hugged him, kissed him, and held him tight. "I bet you're tuckered out from answering all of Johanna's questions on the ride here."

Mark took Sarah's face in his hands as he had done thousands of times before, kissed her, gazed into her eyes, and said, "Yes indeed, we do have an inquisitive child, don't we? Once she woke up, she never quit talking. The entire trip, she asked one question after the other. We sang a couple of songs, but she definitely enjoyed talking the most."

Sarah burst into laughter, with Mark joining in before joining the rest of the family.

Johanna was holding both babies on her lap with Steven sitting beside her, explaining how to bounce them a little to quiet them when they fussed.

"Congratulations, Abby!" Mark kissed her on the forehead. "We were all so excited when Jack told us about Annabelle and Benjamin. I know the rest of the family can't wait to meet the newest members."

"How do you feel now that you're a grandpa?" Ruth asked and chuckled.

"It makes me feel old," Mark replied and grinned. "But not as old as you must feel, Great Grandma," Mark grinned and gave his mother a hug.

Sarah pulled out a chair. "Come sit and have a bite to eat" Knowing Mark was coming, she had everyone packed and ready to return home, plus cooked additional food so Abby would have extra ready to reheat and serve.

Mark and Johanna ate as Steven and Jack loaded the wagon. Abby put the babies down for a nap, and everyone went outside to say their good-byes.

"We sure will miss you, Steven. I don't know what we'll do without your help with the babies and all the chores you did while you were here." Jack said as he enveloped Steven in a hug.

And I don't know what I'd have done without both of you when the twins arrived," Abby said to Sarah and Ruth and then gave them both a hug and a kiss.

A tear escaped down Sarah's cheek. "You two will figure things out for yourselves once we leave," Sarah announced. "I think it's time to let this family get on with their lives. You'll both do fine. You'll have your home to yourselves now and will easily settle into raising your family. You know the babies' routine, and you can manage without us. Remember, taking care of them might not always be easy, but it will always be rewarding. Help each other and take care of those little ones." Sarah wiped away more tears.

Grandma Hewitt gave them each a hug and kiss and said, "The best advice I can give you is to never go to bed angry with each other. Always talk things out, and don't stay mad. Life is too short to stay upset for days. Being upset or mad doesn't do anyone any good anyways." Smiling, she headed for the wagon.

"We must get going. I understand we are dropping Steven off at Billy's, so we best be on our way," Sarah said and then climbed into the back and helped Grandma Hewitt into the wagon where a sturdy armchair tied to the wagon seat awaited her.

Waving good-bye the family headed toward Billy's farm with Johanna and Steven talking up a storm, giving Sarah and Mark a much-needed chance to catch up.

"I assume you planted the garden?" Sarah asked.

"Yes, of course. Everyone helped, and we got the planting all done in a day. And Johanna was such a big help." Mark said loud enough so Johanna could hear.

"I helped plant the garden," Johanna repeated to Steven and Grandma Hewitt.

"I helped plant Jack and Abby's garden, too. We planted beans, peas, carrots, and cabbage." Steven announced.

"We did too, and we planted lettuce and beets," Johanna added.

"We did too, and some onions and potatoes," Steven said.

"Did we plant onions and potatoes Pa?" Johanna interrupted.

"Yes, dear, we did," Mark assured her.

Steven poked his mother to get her attention. "Did we plant squash, Ma?"

"Yes, Steven, we planted squash, as well," Sarah

replied and then said, "Oh look, we're almost to the turn-off road for Billy's."

"I could walk to the farm from the turn-off road if you want, Pa? That way, you could get home earlier to get the chores done," Steven offered.

"No, Steven. That's too far. You'd have to walk a good hour and a half, and you never know what animals may be around." Mark knew Steven would be fine walking to the farm but also knew Sarah wouldn't approve. Delivering Steven, staying to talk for a while, and starting out again would make for a late arrival home.

Mark waited. When he figured they were halfway to the farmhouse, he broached the subject again. "Steven, are you still willing to walk to the house?"

"Sure, I know this road real well. We're close now, and I'd make it to the house before the sun goes down for sure. Can I, Ma? I want to surprise Billy by walking into the house all by myself." Steven said, "Grandma, you think I could walk by myself, don't you?"

"Why yes, I think you'd be perfectly safe to walk. It'd save us time. Not that I wouldn't mind seeing the other children, but it'll make it that much later to get home if we stay and visit." Grandma Hewitt patted his arm. "I can remember Samuel and Mark fishing along the Alleghany River and after dark coming home with their catches and fileting them in the shed by lantern light."

"Oh, all right. I'm outnumbered. You can walk from here," Sarah agreed.

Mark stopped the wagon. Steven gave everyone a quick hug and jumped down to run to the side where his mother sat. "Don't worry, Ma. I'll be fine, and I'll tell everyone you all say hello."

"All right, Steven. Hurry and start walking," Sarah urged, tucking her shawl around her shoulders.

Mark turned the wagon around and headed back down the road with Johanna sitting between her parents.

****

Walking along briskly, Steven knew the farmhouse would come into sight just around the bend ahead. Suddenly he heard rustling in the bushes off to his right. He froze in his tracks and cast about for an explanation. *It's not a little animal like a squirrel or a rabbit. The noise is too loud. Oh, I think it's getting closer. If I stand here, it might smell me. I wish I had a rifle.* He listened as the rustling came closer and got louder. *I think it knows I'm here. I better run. Maybe if I run now, I can get away.* Steven started running, not looking back, and didn't stop until he had the house in sight. Slowing, he caught his breath and decided not to tell anyone about this part of his walk home.

Reaching the farmhouse, Steven lifted his hand to knock so he could surprise everyone.

The door opened before he had a chance. There stood Oat, not Billy, and Oat had a rifle in his hand.

Standing face to face, both boys froze in place for a moment, shouted each other's names, and hugged.

Lydia and Billy came to the door.

"How did you get here? Where are Ma and Pa?" Billy hugged him and pulled him inside.

"They brought me halfway up the turn-off road, and I walked the rest of the way. I wanted to surprise you. They said to say hello and that they'll see us when we bring Lydia home.

"I wish you could have seen your face, Oat. When

you opened the door, you sure were surprised!"

Oat put the gun over his shoulder and grinned, "I was going out to check the chickens. We lost one last night. I better go have a look," he said, heading out.

"Hey, Billy, I passed the garden on my way to the house. How much plowing did you get done?" Steven took a seat at the kitchen table.

"We just started on the corn field." Billy sat beside his brother. "Now you can help Lydia plant and Oat, and I will keep plowing."

"Do you want something to eat?" Lydia held up a plate of muffins. "We were about to have some tea."

"Sure, I'll have one," Steven said, reaching across the table.

"No sign of critters," Oat announced, coming through the door. "I counted the chickens. They're all there."

The foursome talked, catching up on all the news until not one of them could keep their eyes open a moment longer.

****

The Hewitts arrived home safely well past Johanna's bedtime. Mark carried her inside and put her into bed. "I'll take care of the chores and be right in, sweetheart," Mark said to Sarah as she and Ruth stretched from the long ride and headed indoors. Completing the farm tasks, he returned to the house to find everyone had turned in. He paused for a moment before heading to the bedroom and let out a sigh.

It's been eight years since Sarah and I married. So much has happened. Right now, everything is going well. Lord, please help us keep on the right path. Give us the knowledge and wisdom to continue our success with our family and our ranch, and I pray for a prosperous crop. Thank you, Lord, for seeing us through difficult and good times. And thank you for blessing Jack and Abby with a beautiful son and daughter.

Chapter Ten

At breakfast, Mark finally told the family about Emily and Seth expecting a second child. "Emily thinks it's due the beginning to middle of July," he said, looking around at the happy faces.

Sarah smiled and took a sip of tea. "Did she say if she wanted a boy or a girl?"

"No, and I didn't ask," Mark said. "But I did invite them for a visit, and they might come once they get their fields planted."

Sarah took the dishes to the dry sink and sat back down. "Well then, it's probably best that I miss the Fourth of July picnic this year. I'll wait and go to the Fall Festival. The twins will be older, and we can have a family photograph taken with all our newest members to send back east." With the mention of home in Pennsylvania, Sarah pulled out the letters she received in Dead Flats. "I didn't want to say anything when we were at Jack's place. That was Jack and Abby's time as proud parents, but I can share the news with you now. I received two letters. One saying that both my sisters are pregnant. Matilda is due the middle of August, and Emma is expecting her second near the end of November. The second letter was from Matthew, who is now engaged to Lynnette Edwards. I remember her as a little girl. Netty, as Matthew refers to her, lived on Fourth Street and would come to play with Emma sometimes.

They plan to wed in September."

Sarah sighed. "I so wish I could see them all again, but I know that will never happen. I never let on to Samuel when we came west that Mother was against us leaving Warren County. She was afraid we would never see each other again…and it looks like she was right. It's not that I want to go back forever, but it would be nice to visit one last time. I know Mother's fear when we left was that she would never see me again before she died. I assured her otherwise, but I guess she knew better than me. I know a trip home is not likely."

"Now, dear, you mustn't say that," Ruth said. "You never know what can happen. Look at me. I never dreamed I'd be living with my family, but here I am. I could stay with the children, and you and Mark could go back for a visit." Ruth grinned. "You might even decide to take Johanna with you."

"It's not out of the question," Mark agreed. "Let's see how the crops fare this year, and maybe next year, after the planting, we could get away. We may only need to journey to Illinois. From there, we might catch a train the rest of the way."

"Don't say what you don't mean, Mark. I don't want to get my hopes up and be disappointed," Sarah responded.

"I mean it." Mark beamed. "But I wouldn't start packing yet. Let's wait and see."

****

At the Henry farm, while the boys were hitching the horses to the wagon, Lydia packed a mid-day meal to send along. Today she would stay back and do baking. Then, while supper simmered in the warm oven, she would join them in the fields. Two pumpkin pies as a treat for their hard work would be a surprise for dessert.

When Lydia arrived, Billy and Oat were plowing, and Steven was planting corn. She grabbed a pouch, filled it with seed, picked up a hoe, and began planting a row two and a half feet parallel to the one Steven had planted. The work went quickly, with everyone pitching in. After a hot and tiring day, everyone was hungry.

They planted until dusk each night. Once home, Steven would put away the horses while Oat and Billy began the evening chores. By the time they came in and plopped into their chairs, Lydia had supper on the table. Before bedtime, she worked with Oat and Steven on schoolwork. Taking turns, the boys read from a dime novel, and she would fill in the words they couldn't pronounce. After a few chapters, they worked adding columns of digits. The next morning the routine started again.

As promised, Billy gave Lydia a hand with meals when he could. Oat and Steven helped with the evening dishes while playing spelling games or practicing times tables.

Billy didn't have the time alone with Lydia that he hoped. He loved having her there and often caught himself watching her and daydreaming about what it would be like if they married. He occasionally picked flowers for the table and hung up the laundry with her a few times. Other than small acts of kindness, there was little time to talk without the boys around. He decided the family needed to take a break and have some fun.

After sending the boys out to hitch the horses, Billy took Lydia aside. "We've been working the fields for three weeks now. I think everyone deserves a break. What do you say we quit early today? We could take a picnic, go to the creek fishing, and take a swim."

"That's a wonderful idea," Lydia agreed. "I'll pack a special meal, and you can surprise the boys and tell them your plan."

Mid-morning, Steven began looking for Lydia to join them. Finally, he asked. "Isn't Lydia gonna come help today?"

Billy grinned. "No, because we're taking a break today. Lydia's packing a picnic. We're going fishing and for a swim. Come on. We'll take the horses back, get Lydia, and be on our way."

****

Arriving creek side, Oat called, "I'm heading downstream after I dig some bait."

"All right, I'll go upstream, and I'll still catch more fish than you," Steven boasted.

Lydia lifted the basket of food from the back of the wagon. "Don't you boys want something to eat first?"

Steven grabbed the shovel. "It won't take us long to catch enough fish for supper. We'll eat when we get back."

Billy unhitched the horses, led them to the creek to drink, and hobbled them in a grassy spot to graze. He checked to see if the boys had enough bait. "You'll each have to catch at least four before you come back because I'm not fishing today."

"I'm going to catch five fish," Oat bragged.

"Well, so am I, and I'll be back to the wagon before you," Steven said as he took off running to get his line in the water first.

"Be careful. No fooling around like walking out on logs or falling in and getting hurt. Ma would skin us alive if anything happened to you," Lydia called out as the boys scurried out of sight.

Once Steven and Oat left, Billy spread a quilt in the shade of an old Elm tree, and he and Lydia sat down to enjoy the day. "I can't believe how competitive the boys are. Who do you think will be back first?"

"I don't know." Lydia giggled. "They both sound pretty determined. Don't you remember a few years back when you and Jack had to see who could catch the most fish? Competition must be a boy thing. Girls don't compete like that." Lydia stretched out her legs and leaned back on her elbows.

Billy glanced her way. "How do you do it?"

"Do what?" Lydia asked.

"How do you look so beautiful lying there? You always look beautiful no matter what you're doing. You even look beautiful when you're planting the fields."

"You're joking with me." Lydia laughed and rolled her eyes.

"No, I mean it," Billy said. "And I mean this too. We make a good team, don't you think?

"Why yes, yes we do. We're getting the crops in and taking care of our family. You know Billy, you're more than a big brother to Steven and Oat. You're like a father. They respect and listen to you."

Billy scoffed. "They listen to you too, Lydia. And I want to thank you for helping Oat with his reading and writing. He's come a long way. He picked up math in no time, thanks to you, and I love hearing Steven and him rattle off their times' tables and count by twos and fives together.

"Come on, let's go for a walk before the boys get back." Billy stood and reached out his hand to help Lydia up.

Lydia took his hand, and he pulled her to her feet. "Why didn't you go fishing with the boys?" she inquired.

"Because I didn't want to leave you sitting around by yourself, and besides, we haven't had much time to talk without the boys around since we left home. I know I haven't helped you out much with the work around the house or with the cooking like I said I would. By the time we're done in the fields, I can hardly keep my eyes open. Hopefully, we'll be done soon." Billy picked a daisy and handed the flower to Lydia.

"I know what you mean. I'm exhausted too, and I'm sure the boys are, but they don't let on." Lydia tucked the flower into her hair.

"Having Steven and Oat helping makes a difference. We added a good ten to twelve feet to each field this year. I have four head of cattle at the family farm that I'll bring back when we take you home. Now with Oat to feed, I'm thinking of buying one more."

Billy looked up, and Oat ran past, heading toward the wagon carrying five fish.

"Why Oat, you're all out of breath." Billy grinned.

"Is Steven back yet?" Oat called over his shoulder.

"We haven't seen him," Billy said. "You're the first one back. I'll help you get them gutted and scaled."

Five, ten, fifteen minutes passed, and Lydia said, "Maybe we should check on Steven. Something might have happened. I know how much he wanted to win and be the first one back."

Billy washed his hands in the creek. "We'll give him five more minutes. If he's not back by then, we'll go find him."

A few minutes later, Steven came running, calling out, "Did I win? Did I win?"

"Not this time," Oat said with a big grin on his face as he stepped from behind the wagon holding his fish strung on a stick. "Come on, hurry up. I'll help you gut and scale yours. I'm hungry, and I want to go swimming."

Lydia reached for the basket of food. "Why don't you three go swimming now, and I'll get things ready. When you're done, we can eat, and you won't smell like fish."

"Last one in is a rotten egg," Steven said, ripping off his shirt, shoes, and socks. "The swimming hole is down by that tree. I'll show you Oat."

The threesome took off. Lydia joined them at the swimming hole after preparing for lunch and spreading another quilt.

"Lydia, why don't you at least get your feet wet? You can go up a little ways where it's not as deep, hike up your skirt, and wade in to your knees," Steven suggested. We won't even splash you and get you all wet."

"Oh, all right." Lydia took off her shoes and stood. "Is the water warm?"

"It's not bad," Billy assured her.

Wading into the creek, Lydia watched as her brothers frolicked downstream. She had good footing about five feet from the shore, when something brushed her leg. *Oh, a fish*, she thought, looking down. But nothing was there, and she forgot about it.

Steven yelled, "Watch me stand on my hands and walk across the bottom."

"I'm watching," Lydia called back and waved. As she waved, she felt something brush against her legs again. This time whatever swam past had a sharp edge.

Startled, she lost her footing and fell with a splash, letting out a scream.

Billy leapt out of the water and ran to Lydia. The boys followed.

She was thrashing about when Billy waded in, scooped her into his arms, and carried her to shore.

"Are you hurt anywhere?" Setting her down in the grass, he checked for broken bones as the boys huddled around her.

"No, I'm not hurt. Whatever brushed against me just scared me. A catfish must have grazed my leg. I felt something sharp and was startled. I lost my footing. I'm fine. I'll sit here for a minute. Thanks for coming to my rescue." Looking down, she noticed blood on the back of her leg. The bleeding had almost stopped. Not wanting to spoil the boys' fun, she suggested, "Boys, why don't you go back in and swim before we have to eat and head home."

"Go ahead," Billy insisted. "Lydia and I will come watch you for a while." Billy assured them, and the two boys took off for the swimming hole. He looked at Lydia and then her legs. The cut wasn't deep. "Are you sure you're all right? You're not hurt anywhere else, are you?"

"No. I'm fine. I'm sure. Can you help me to my feet? Lydia stretched out her arms, and Billy helped her up. "It happened twice so quickly I couldn't get a glimpse of whatever it was. The cut isn't bad."

Lydia took a few steps, but she nearly fell. Billy stretched and caught her. "Sit back down and let me check you out again," he insisted.

"I'm so embarrassed. It's my ankle. I must have twisted it somehow." Lydia reached to rub the pain away and noted redness and swelling.

"Maybe we should get you in to see Doc Glasgow." Billy raised an eyebrow.

Lydia shook her head. "No, nothing's broken. Let's give it a couple of days and see how it feels. I'll stay off my feet and give the swelling a chance to go down. Now help me over to watch the boys for a while, then we better eat and get home."

Instead of letting Lydia use him as a crutch, Billy scooped her up in his arms again and carried her to a fallen tree log. "Ten more minutes," Billy called to Steven and Oat.

****

Once home, Billy carried Lydia into the house, and helped her prop her foot on a pillow. "All right, boys. You have time to weed the garden, do the evening chores, and clean out the chicken coop. I'm cooking tonight, and I'll call you when it's ready."

Under Lydia's instruction, Billy prepared fried potatoes and fish. Proud to have cooked the meal himself, he called out the door, "Time for supper."

Lydia's cooking lessons had paid off. There were no leftovers.

Chapter Eleven

Lydia had to admit, *the other day, when Billy carried me into the house, I didn't want him to put me down. I could have stayed in his arms forever. He's so gentle and understanding.* Thankfully her ankle wasn't broken, only sore. She took the next few days easy until the swelling went away, and by the end of the week, she was walking as though nothing had happened.

"It's time to help in the fields again. If my ankle starts hurting, I promise I'll stop. But we need to finish the work," Lydia insisted.

In the middle of the next week, while everyone was in the fields, Lydia spotted Jack riding in. Being almost midday, she suggested taking a break. Jack joined them at the wagon parked under a shade tree.

He took saddlebags filled with leatherwork that needed to be stitched and placed them in the back of the wagon. "You have plenty of work cut out for you, Lydia. Hopefully, you'll be able to take the finished work to town a few days ahead of the Fourth of July. You can put price tags on them. You know the prices. Abby and I discussed it, and we've decided not to take the twins anywhere yet. So if you could get them to town, I'm sure sales should be good the weekend of the town picnic.

Lydia looked at Billy.

"I'll make sure she gets the goods there in time," Billy agreed. "The fourth is on a Wednesday this year.

We'll stop by on our way home and drop off the money from sales and see the twins."

"To town? We're going to town for the picnic?" Steven said with a big grin on his face. "Are we going to stay for the picnic and the dance?"

"Not so fast, Steven. We're going early. I don't know yet, so don't get your hopes up." Billy corrected him. "I'm not planning to shoot in the contest this time so there's no reason to stay. We may run the leather goods in, pick up supplies, and come home."

"Oh, that's all right, I guess. At least we get to go to Dead Flats," Steven said. "I can show you around town a little, Oat. You'll like it."

"How are Anabelle and Benjamin? Are they sleeping all night yet?" Lydia inquired.

"Almost. Once one starts fussing, the other wakes, and they both carry on until they're fed or changed and rocked back to sleep. We know they'll outgrow that stage soon, but we also don't want them to grow up too fast."

Jack ruffled Steven's hair. "Well, I hate to leave so quickly, but I promised Abby I wouldn't stay long, and you need to finish planting. I sure wish I could help." Jack snickered. "We'll look for you the week of the Fourth."

"All right, let's get back to work, boys," Lydia said. "Please give my love to Abby, Jack."

****

Billy walked with Jack back to his horse Dusty. "Jack, do you have a minute? I'd like to talk with you about something."

"Sure. What's up?"

"What would you say if I told you," Billy looked around to make sure everyone was out of earshot, "that I

77

think I'm falling in love with Lydia?"

Jack's eye's widened.

"I'm not kidding," Billy said. "Ever since she took the bullet out of my shoulder, we've had a closer relationship. I've thought a lot about us. I know we've grown up together, but Lydia and I are not related by blood. We could always talk to each other about things that bothered us. I have special feelings for her, Jack. I don't know if her feelings for me run as deep as mine for her." Billy sat on the back of the wagon.

"Wow, this is a surprise. Are you sure you're feeling love and not gratitude for her helping you when you were shot?" Jack asked and sat down beside Billy.

"No, it's not gratitude. It's much stronger. I've felt this way for quite some time. I'm sure I love her. I have more feeling for Lydia than I ever did for Elizabeth, but what if she doesn't love me?" Billy lowered his voice and then hung his head.

Jack said, "Looks like you have to talk with her about it."

"Of course, you're right." Billy tensed. "I was thinking that maybe when we get done with the planting, I'll suggest we go for a walk so we can talk in private."

"That sounds like a good idea, Billy. You know, Lydia isn't experienced when it comes to men. I know you would never hurt her, but this could make things awkward if she doesn't feel the same as you. Be careful how you share your thoughts. Have you considered talking with Pa first?"

"Maybe I should talk to Pa. He always gives good advice. At least I know you're all right with it, Jack."

"I can't think of anyone else I'd rather have for a brother-in-law, Brother. Regardless of Lydia's response, don't let sharing your feelings with Lydia ruin our family. You know what I mean, Billy. Ma and Pa love you and Steven very much. I wouldn't want to see anything happen to that relationship."

"Courting could be difficult. With Grandma at the farm, the Hewitt house is full. Oat will be living with Steven and me here. I'm not sure when or how we'll find time to spend together."

"I understand what you're saying. I'm sure you'll think of something." Jack nodded and jumped down from the wagon. "I better get going. Good luck. I'll be rooting for you."

****

In the mornings, Lydia stayed at the house working on leather pieces. At noontime, she'd bring a meal to the fields and stay to help for a while, and then head back to sew and prepare supper. Billy took over the schooling of Oat and Steven while Lydia sewed long after everyone else was in bed. As she worked, she thought about dress patterns. Her dream was to start a business where she could offer original dress designs. She was looking forward to making that plan come true.

Ever since the day the lady at the dress shop let her sew on their new treadle machine, she'd wanted one of her own. She bought her own sewing machine last fall. Soon she would have enough money saved to order material, and her business would become a reality.

Lydia planned to talk to the ladies at the dress shop while in Dead Flats. Secretly she hoped that if she told them that she had her own sewing machine, they might ask her to join them in their business. A shop of her own was out of the question at this time. Perhaps a mutually beneficial arrangement would be the answer.

Chapter Twelve

"Thank you for all your help, everyone," Billy said at the end of the final day of planting. "I couldn't have done all of this without you." All the fields were planted, and the clover pasture was reseeded. "The garden is in, and I think we all deserve a day off tomorrow to relax. We have to take Lydia home so she can get some different clothes before we go to town for the fourth. And I'm sure Johanna is missing her big sister."

Tears welled in Lydia's eyes. "With the three of you living here, we'll miss you. You'll have to come visit as often as you can. Maybe we could meet halfway and enjoy a picnic now and then." She said, wiping away tears before they could spill.

"I like the idea of the two households meeting halfway." Billy agreed.

"A picnic," Steven said. "The whole family can come. Ma and Grandma are good cooks."

Lydia put her hands on her hips and gave him a look.

"You know what I mean," Steven said quickly. "I like your cooking too, Lydia."

"All this talk of food makes me hungry," Oat said. "My ma used to make potato sticks. That's what she called them. If I explain them to ya do ya think you could try to make them sometime, Lydia?"

Lydia smiled. "Sure, I can try."

"Ma used a slaw cutter to cut the potato and fried

80

them in bacon drippings. They sure were good." Oat picked up a rock and chucked it away.

****

The following morning, Billy asked the boys, "What are you two doing on your day off? Any ideas?"

Oat spoke up, "I want to spend time at Davey's grave. I have lots to tell him, and I'd like to tell him by myself. If we had my horse here, Steven and I could go for a ride. Can we bring them back with us this trip, Billy?"

"I don't see why not," Billy assured him. What are you doing today, Steven?"

"Well, while you talk to Davey, Oat, I'll patch the hole in the chicken coop before we lose any more chickens. And if the wild berries are ripe, I'll pick some, and Lydia can turn them into sauce for over cornbread."

Lydia reached for an apron. "I need to do some baking, and Billy, you better help. I know you can mix up muffins and make biscuits, but you never helped make bread, and you have to learn. If you don't, you're not going to eat well. It's not hard, it just takes time, and you have to make bread in steps."

Billy put on an apron, too. "All right. I'll make bread with you, but while it's rising, what about taking a walk with me?"

Lydia chuckled. "A walk would be lovely. Since you'll be taking me home tomorrow, this afternoon, we can clean out the back of the wagon and weed the garden. With me gone, you'll be on your own. All three of you are going to have to pitch in and help around here. And you should probably take baths before we leave, too."

Steven opened his mouth, but before he got a word out, Billy suggested, "Maybe we could stop at the creek and take a quick dip on the way tomorrow."

Steven and Oat quickly agreed and ran out to enjoy their day of leisure.

Bill wrote down the ingredients and measurements to make the bread and caught on to the kneading easily. The first rise would take at least a couple hours, so as soon as they set the bowl in the warming oven, Billy pulled on the bow of Lydia's apron and suggested, "Let's take that walk."

Walking down the lane toward the turn-off road, Billy picked Lydia a flower for her hair, and then turned and asked, "Lydia, do you think you could ever think of me as more than a brother?"

"You asked me that once before, Billy, but I didn't know what you meant. Now I think I do. You mean love you like a man and woman, like a husband and wife? Is that what you're asking?"

"Yes, exactly. Like a man and woman, as in husband and wife. We could be more to each other if you think that's what you'd like. And I'm not saying everything has to happen right away. I would like to court you. We know each other pretty well, but I'm sure we both have more to share and learn about the other. Would you let me court you, Lydia, and we could see what happens from there?"

"But Billy, you've been married. You know about things I don't." Lydia stopped walking, stopped talking, and looked away.

Billy took her small hand in his and with his other gently lifted her chin. "I don't want this to feel uncomfortable for you. If you're not interested in me other than as a brother, I understand. We can forget this conversation ever happened. But I liked having you near the night you lay beside me after taking the bullet out of my shoulder."

Lydia squeezed Billy's hand. "I liked that too, Billy. I never felt that way before. You make me feel safe and special. I've shared things with you I've never told anyone else."

"I know what you mean," Billy said. "You helped me when my wife Elizabeth died. I've also told you things nobody else knows."

Lydia let out a small sigh, rested her head on Billy's chest, and they stood there in silence for a few moments. "Billy," Lydia whispered. "What do you think Ma and Pa will say if we ask them to let us court?"

"I think they'll be happy for us. So…what do you think? Would you let me court you? And remember, if at any time you want to stop or you change your mind, I promise there will be no hard feelings. We'll still be sister and brother, and you can always count on me."

"Well, I'm not sure how I truly feel. Taking Elizabeth's place would be awkward."

"Don't think that way. I certainly don't. In fact, I hardly think of Elizabeth anymore. I want to start over, marry again, and start a family. Just promise me you'll think about us, and we can talk more about possibly courting when I take you to town."

Lydia said, "I must admit I enjoyed being with you and the boys. We all get along so well. What do you think Steven will say if we start courting?"

"It will be hard to keep our secret from Steven and Oat, but I think they'll feel the love between us long before they see our outward affections. Steven may not understand at first, but I think we can show him our being together will make our family happy and stronger. He loves you, and if we show him how happy we are, I think he'll understand.

"Remember, Lydia, you can end everything at any time if you don't feel courting is right for you…or for us. You have my promise that I'll honor your wishes." Billy took her hands in his and softly brushed her fingertips with his lips.

Lydia returned the gesture with a gentle squeeze, and said, "I'm not saying no. I'll think about what you've said. You know I'll be busy soon. I've given lots of thought to starting my own business sometime this year. Do you mind if I talk to Grandma about us? I don't think I could tell Ma until I've made a decision about us courting, but I feel Grandma would give good advice."

"No, I don't mind. I already asked Jack what he thought about me courting you."

"Oh, Billy. You didn't! What did he say?"

"He said he could do worse for a brother-in-law."

"You're joking? You mean he's all right with us being together? What made you ask him?"

"Well, I figured if he wasn't good with the idea, Pa and Ma wouldn't be either. He encouraged me to ask you and said you could talk to him if you wanted.

"Knowing Jack's opinion means a lot. Sounds like he's happy for us. I'm not sure what Ma and Pa will say. I'm not saying no, but I want to think on it."

"I understand, Lydia. Take all the time you need. Just know my feelings for you are real."

"I guess we better head back and punch that bread down for the second rise." Lydia gazed at him off and on as they walked back to the house."

Chapter Thirteen

When they arrived at the creek on the way to take Lydia home, the boys and Billy jumped down from the wagon with soap, towels, and a clean change of clothes.

"Don't be all day," Lydia said. "And make sure you wash your hair. I'll go upstream a ways and wash up."

Steven said. "Don't worry, we'll hurry. I want to spend time with Pa and Johanna. I haven't seen them in a long time." Everyone took off for the swimming hole and returned shortly, clean and refreshed. Billy dug out a comb, and everyone ran it through their hair and put their dirty clothes in the back of the wagon.

Lydia returned with towel-dried wet curls. When Billy noticed her from afar, she took his breath away. He handed Lydia the comb, and she started untangling her unruly curls. Before long, they arrived at the Hewitt farm.

Climbing down, Oat said, "Don't forget, Billy, Steven and I are riding our horses back to your place."

"I remember, Oat. But you remember, it's not only my farm, it's yours and Steven's too. You're part of the family now. We'll be taking our cows back with us, too."

Oat grinned as Johanna ran toward them to give hugs. "Oh, I'm so glad you came to visit. I missed you. Come on, I want to show you the baby calves and the new foals." She took the boys by the hand and set off to the barn.

Billy and Lydia joined the adults in the house.

"We figured you might show up sometime this week," Mark said as he rose from his chair to shake Billy's hand. "Everything planted?"

"Yup, and we even re-seeded half the clover pasture. The garden is doing well. Looks like we could have a good crop this year." Billy kissed Grandma and Sarah.

Lydia caught them up on their plans. "After the noon meal, we'll return to Billy's. The boys will ride their horses back, and Billy wants to take his cows back home now that he's living there permanent. And I need to pick up my dress designs.

"I've completed the sewing on the leather projects Jack brought, and Billy said he'd take me to town to drop them off before the big Fourth of July doings.

"While I'm in town, I plan to talk to the ladies at the dress shop, show them my dress drawings, and see if I can make my dream come true getting my business started. Don't you think I'm ready, Ma?"

"Yes, Lydia dear, that sounds like a good plan," Sarah said. "You have your sewing machine now, and your designs are wonderful."

Billy sat beside Ruth at the table. "You're planning on going through with your dream of being a seamstress, aren't you, Lydia? I guess I didn't realize you were this close to making it happen."

Lydia handed five sketches to Billy. "I've spent hours designing these. I hope they're good enough to sell. My designs are a step up from an everyday dress and good enough for a Sunday go-calling dress. I can't wait to show the ladies and get their opinions. I already have the pattern pieces drafted to size and ready to cut."

Ruth pointed to the collar on the sketch Billy held.

"I love the lace you've added here, Lydia. Lace softens the neckline and adds grace to the dress."

"It looks real nice, Lydia," Billy agreed. "I wish you the best. I'm sure the dress shop ladies will be interested. Once they see your designs, they'll be happy to have you join them."

"I hope so. I know you've wanted this for a long time." Sarah interjected, "Billy would you get a jar of pickled beets and one of pickled beans from the root cellar to have with dinner, please?"

Laying the sketches on the table, Billy left to fetch the canned goods.

Mark followed Billy out the door and asked, "You seem genuinely happy for Lydia about her dresses, but I can tell something's on your mind."

"You're right, Father. I wonder how she'll manage her business this far from town. Wouldn't living closer be helpful? I don't want her to move to town. That's not what I'm saying. But living closer would be better, don't you think?"

"True, living closer would help. I can't take her every time she needs to pick up fabric or drop off dresses, and if she thinks I'm letting her take the wagon to town by herself, she's mistaken. There's still too much bickering about the war. It's not safe for a woman alone on the roads. I'm glad you said you'd take her this time. She's too young and too naive to travel by herself."

Billy quickly asked, "Is there anything you need in town? I'd be glad to pick it up for you."

"Why yes, actually, there is. I'll ask your ma to make a list. I know she needs canning supplies. You might want to get some canning supplies and a few extra crocks for your harvest too."

87

"Good idea. I hadn't thought of that."

"Are you going to shoot in the contest this year since you're going to town?"

"Well, I wasn't gonna. We'll see. I guess if I win, I could give the rifle to Steven or Oat. I thought we could attend the picnic and then stop at Jack and Abby's on the way home. Jack told us when he dropped off the leather goods that they didn't want to take the babies anywhere yet, so they wouldn't be going to the celebration this year."

"Perhaps Grandma would like to go along," Mark suggested. "I know she'd enjoy being with everyone and love the chance to see the twins."

"That's a good idea. We can take Johanna too and give you and Ma some time to yourself. You don't get much of that anymore. Well, Mother will be looking for those vegetables." Billy took off for the root cellar.

Mark called to him, "I'll ask Grandma now so she can pack if she says yes. I'll come out and help with the cattle and horses in a few minutes."

"Thanks, Pa. I'll be right back," Billy called.

Mark proposed the plan. "I know how much you'd like to see the twins, Mother. Do you think you'd be interested in going along?"

Ruth's eyes lit up. "Of course I'll go. I'll pack a bag, and maybe Ja--, maybe Doctor Glasgow and I can meet for supper while we're in Dead Flats." She looked at Lydia and smiled. Lydia winked back.

Putting his arm around Sarah, Mark whispered. "Billy said if Grandma went, Johanna could go too, giving us some time to ourselves. How does that sound, my dear? We won't know what to do with a few days alone."

Sarah grinned. "Don't you worry, I'm sure we'll find something."

Placing the jars on the table, Billy looked around and asked, "Where is everyone?"

"Grandma said she'd love to go, and she and Johanna are packing." Mark chuckled. "Now, let's go get your livestock ready to leave."

After saddling two horses, Mark and Billy grabbed their lassoes and headed for the pastures where the cows and horses were grazing.

"I'll get the horses back to the barn, and you find your cows and pen them in the corral," Mark suggested.

"Can we help?" Steven asked.

"You can take the top three rails off the corral fence and help keep them in while I fetch them all. That would help. I don't want you beyond the corral, though. I'll have the first cow there by the time you walk out and get the rails down." Billy took off at a gallop.

Mark lassoed each horse and tied them in the barn while Billy roped and corralled three of his four cows without a problem. The last one gave him the most trouble. He lost his hat and had to pick it up off the ground, and the cow dodged the noose a couple times. Frustrated, finally Billy outsmarted her. He got off the horse with the lasso in his hand and roped her standing instead, tied her to his saddle horn, and persuaded her to follow his horse to the corral. With the boys' help, it didn't take any time at all. They were all out at the corral when they heard Johanna call, "Time to eat!"

****

Sated with Sarah's cooking, the boys saddled their horses.

"Come on, Billy," Steven called as he mounted

Cloud. "We have to get these cows home."

"I'm coming. Thanks for everything," Billy said as he climbed up onto the wagon seat.

"Have a good time in town, and thanks for getting the supplies," Sarah said as she and Mark linked arms and watched as the cows, horses, and wagon pulled away.

Arriving at Billy's before dark, Lydia pulled together a light supper while the boys got the cows in the corral and showed the farm to Johanna as they did the evening chores.

"Tomorrow the boys and I will ride to the neighbors and ask if they could come do the chores for a few days while we'll be away," Billy said. "It's a good opportunity to introduce Oat. We'll only be gone for a couple of hours."

Chapter Fourteen

After the boys left, Johanna went outside to play, and Lydia asked, "Grandma Hewitt, I wonder if we may talk a while."

"My goodness, dear, this sure is a surprise. How did all of this come about?" Grandma took a sip of tea.

"For me, my feelings began the night I took the bullet out of Billy's shoulder. He was thrashing about and opened his wound, so after a few times of having to hold him down, I crawled onto the bed beside him to quiet his movements. Being next to Billy that way made me feel different." Lydia's face flushed with sudden heat, recalling that night.

"Did he try to force himself on you?" Grandma asked.

"No, of course not!" Lydia said. "Billy wouldn't do that. I've danced and held hands with other boys before, and I've even been kissed a few times. But with Billy, it's different. He is caring and treats me like a lady. He'd never hurt me. I know that. And he said if I change my mind about us, to tell him, and we can always go back to being just brother and sister."

"And do you think you could do that if your relationship doesn't work out, go back to being just friends and brother and sister?" Grandma asked.

"I'd like to think we could. I wouldn't want to hurt him, and I know he'd never want to hurt me. What do you think about us, courting, I mean? I'd like to see what it's like." Lydia twirled a piece of hair around her finger.

"Darling girl, courting isn't something you try on to see if you like it. Courting is a serious commitment. If you question any part of your feelings now, I say it's not a good idea. You need to give this much thought. What about your plans to start your own business? Have you and Billy talked about what this might mean, the adjustments you'd have to make? How will he feel about the time your work would take away from you caring for him and the boys? These are things you have to consider before you commit to courting."

"I mentioned my business plans briefly, but we didn't talk out all the details. It would be difficult with Billy here and me at home." Lydia mused.

"It might not be easy, but you could try. Billy and the boys could come to the farm occasionally, or we could meet halfway for a picnic once in a while." Grandma suggested.

"Do you think Ma and Pa would agree to us courting?"

"I can't say for certain, but I don't see why not. They know what being young and in love was like. But first, you and Billy have to speak with them and get their blessing to proceed. What you two are suggesting would certainly change things." Grandma smiled.

"I've never been in love before. I know Billy was married once, but Elizabeth hurt him terribly. You didn't know Elizabeth, but she always wanted her own way, and Billy usually gave in. The one thing he didn't give into was when she wanted a baby before he left for war. Having a child was all she ever talked about. With all the uncertainty of the war, Billy said he wanted to wait to have a child. I know he's glad he waited." Lydia took a sip of tea.

"I'd never hurt Billy or him me. I have given this a lot of thought," Lydia said. "I'll talk to Billy about my business plans, but I'm sure he'll want me to follow my dream. At least, I hope so. He knows how excited I am about designing and sewing. He's seen firsthand how hard I've worked with Jack on his business. We'll talk things over before I give him my answer about courting. I want Billy, and I want my business too. Oh, that reminds me. I have letters to mail tomorrow to some suppliers."

"Did you say when you'd give him an answer?" Grandma asked as she took Lydia's hand.

"I said I wanted to talk with you first, and I'd let him know. We never have any time alone. Someone is always around, and we can't talk like we need to."

Grandma looked at the family photograph on the side table. "Have the two of you discussed how this will change Steven and Oat's life? They will be affected too, you know."

"We talked about them a little," Lydia admitted. "We know Steven may not understand at first, but we hope he will see how happy we are together and how much he and Oat figure in our plans. Being together will only make our family better."

Grandma nodded. "Well, it does sound like you've given this whole thing some thought. You know, of course, that you and Billy cannot proceed until you've spoken with your mother and father."

"I know, Grandma. We must have their blessing before anything can take place. We thought we'd talk to them together when we return from town." Lydia nodded.

"Sweetheart, I'll pray that things work out the way you and Billy want. Be thoughtful and be patient. If it's meant to be, you'll work things out. As I told Jack and Abby, remember never to go to bed angry or upset. Life is too short. Being upset doesn't do anyone any good anyway. It's the key to a good marriage which your grandpa and I always abided by."

Chapter Fifteen

Arriving in Dead Flats mid-afternoon, Lydia got out at the hardware store with her huge bag of leather goods, Grandma Hewitt walked to visit Doc Glasgow, and Billy, Oat, Steven, and Johanna went on down the street to the dry goods store.

Quinn spotted the Hewitts' wagon come into town. He thought, *this is my chance to get back at Billy Henry, that dog who stole my Elizabeth! And that black boy is with him again. I'll do something about that.* Ducking into the saloon for a shot of courage, he spotted his friend John and a couple other men drinking at the bar.

"John," Quinn said, "how would you like to have some fun and help me with a problem? I'll buy you and your friends a bottle if you help. I want to put the fear of God into a black boy and run him out of town. Billy Henry has gone too far. Blacks have no right living with white folk."

John said, "You're right, Quinn. Scarin' him off should be easy. Come on, men. Get your ropes. I have an idea."

In front of the dry goods store, Billy jumped down from the wagon and said to the youngsters, "I'll only be a few minutes. You three wait here," he disappeared inside the store.

Fidgeting in the hot sun, Steven asked, "Can we get down and look in the window, Oat?"

"I suppose," Oat said, clambering down from the wagon, "as long as we stay right here." Moving toward the storefront, Oat pointed through the window at a straw hat with a wide brim that he announced he'd like to buy someday. The reflection in the glass of a group of men walking determinedly across the street caught his attention. He turned to see what they were up to. Without warning, one of the men grabbed him by the front of his shirt and dropped a rope around his chest, pinning his arms to his sides. Next, he tied Oat's hands behind his back and handed the rope to one of his companions. The other men laughed as Oat kicked and twisted his body every which way to free himself. Oat's terror was real. He had seen scenes like this too often when he lived in the south. He knew he was in danger, and he was scared.

Unexpectedly, a hard yank on the rope made Oat's chest feel like collapsing. As he struggled to take a breath, a rag was shoved in his mouth. He stumbled but managed to stay on his feet.

Steven jumped on the back of the ruffian holding the rope and yelled, "Let go! Let go of my brother!"

The man shook Steven off like a cat playing with a mouse. He flew into a barrel of brooms and axe handles, leaving him a crumpled form on the boardwalk.

A third man put a sack over Oat's head. The flat blade of a knife pressed against his ribs. "Keep on your feet, or we'll drag you," a fourth man said, his breath hot on the base of Oat's neck.

Johanna started to cry and then screamed.

Traces of flour in the sack made breathing difficult for Oat. He struggled to keep his footing as the men half-dragged, half-forced him down the street. Tripping, he went down on one knee, and the rope cut in tighter. *I have to do what they say. Billy, where's Billy? Why isn't anyone helping me? Where are they taking me?* Finally, everyone stopped. The men were still laughing as they pulled the sack off his head. Blinking in the sudden sunlight, Oat realized he was standing among headstones in the church cemetery, his kidnappers surrounding him.

The man holding the rope looked around. "We're in luck. There's nobody here." Throwing the rope over a low-lying limb, the man said, "Let's get on with this." He kicked the back of the boy's legs, forcing him to land hard on his knees.

Oat struggled, knowing with certainty what was about to happen next. His heart pounded, his chest tightened, and each breath seemed a gift from God. *I don't want to die. I don't want to die!*

****

Billy was reaching for a case of canning jars when a scream from outside got his attention. *That sounds like Johanna!* He charged down the aisle and out the door to see a dazed and confused Steven holding his ribs. Billy helped him to his feet asking, "Are you all right? I have to help Johanna. Where is Oat? What happened?"

"I'm all right," Steven whispered.

Johanna whimpered as she lay on the ground bleeding from a cut near her eye.

Billy lifted her up from the dirt. She was limp as a ragdoll.

"Help! I need help!" Billy called.

The store clerk ran to his side.

Billy handed Johanna to the clerk and said, "Hurry, get her to Doc Glasgow."

"Where's Oat?" Billy yelled.

A man standing across the street where people stood

whispering called out, "There were four men. They tied up the black boy and ducked down the side street, probably headed toward the church, I'd guess. There's a big tree there."

"Steven, fetch Sheriff Sloan. I'm going after them."

Billy grabbed his rifle from the wagon and raced toward the church, rounding the corner in time to see the rope being thrown over the limb. He fired a shot into the ground close to the men's feet. Three men swung around. Billy shouted, "You cut that boy down right now, or my next shot won't be so considerate! Nobody's hanging today unless it's you!"

Seeing only the lone figure of Billy, one man shouted, "Go on, and get out of here."

"Yeah, mind your own business," another taunted.

"This *is* my business! That's my brother you're fixing to hang," Billy called out spitting mad.

"Your brother, hardly. This one ain't got no rights. He should stay with his own," another retorted.

"Yeah, he belongs with his own kind. If he don't know his place, we'll show him," one said, threatening to pull the rope.

"If you think I'm going to let you hang my brother, you're wrong. Dead wrong! Now get that gag out of his mouth." Billy moved a few steps closer, pointing his rifle at the man closest to Oat.

"We wasn't going to hang him, Mister," the bully said, suddenly subdued as he pulled the gag from Oat's mouth. "Just scare'm and run'm out of town," added a voice in the back, obviously trying to hide his face.

At that moment, Sheriff Sloan strode up, shotgun in hand. "What's happening here, John?" he said, addressing one of the men.

"We're having a little fun, is all, sheriff," John replied.

"Which one of you hurt my little sister?" Billy gripped his rifle tightly to control his anger. "She's at Doc's right now. You call that having fun? You all belong in jail for hurting a little girl and an attempted hanging."

"Take that rope off the boy, John," the sheriff demanded.

John complied.

Free of the rope, Oat moved to Billy's side, breathing in ragged gulps.

Billy slipped his arm around the young boy's shoulder. "Are you all right, Oat?"

Oat nodded, still unable to speak.

"So help me, I'll see that you pay for what you've done!" Billy said. "And if I ever hear anything like this happens to any person whose skin isn't white, you'll be the first I'll come looking for. Wait a minute. The man at the store who saw what happened said there were four men that took Oat. Someone is missing, sheriff."

"Don't worry," Sheriff Sloan said. "I'll get this sorted out. You men are under arrest. Get along."

The men protested.

Raising his shotgun, Sloan said, "Don't make me use this."

Sloan herded the trio out of the cemetery and down Main Street toward the jail. People stopped to gawk. Protesting, one of the men finally spoke up, "But we weren't the ones who backhanded the little girl when she started to cry."

"Will you testify to that?" Sheriff Sloan asked.

"Sure, we'll all say that's what happened," a second

man said. "We was only to shake up the boy, and run him out of town so he'd never come back. That's what he told us to do."

Corralling the men into his office, Sloan said, "Who told you what to do, and how did this start? Who is this 'he?'"

John said, "Quinn Harris came into the saloon, sheriff, and started talking against blacks. Said he saw Billy Henry with a black boy. Got us all riled up. He was with us when we jumped the boy and must have slipped away once we got to the cemetery."

"In those cells, all of you, now!" Sloan ordered. "You're staying until I find Quinn. We'll sort this out when I bring him in."

****

Still in the cemetery, Billy grabbed his brother and gave him a hug. "Are you sure you're all right, Oat?"

Trembling, Oat said, "I think I'm good, jist a little sore. But I was scared they was gonna hang me. I saw a hangin' once. White men were laughin' and shoutin', jist like them men. Thank God you got here. They was gonna kill me 'cause I'm black. Jist 'cause my skin is different. I never done nothin' to them. Thanks for sticking up for me, calling me brother. That means a lot." Oat grabbed his shoulder where one of the men had punched him. "We best go check on Johanna. I heard her scream. Is Steven all right?"

"Yeah, Steven's okay. We brothers stick together. So help me...whoever hurt you and Johanna, I'll make them pay." Billy put the rifle over his shoulder and his arm around Oat as they headed to the Doctor's office. "If anything happened to Johanna, Mother will never forgive me. I'm gonna have Doc check you out too. I'm sorry for what those men did. You'd think with the War over, people would accept each other. The color of your skin shouldn't matter now or fifty years from now."

When Oat and Billy walked through the door at Doc's office, Lydia was there as well. Steven hurried to Oat's side and gave him a bear hug.

"I'm glad you're all right. I was worried sick they were gonna hurt you," Steven said. "Grandma's in with Doc and Johanna. Doc said something about stitches."

Billy began pacing the floor, stopped abruptly, and whispered to Lydia, "I'll make them pay for what they did. I'm going to the Sheriff's office right now."

Lydia clung to Billy. "No, don't go until we see how Johanna is doing. Stay with us. I don't want any more trouble. There'll be time to talk to Sheriff Sloan later."

Billy took a deep breath and exhaled. "All right. I'll wait."

Minutes later, Grandma Hewitt came out to tell them, "Johanna will be fine. Doc put in three stitches to close her deep cut. He gave her medicine to calm her. We should get her to Jack and Abby's tonight and let her rest. You can come back to town tomorrow and finish your business."

"I'll go get the wagon and pick up the supplies I gathered. Grandma, would you ask Doc to check on Oat? He mentioned his shoulder was sore." Billy walked to the dry goods store, thanked the clerk for fetching his sister to the doctor, and paid for the supplies.

Grandma Hewitt helped Oat out of his shirt. He was bruised and sore, but Doc Glasgow determined there were no broken bones.

Rubbing liniment on Oat's chest, Doc said, "You've got a few bruises, young man. You'll be sore and will need a few days to rest and heal."

"Thanks for everything," Billy said and shook Doc's hand. "What do I owe you for all you did for us?"

"Nothing, Billy. Glad to help." Doc patted him on the shoulder.

"Thanks, and would you tell Sheriff Sloan I'll be back tomorrow morning, and I expect to see those responsible behind bars for what they did."

"I'll tell him for you, Billy. And Ruth is right. Johanna was more frightened than anything. Her cut will heal, but she will have a scar by her eye. Looks like a ring might have caused the cut."

****

Grandma held Johanna on her lap for the ride to Jack's place. "There, there, sweetheart. You're safe. I know your stitches hurt. Rest now. You'll forget all about the hurting. I'm so sorry this happened. Everyone feels terrible you had to go through all this. You were such a brave girl at the doctor's office. Your pa had to get stitches once. As I recall, he got into a fight, and a doctor had to stitch him up, too. You rest, dear. We'll be to Jack's soon."

"How much further?" Johanna called out to Billy.

"Not long, Johanna. Why don't you try to close your eyes and think about getting home tomorrow and playing with Momma Kitty, Muzzy, and the chickens? I bet the cats miss you."

Grandma held Johanna close, and she closed her eyes while Billy talked to Oat.

"I hope you know how sorry I am that all this happened to you, Oat. I never thought leaving you children alone while I went in for supplies would turn out this way. I'll never leave you alone again. I want you to feel safe with our family. And don't worry about those men trying anything like that again. They're in jail right now for what they did to you. Pa and I will see to it that they are punished. I assure you it'll never happen again." Billy put his arm around Oat's shoulder.

"It weren't your fault. I don't blame you. I's a slave, and now I ain't. Those men don't like me bein' free." Oat stared down at the ground.

Billy placed his hand under Oat's chin and raised his head until it met his gaze. "You're more than free. You're your own person now, and my brother. And brothers stick together, don't we, Steven."

"Yup, we sure do," Steven said, smiling at Oat. "We sure do."

Chapter Sixteen

Horse's hooves pounding the dry ground gave Jack warning of someone coming. He grabbed his gun and dashed outside to see a wagon with Billy, Oat, and Steven on the seat. He ran to meet them.

Billy called out, "You won't need that rifle, but you'll need to help Lydia and Grandma with Johanna. She's in the back. It's a long story." The horses came to a stop, nostrils flaring from the fast-paced trip.

Lydia handed Johanna to Jack, and he carried her into the house while the rest of the family followed.

After recounting what happened in town and reassuring Oat and Johanna that nothing like this would ever happen again, Jack helped Billy care for the horses and do the evening chores.

In the barn, Jack asked, "What are you going to do about those men?"

"I'm thinking about talking to a lawyer to see legally what I can do about their assaults on Johanna and Oat. They pushed Steven out of the way, but he wasn't hurt, only frightened. Three men are behind bars right now. I'd like to keep them there." Billy grabbed the pitchfork and stabbed at the hay as he cleaned the milk cow's stall.

"Do you want Oat to have to relive the scene in court? He's been through a lot. I'm not sure what Ma and Pa would say. Did Grandma and Lydia give you their thoughts?" Jack questioned.

"They agree the men should have consequences. They just don't agree with my idea of taking them to court for what they did," Billy said.

Jack grabbed the pail of milk. "It sounds like you want to get even with them."

"I don't want them to get off easy." Billy hung up the pitchfork. "You weren't there. I'll never forget the look on Oat's face. He was terrified. And hearing Johanna crying while Doc stitched her up was hard. No, they should pay for what they did, all four of them."

****

Early the next morning, Billy and Lydia drove back into town. They rode in silence as Billy contemplated what to do about Oat, and Johanna and Lydia rehearsed her presentation to give the dress shop owners in her mind.

After dropping Lydia at the dress shop to finally talk to the owners, Billy headed to the jail to see if Sheriff Sloan had caught the fourth man. Walking into the office, Billy spotted four men lying on cots behind bars and then took a closer look.

"Was Quinn Harris the fourth man? What rock was he hiding under, sheriff?" Billy said, referring to Quinn in the cell. He slammed his fist on the desk and asked, "Did he admit he was part of the whole thing yesterday? He must have, or he wouldn't be behind bars."

"Maybe you should let Quinn explain and ease up a little, Billy," Sloan said.

"No, sheriff. You don't know Quinn like I do. He's a piece of dirt," Billy said looking at Quinn with disgust. Noticing the large ring on Quinn's left hand, Billy said, "You hit my sister. I know you did it. She had to get her face stitched up because of you." Billy grabbed the bars of the cell and stared Quinn down. "And you had your thugs scare an innocent boy half to death, threatening to hang him."

Quinn jumped to his feet. "Believe me or not, all I said to them was to scare him and run him out of town. They're the ones that took the threat too far."

"Yes, and you were nowhere around when I and Sheriff Sloan arrived."

Sloan interrupted, "The other men said they'd testify that Quinn was the one who started the whole thing."

"We'll testify. We'll all testify. Quinn planned everything from the beginning," John said.

"Yeah, it wasn't our fault he hit your sister," another man added.

"That wasn't my intent," Quinn insisted. "They were only supposed to throw a scare into the boy."

"Intent or not, you're the one who must have gotten them all riled up. What'd you do, buy them drinks at the saloon? What I want to know is why?" Billy shook with anger.

"You know why," Quinn retorted venomously. "You took Elizabeth away from me by marrying her. If I had been here, she'd never have married you. I wanted to take something away from you the same way you took Elizabeth away from me."

"I didn't take Elizabeth from you, Quinn. She decided on her own to marry me. Then, while I was away at war, she had second thoughts and turned back to you. I found out when I came back that she was planning on leaving me. She confessed with her dying words that she had been with you and had planned on leaving me. I guess she wanted whoever was around at the time. It looks like we both shared the same experience."

Quinn took a deep breath. "I admit I wanted you to know Elizabeth was with me. I never hid my affection for her from you or anyone else. I believed she loved me."

"I believed she loved me too. I've let go of her, and so should you. She's gone. Maybe she did love us both, but I finally figured there was no sense living in the past and moved on."

"I shouldn't have started anything," Quinn admitted. "I promise if you let me out, I'll stay clear of you and your family. You said your little sister had to get stitches. Will she be all right?"

Billy stepped forward. "Doc says she'll have a scar she'll have to live with the rest of her life because of you."

Quinn hung his head. "I didn't mean to hurt her. Really, I didn't. But when she screamed, I panicked. I'm sorry. I'm sorry for everything. I hope the black boy is all right too."

"The black boy's name is Otis. He has a lot of bruises and was really shaken, but he's tough."

"All I can say is I'm sorry," Quinn extended his hand through the bars. "And I'll respect your family from now on. What do you say?"

Billy turned his back to Quinn and addressed Sheriff Sloan. "I'm going to talk to a lawyer and see how strong a case we have for pressing charges."

Billy turned quick and grabbed the bars. Staring Quinn in the face, he said, "I want you to pay for what you've done. All of you. I want you to pay. You need to stay away from my family and never come near us again."

Quinn took a step back. "I won't bother your family

again. I won't. I promise. There's no need to press charges, Billy."

Billy turned to the sheriff and said, "Can you hold them here until I can get home and bring my father back with me? When is the traveling judge in the area?"

"You have a week before the judge arrives," Sloan said.

"I'll be back before then. You boys enjoy your stay in jail," Billy said sarcastically and walked out.

One of the other three men shouted, "Come on, we didn't do nothing. This was all Quinn's idea. I have a family."

Billy went from the sheriff's office to see Mr. Brooks, Town Prosecutor. Sitting in the lawyer's office, he explained the circumstances. "I want to spare Otis from having to relive everything if possible."

"Tell your folks we have options," Brooks said. "But regardless of what we do, there's no way to keep Otis from having to tell his side of the story to the judge. He'd have to give a detailed description of what happened, and even then, there'd be no guarantees. If the case does go to trial, a jury of twelve white men will be listening to a black teenager, and they may not convict the perpetrators because Otis is black. Quinn knew what he did when he slipped away after the hardware store. We have some options with Quinn causing injury to your little sister, but I'd like to discuss them with you and your father."

Billy shook his head. "Sheriff Sloan said the judge won't be here for a week. Can you keep them locked up until I have a chance to bring my Pa to town? I know Doc Glasgow will testify to the injuries Johanna and Oat received if you need evidence of wrongdoing."

"Yes, under the circumstances, we can have them held until your Pa can get here and we talk things over," said Lawyer Brooks. "I'll talk to the sheriff, and while I'm there, maybe one of the other three men will say something to give me a better idea of how to approach all of this."

"Thank you for your assistance," Billy said. "My real father was a lawyer in Kansas City. I spent a good many hours in his office helping…filing paperwork. I know your work isn't easy, and you spend long hours preparing for court. Thank you for listening to me."

"You're welcome, Billy. When do you think you and your father can get back to town?" Mr. Brooks asked.

"We'll be back in three or four days." Billy shook the lawyer's hand and headed to the postal office.

****

At the dress shop, Lydia laid out her five pencil-sketched dress designs for the ladies and one of the designs she had sewn up to show them her sewing skills on her new machine.

"They look lovely, dear," the oldest woman, Violet, said. "I like the square neckline and lace you added to the sleeves on this one, and the round shoulders and the belt you added are all the style in the magazines." She raised an eyebrow. "What do you plan on doing with them?"

"All I need is the fabric, and I'm ready to sew my patterns into ready-to-wear dresses from my own designs. I'd hoped you'd let me sell the dresses on consignment of course, through your shop." There, her proposal was made. She exhaled with a sigh of relief.

"What do you think? I will make them in three

different sizes, and women could come in and buy them off the rack. They wouldn't be custom-made like your dresses, but if they needed a tuck here or there, if the woman sews, she should be able to make adjustments. Or you could offer to alter them with little effort. They wouldn't be custom, so they wouldn't compete with your dresses. I think I've located a fabric supplier that I can buy material direct from, so our fabrics wouldn't be in competition either."

"Well, different fabrics would be good," Violet commented.

"By October, I should have the first dresses ready for sale. I've been practicing since last fall, and I'm very good with my machine now. My mother will help cut out the patterns, and I will sew them together."

"I like your designs," Josephine admitted. "I'm not sure I agree with your theory that we wouldn't be in competition. Every dress they buy off the rack is one fewer we may not be asked to make."

Lydia started to perspire and asked, "Do you have time to sew ready-to-wear dresses? Have you even considered ready-to-wear before?"

"Well, we do have some slow times, but that's when we restock and order for the next season." Violet picked up one of the designs and asked. "What made you want to get into the dress designing business in the first place?"

"When you first opened, I was in your store looking around. I heard the sewing machine running in the back and you, Violet, let me try it. You showed me how to pump the pedal, and let me sew a little bag. The bag sits on my bureau as a daily reminder of my goals. Ever since that day, I began designing dresses with the intent of becoming a seamstress and starting my own dress business."

Violet nodded. "I do remember a young girl coming in all wide-eyed and fascinated with the machine. We had just opened and were doing all kinds of sewing to get started."

"Yes, I watched you take in the legs on a pair of trousers. I was amazed at how quick that task was completed and with such strong, neat stitching. What would have taken me a half-hour to hand sew was done in moments." Lydia smiled to think Violet remembered her.

"We know we need to expand. We aren't sure into what yet." Let us think about your off-the-rack dresses idea and check back next month. We'll have an answer for you then." Violet stood and gathered the sketches from the table. "I do like your designs, dear. I can tell you have put a lot of thought and time into them. Josephine and I will think over your offer."

"You are the first to hear my proposal. The thought of opening my own storefront even crossed my mind. I plan to order my fabric by the end of this month, so I would appreciate a decision then. We can talk terms at that time if you're interested." Taking her designs, Lydia said, "Good day."

Lydia was barely out the door when her legs wobbled as she walked to the bank with a deposit from the sale of Jack's leather goods. Had she been too direct, too demanding, too unwavering in wanting an answer by the end of the month? *The ladies did say they liked my designs and admitted they needed to change to keep up with the growing town.*

Lydia turned her thoughts to Billy and wondered

what happened at the sheriff's office. As she stepped out of the bank, Billy came out of the postal office. "Billy, Billy Henry, wait up," Lydia called.

She crossed the street to join him. "Did you mail my letters? Any mail for me?"

Billy cocked his head. "Yes, I posted your letters, and you got this letter from New York City. Do you know someone in New York?" He handed her the large bulky envelope.

"A textile company. I hope it's good news." Lydia folded and tucked the envelope under her arm. "Now, tell me. What happened with those men at the jail?"

"Not now. I'm still fuming mad, but I will say I talked to a lawyer. I'll tell you everything when we get back to Jack's." Rubbing his belly, he said, "I'm hungry. Are you?"

"Yes, I'm starving. Let's eat at the café and then pick up the rest of the supplies."

****

At the café, Lydia told Billy about her business plans and recalled the details of her meeting with the dress shop ladies. "I'll be doing a lot of sewing, and I'm not sure how much time I'll get to spend with you until my business is up and going. I hope you understand."

Billy nodded.

"Grandma and I talked when you and the boys visited the neighbors the other day. I told her I love you." Lydia took his hand. "She was supportive of us courting. I've given us a lot of thought, Billy. I'm not going to have the time to spend with you that I'd like, especially in the beginning."

"I can deal with everything as long as you're sure you love me. I was afraid you'd see your business plans as an obstacle we couldn't handle." Billy said.

"Don't tease me," Lydia said. "We can handle anything together. Let's not wait to talk to Mother and Father. Let's tell them our plans as soon as we get back. That way, when we do get to spend time together, we can be open about everything." Looking around to make sure nobody was watching, she gave Billy a quick kiss on his cheek and squeezed his hand.

"Good idea. We said we'd take things slow." Billy gazed into her eyes. "This will work. As long as we are always honest with each other, Lydia, we'll be all right."

Chapter Seventeen

Returning to Jack's place, Lydia's first concern was checking on Johanna and Oat to make sure they were all right. Abby was reading to them. The children were fine, so she whisked Grandma off to talk in private while the men unhitched the team and tended to the horses. "Billy and I talked everything over, and even though a lot of my time will be taken by starting my business, we've decided to start our courtship. We'll ask Ma and Pa for their blessing and let them know our plans."

That's wonderful, dear." Grandma Hewitt grinned.

Lydia nodded. "We'll talk to them right after we tell them about the ordeal that happened in town."

"And what did the ladies at the dress shop say? Are they interested?" Grandma asked.

"They liked my designs and are considering my offer. They'll have an answer for me by the end of the month," Lydia replied.

When Jack and Billy came into the house, Lydia said, "Now, Billy, tell us what happened with those men who hurt Johanna and Oat.

"Were they at the sheriff's office?" Grandma asked, anxious to hear what Billy had to say.

"Did the sheriff find the fourth man?" Jack asked.

Billy let out a long sigh. "Yes, the sheriff found him, and you'll never guess who it was."

"Come on, tell us. Don't make us guess," Lydia said

impatiently.

"Turns out, Quinn Harris was the fourth man. He set the whole thing up and got the men to go along with his plan to frighten Oat. He claims he only intended to scare Oat and run him out of town. He said he wanted to take something from me like he thought I had taken Elizabeth from him. I wanted to reach through the bars and shake some sense into him." Grandma and Lydia listened intently.

"Long story short, I decided to talk to a lawyer. The sheriff can hold them in jail until Pa, and I talk to the lawyer and decide what to do next. Like me, Pa will be spitting mad about the attack on the children. We must deal with this straight on. It's a matter of Oat's right to live as free as any white boy. The color of his skin shouldn't matter, although the lawyer said convincing a jury of white men to take a black boy's side in court won't be easy."

****

"What happened? What happened to my baby?" Sarah asked, seeing the bandages on Johanna's face once the wagon pulled into the yard of the Hewitt farm.

"I'm fine, Ma. My stitches only hurts a little now, and Doc told me not to touch them," Johanna said.

And Oat, you have bruises on your face. What happened?" Sarah demanded.

"It's nothin'. Don't worry 'bout me, Ma. I'm good," Oat said and looked away.

Billy sent the children out to play and to Mark and Sarah's horror gave a lengthy report of everything that had occurred in town.

Mark said, "Billy, I'm proud of the way you handled the situation with the children. It sounds like we have two separate but related cases. One is Quinn hitting Johanna. The other is Quinn inciting a riot to scare Oat and run him out of town. Certainly, that could have gone too far if you hadn't shown up. Thank goodness you did. We need to get to town. Oat can stay and help here, and Lydia and Steven can go to your farm until we get back. These are my children. Those men must be held responsible for their actions."

Grandma said, "I think we should also consider extending mercy if they repent." She quoted Luke 17:3. "'If your brother or sister sins against you, rebuke them; and if they repent, forgive them.' You don't want to upset Oat again. I know he was shaken by this event. I'd like to see the men pay for their actions, but more so to teach them a lesson. I know I'm an old woman, and you'll take my words with a grain of salt, but there have been things that I've done in the past that I regret now. Think everything through before you make your final decision."

"We will, I promise," Mark said, as Billy nodded his head in agreement.

"Your father's right. I think those men should be punished, but I also agree with Grandma." Sarah said. "Don't be hasty in your decision making."

****

Waiting for a more relaxed moment after the furor about the incident in town died down, Lydia shared her news about speaking with the owners of the dress shop. Sarah and Grandma were particularly interested. Sarah spoke up, "Lydia, dear, you showed strength and determination. I'm proud of you for letting the ladies know your plans. Now it's up to them whether they want you to join their business or not.

Billy gazed at Lydia, smiled, and said, "We have something else we want to talk to you about too."

Lydia looked at Grandma Hewitt, who understood what to do next.

Grandma stood and made a sweeping motion with her hands. "Come on, children. Let's go outside and find something to do. I'm sure the garden needs weeding, and after that, we can go to the swimming hole to wash up."

"Me, too? Johanna asked.

"Yes, you too, dear, but you won't be able to get your face wet.

Once everyone was out of the house, Sarah and Mark looked at the couple expectantly. Billy said, "I've thought about the best way to say this but didn't come up with a speech like I thought I should. I know it's customary to ask the father for permission first, but since Lydia and I grew up together, and you're our parents, I'm just going to ask. Lydia and I would like to be much more than sister and brother to each other. We are asking your blessing to start courting. Lydia and I love each other."

"Before you say anything," Lydia added. "I want to add that we realize we won't have a lot of time to spend together with me starting my business and all, but we wanted to get your blessing so that when we are together, we can enjoy our time courting. We also considered how Steven and Oat might feel when we explain everything to them. We believe they will be happy for us. Yes, our courtship will change our family, but it will be for the best. I really do love Billy."

There was silence for a few moments before Sarah finally said, "I must admit. I didn't see this coming. Are you sure this is what you both want?"

"Oh, yes, Mother, Billy and I have always had a

special connection. And we discovered that connection is true love. He's the man I want to spend the rest of my life with."

"I remember when you came to live with us," Mark recalled. "You've grown into a fine young man. And Lydia, you know I'm proud of you always. I want you both to live your lives fully. If that means you are sure about loving each other and being together, that's what you should do. I'm happy for both of you."

"Thanks, Pa. You changed my life when you brought me here to join the family. I know I've made some mistakes in my life, but loving Lydia isn't one of them."

Mark was quiet for a few moments, deep in thought. "Have you considered how your being together will look to others? What people might say? I wouldn't let the opinions of others change your decision, but some may not be so kind."

"We know some townspeople will turn up their noses because we were raised as brother and sister. But I've never let those people bother me before, and I'm not going to start now." Billy said, sure of his intention.

"They won't bother me either," Lydia boasted. "Let them think what they will. Billy and I love one another, and we want to be together. And hopefully have a family of our own."

"Then we have both your blessings?" Billy asked.

"You have mine," Sarah said.

"Mine too," Mark added, with a big grin on his face.

Hugs were exchanged. Billy and Lydia were relieved their announcement was so well met. "I'm so happy. I can't wait to tell the rest of the family," Lydia said as she drew her hand across her cheeks to brush away tears. Sarah's eyes glistened as well, and the two women, mother, and daughter, embraced one another.

Kissing Lydia on her forehead, Sarah said, "I take it Grandma already knows of your plans?"

"Yes, we confided in her first," Lydia smiled. "We figured if she was fine with us courting, we might have a better chance putting our case before you and Pa."

"I should have known my mother would have taken your side," Mark said, smiling. "She's so good-hearted. Remember the letter she sent when we told her about us, Sarah? She couldn't have been prouder. She knew you made me happy and that your family was my family. I know you will treat Lydia with honor and respect, Billy. That is the one thing I am going to demand."

"Yes, of course, Pa," Billy agreed.

Lydia said, "I wouldn't have it any other way."

Sarah gave her daughter another hug. "Well, then, we're all in agreement. You may begin your courtship."

Billy put his arm around Lydia and drew her close. "Pa, we better go help Grandma. When she said wash up at the swimming hole, Steven probably talked her into going swimming, if I know him."

"Good idea. You two go help with the children," Sarah said, shooing them toward the door. "Lydia and I will start dinner."

Lydia hugged her mother, and Sarah whispered. "I can see from the glow on your face that you're in love. It won't be easy with the distance and your work, but you'll do fine."

"I know, Ma. I really do love him. Billy and I enjoy doing things together and being together so much. I like doing special things for him, and he is always surprising me with what he knows and can do. I know we're good for one another and that we'll do a good job raising Steven and Oat together. They'll still be my brothers. Hopefully, Billy and I will have our own children someday. I wish we could get married right away."

"Don't get ahead of yourself, sweetheart," Sarah said, getting plates out of the cupboard to set the table. "You're a beautiful young woman, and there will be time for marriage and children. Right now, though, your business should come first. Being successful will mean income for your family, so it's worth waiting while you focus on your plans. Grandma and I will help whenever we can. You have a promising future ahead of you. Billy will wait. I saw in both your eyes the love and compassion you hold for each other. When will you tell the children your plans?"

Lydia sighed, "Not until Pa and Billy get back from town and figure out what they're doing about Johanna and Oat's ordeal. Oat can stay here and help with the chores, and Steven and I will go to Billy's. Don't worry. I can handle a gun, and we'll be fine. I'm sure the men won't be gone long. Steven and I can handle the chores."

Chapter Eighteen

The following morning, shortly after Mark, Billy, Lydia, and Steven left for Billy's farm, Seth Frazer rode in. "Hurry, Sarah, grab a bag. We have to get back. Emily is having pains and said to fetch you right away."

"Oat, please saddle a horse for me," Sarah instructed. "It will be up to you and Grandma to keep everything under control here. I'll take Johanna with me. Now hurry."

"Sit and rest a minute, Seth," Ruth said as Seth paced the floor. "Sarah will hurry, but you have time for a glass of cool tea. Did you pick out names yet?"

Collapsing gratefully into a chair, Seth replied, "Emily is hoping for a girl. She wants to name her Laura after her grandma on her mother's side. I'm secretly hoping for a boy, but not a word of this to Emily. I'll be happy with either as long as it's healthy and Emily is all right," Seth confessed.

"We're almost ready," Sarah said, rushing out of the bedroom and up the ladder to gather clothes for Johanna.

Oat yelled in the door, "The horse is saddled."

"Johanna can ride with me," Seth offered.

Sarah looked around and said, "Yes, as soon as we find her. Has anyone seen Johanna?"

"I think she's with the chickens. I'll fetch her," Oat said and sped off.

Sarah tied her bag on the horse and swung herself

into the saddle. Oat returned and quickly lifted Johanna up to Seth.

"Oh boy, Mrs. Frazer is having her baby, and I get to go," Johanna chirped from her saddle perch.

"Yes, and we're going to move fast, so you hold on to the saddle horn," Seth said as he put his arm around the little girl's waist. "Don't worry, Sarah. I'll hold on to Johanna the whole time."

Grandma stepped onto the porch to wave them off.

"Please take good care of Grandma, Oat," Sarah called.

"Don't worry, Ma. I's a good shot. Billy taught me." Oat grinned.

****

Emily Frazer laid in bed, glistening with sweat and exhausted. At the sound of the door opening and Seth's voice calling her name, she replied, "Oh, Seth, is Sarah with you?"

"I'm right here, Emily." Sarah moved swiftly to Emily's side. "Seth, please take the children outside, put some water on to boil, and then you can go out too. I'll call you when the baby is here." Turning her attention to Emily, she wiped her friend's face with a towel and assured, "Don't worry, Emily. We'll get you through this, and you'll be holding your son or daughter soon. How close together are the pains?"

"They come about every two or three minutes. I prayed you'd come soon, and God answered my prayers. I haven't pushed yet, but I want to," Emily answered, a contraction stealing her breath.

Looking into her friend's eyes, Sarah explained, "I'm an old hand at this, you know. Turn your body so you're lying across the width of the bed and put your feet so your toes are on the edge of the mattress."

"Try to relax, Emily. I'll be right back." In the kitchen, Sarah scrubbed her hands and brought a chair from the table to place by the bed at Emily's feet.

After supporting Emily's back with pillows, Sarah sat in the chair and said, "Now, let's see how you're doing."

Emily cried out. "I have to push. This baby wants to come out."

"Go ahead. Push and remember to breathe," Sarah reminded her.

Another contraction engulfed Emily's body. "Grab the blanket and push. I can see the head already. Thank God it's not breech."

"Yes, and thank God you're here," Emily panted.

"Take a breath and push as hard as you can. Bear down. Push. Take another breath and push again. The head is out. You can do this, Emily. Focus. Breathe, and one more long push. You're doing fine. The shoulders are out. Breathe. Come on, stay with me and push…"

As the baby slid into Sarah's capable hands, she said, "You did it, Emily." Holding the newborn, Sarah assured her friend, "Your daughter is perfect."

Sarah cleared the baby's airway, held the tiny form face down as she had seen Doc Glasgow do with Abby's babies, and rubbed the little one's back. A tiny gasp for breath followed by the sweetest cry a mother wants to hear filled the room. After swaddling the infant, Sarah handed Emily her daughter and made the two of them comfortable before announcing to Seth, "Come meet the newest addition to your family."

****

After a night of deep discussion at Billy's place

about what to do about Johanna and Oat, Billy and Mark rode into town and went directly to the prosecuting lawyer's office.

"Good to meet you, Mr. Brooks," Mark said, offering a firm handshake. I hope you can tell us what our options are with this unfortunate situation. My family is of the mind these men should be punished for their actions."

Mark and Billy sat down in the high-backed chairs placed near the lawyer's large walnut desk and bookshelf.

"I see you didn't bring Otis with you," Brooks said. "If you want restitution from all four men for their involvement in the assaults against him and your daughter, the judge is going to want to talk to the young man. I already spoke to Doc Glasgow, and he'll testify to the fact that your daughter needed several stitches to close the wound on her face. He also said she was traumatized by the event, as was Otis, who also had cuts and bruises. How are they both doing?"

Mark straightened in his chair and said, "Johanna is doing much better now. She's young and says the injury doesn't hurt anymore. Otis, on the other hand, is nervous about coming to town ever again. He doesn't talk about the ordeal, but the attempted lynching shook him up. He has nightmares that jolt him out of sleep, but it helps him to know his family loves and supports him, and we'll never let anyone harm him again."

"Well, like I told Billy, with the strong feelings on both sides around here about abolition and slavery, there's not much chance a white jury is going to accuse four white men of wrongful doings to a black boy, even with the boy's testimony. I'm sorry to say the odds are not in your favor. Although Judge Bennett is sympathetic to Blacks, I don't see him taking this to trial. The best we could do is ask for restitution for Otis and Johanna."

"Restitution would be a good start, but what about an apology? Even better, a public apology?" Mark asked.

"Well, it's never been done in this town before. We can try and ask the judge if he'd make an apology a condition for their release. I don't know if he'll go for it or not," Mr. Brooks offered.

Brooks added. "Maybe I could convince Quinn and the others to make a deal with you instead of taking them in front of the judge. I told them all to get a lawyer. Quinn is the only one who can afford to pay someone. The others said they'd talk to Mr. Martin, who works at the telegraph office for advice. He knows a little law."

"You're right," Billy said. "If Quinn's remorseful, it might work better if we deal with him ourselves."

Mr. Brooks leaned back in his chair and said, "I doubt he's going to want the public to hear he struck and caused permanent injury to a little girl. Yes, I believe Quinn might want to keep this private. What do you feel a fair amount would be for keeping this between you and him? If that's the way you want to handle this, of course. If he's unwilling to negotiate, we can always take him before the judge."

"What do you think, Billy?" Mark asked.

"I'd like to see him pay with more than money, but that's because of other dealings between us. If he's willing to pay instead of going in front of the judge, make it enough money to benefit Johanna. She'll have that scar and those memories for the rest of her life." Billy turned in his chair toward Mark. "I'd ask for one hundred dollars. He has money. He can afford it. And if he wants to keep his good name in town, that's a small price to pay."

"I agree. Can you talk to Quinn for us, Mr. Brooks?" Mark asked.

Brooks nodded. "I can. And what if the other men want to make deals too? I can't guarantee they will, but I want an answer for them if they do. They might be willing to pay something to Otis as well if you don't take this to court. Keep in mind they don't have the money Quinn does. And whatever you ask, Quin would have to pay in addition to the hundred dollars to Johanna."

Billy stated, "What about twenty-five dollars each? If need be they can pay the sheriff over time, say three months. And I insist on a written apology to Oat from each of them. That seems fair to me. Or they take their chance with Judge Bennett."

"And let them know if they don't hold up their end of the deal, the letters of apology will go public," Mark added.

"If that's what you think is appropriate, I'll make them the offer." Brooks picked up his pen.

"If Billy thinks that's fair, I'll go along with it," Mark said.

Mr. Brooks read the agreed-upon conditions to the men from the document he drafted. "Did I miss anything?" he asked.

"No," Mark and Billy said in unison. Then Mark added, "Don't come down from a hundred dollars for Quinn hitting my daughter. That's the offer. He either takes it, or we talk to the judge."

Mr. Brooks folded the document and tucked the paper into his pocket. "I'll confer with them right now and have each sign this paper if they agree. Should we give Quinn three months to pay, too?"

"Sure. That's more than fair," Mark said.

"I'll meet you back here in a half-hour or so. It shouldn't take them long to decide. If they accept your terms, I'm sure they won't want to spend any more time in jail than they have to."

"If they agree, I want those written apologies today, before they're released. And they better sound good," Billy demanded. "We'll see you in a half-hour, Mr. Brooks. Let's go have a cup of coffee and a piece of pie. How about it, Pa?"

****

Mr. Brooks swung open the heavy door to the sheriff's office and walked in. The four men looked up from their cell. When they noted it was Brooks, they sat on the edge of their cots waiting for what came next, except for John who began pacing.

"Good day, Sheriff. I wonder if I could talk to Quinn Harris in private," Brooks said.

"As private as I can get ya, is to move him down a cell," Sloan replied as he grabbed the cell keys.

"That will do. We'll keep our voices low so as not to disturb your other guests." Brooks smiled and took a seat in the third cell as the sheriff brought Quinn to join him.

"I have an offer for you from Mark Hewitt and Billy Henry," Brooks spoke softly. "Are you interested?"

"Let's hear it first. Then I'll tell you if I'm interested or not." Quinn glared at Brooks and leaned back against the bars while the lawyer spelled out the conditions.

"So if I pay one hundred dollars for the little girl, write an apology to the black boy, and pay twenty-five dollars to him, this all goes away? That's the bottom line?" Quinn clarified.

"That's it. You take the deal or take your chances before Judge Bennett. I believe you've played poker with Judge Bennett, haven't you? You want to take your chances going up against him? There's no guarantee what the Judge will sentence you to, or if he'll want to take this case to trial. Are you willing to take your chances, or do you want the deal you've been offered?"

"What about the other men?" Quinn asked.

"Well, their deal's a little different. They didn't hit the child, and they're going to say you talked them into running Otis out of town. They'll try to pin this all on you."

"Yeah, they already said as much. They're pretty upset with me. Is their deal the same as mine?" Quinn asked, glancing at the other cell and rubbing his forehead.

"I can't share that with you, but I can tell you this. If they don't agree, you'll all go in front of Judge Bennett for the attempted lynching and assault charges. And at that point, a public apology would still be on the table. And if you take my offer and any retaliation is ever made on the young man or the family, the letters you write will be made public," Brooks said. "Now I need an answer. What's it going to be?"

"I should talk to my lawyer," Quinn said. "I don't want to have to publicly apologize, if it comes to that. And you don't have to worry. I already told Billy Henry I'd never go near his family again."

"I'm sure you've already talked with your lawyer, and he listed all your options. I'll fetch him for you if you want, but right now I'm making you an offer that could go away at any minute. It's up to you."

Quinn paced the length of the cell a couple of times, turned, and said, "Yes, all right. Yes, I'll pay and write an apology. Now you need to get those men to do the same. Let me talk to them with you. Maybe I can help persuade them," he added in a whisper.

"No, this is their own decision. It's all or none." Brooks raised his voice and said, "Sheriff, I need to talk to the other men now."

Sloan let Brooks into the cell, where the three men waited anxiously to hear what he had to say.

"Are we getting out of here?" one asked.

"Yeah, we only did what Quinn told us to do," said another.

Brooks raised his hand to quiet them. "Let me start from the beginning, and then you can make a decision. But keep in mind, you all have to agree to my offer and follow through, or you take your chances in front of Judge Bennett. Attempted lynching and assault are criminal offenses. That boy had bruises that Doc Glasgow will testify to. Three grown men against one young boy. You roughed him up real good. What were you thinking?"

"We only did what Quinn told us to do," John said. "He bought us all a round of drinks and said he'd buy another after we had some fun with the boy."

"You know what Judge Bennett would do if you attempted to hang someone for horse stealing without bringing him in for justice first. A lynching is a lynching," Brooks said.

The men got quiet. One man asked, "So you have a deal for us?"

Brooks spoke in a low voice again to relay the terms. One man summarized, "So we each have three months to pay twenty-five dollars each, and we have to write an apology to the boy, or we'll go in front of the judge. Is that right?"

"Yes, and your answers must be unanimous. Quinn already accepted the deal about the boy. Now it's up to the three of you." Brooks looked them in the eye and said in a louder voice so Quinn could hear. "It's your choice. I'm not telling you what to do. You can talk this matter over with your wives or with Mr. Martin if you want. Do you want me to fetch anybody?"

Quinn called from the other cell, "I'll pay half of whatever your restitution is. That goes for all three of you. That's fair. Tell them, Brooks. That's fair."

As the men talked, Brooks gave them some space. After a while, he said, "Judge Bennett will be here the day after tomorrow if you want to talk to him. But if you do that, this offer goes away. What's it going to be, gentleman? I need your decision, and I'd like partial payment today to show your good faith. Also, you must submit your written apology before Sheriff Sloan turns you free." Looking at the sheriff, he asked. "Can you hold the money during the three-month period?"

"That's all right with me," Sloan said.

As the three men discussed their options, one man admitted. "I don't know how to write."

"You tell Sheriff Sloan what you want to say, and he'll write your words for you," Brooks told him. After a few minutes, he turned to the men and asked for the final time, "What's your decision? You either all agree, or you all, including Quinn, go before the judge."

John spoke up. "Well, if Quinn's willing to pay half the money, we decided we'd all write the apologies and pay our share instead of facing Judge Bennett."

Brooks nodded. "I trust none of you will try skipping town. You all live in the area, and if you've not paid up in the time allotted, the sheriff will come looking for you. That's the deal. Now each of you needs to sign this agreement that says that. Your signature makes this a binding document. Sign, or make your mark. Sheriff Sloan is your witness to the fact that I gave you all the information and answered your questions. There shouldn't be any retaliation against the boy or his family. If there is, instead of keeping your letters of apology private, I'll have them printed in the newspaper. If there is ever another attempt to lynch a black man in this town, the sheriff may shoot first and ask questions later."

"Your right, Mr. Brooks," Sloan said. "If it hadn't been for Billy Henry being there, that's exactly what I would have done."

Brooks nodded to the sheriff. "I'll be back in two hours to pick up a down payment and the apology letters. The boy's name is Otis Daily. The Hewitts took him into their family, and he lives with Billy Henry now. All I can say is that your apologies better be good."

Chapter Nineteen

Catching sight of Mr. Brooks walking back from the jail, Mark turned to Billy and said, "Finish your coffee, Son. It's time to go."

Following the lawyer into his office, Mark asked, "Did they all agree?"

"I'm surprised. I can't believe it, but yes, they all met your demands. They'll have their letters written to Otis before the sheriff releases them. By the end of October, Sloan will have all the money for you. I'll hold this document they all signed until the transaction is finalized." Mr. Brooks took the signed paper from his vest pocket and showed Mark and Billy the signatures. "Here's their signed admissions to the acts they committed. I told them any retaliation, and I'd have their letters printed in the newspaper. They certainly don't want their confessions to become public."

"We'd also prefer if they didn't but will use them if they cause us any more trouble. We'll stay out of town for a few months to let tempers cool off. In fact, we probably won't be back until the Harvest Festival in September. Mr. Brooks, you must have been very persuasive," Billy acknowledged.

"I must admit, I am pleased that they agreed to your terms. I'm sure after writing Otis an apology, they'll think twice before getting involved in anything like this again. I told Sheriff Sloan I'd be back in two hours to collect the letters. You can pick them up at my office then."

****

Outside, standing on the wooden sidewalk with Mark, Billy said, "I have a few errands to take care of while we're waiting."

It seemed strange knocking on the door he had entered freely so many times before. When Mrs. Parker, Elizabeth's mother, appeared, she stared at Billy for a few moments without speaking.

"Mrs. Parker," Billy said, "I do not wish to bother you. I'm sure you still have the engagement gift I gave Elizabeth. I'd like my mother's brooch back."

"Well, you are the last person I expected to see at my door. After the way you talked to my husband and me, you have no right coming or asking us for anything," Mrs. Parker said, preparing to slam the door.

Billy placed his boot in the way. "Maybe you didn't understand me correctly. I want my mother's brooch. I'm sure it's here. I know I gave it to Elizabeth, but it obviously didn't mean as much to her as it meant to me. I have so few items of my mother's to cherish."

Mrs. Parker mused aloud. "Yes, it's here. I remember when Elizabeth wore the brooch every day. She was happy then. Or at least I thought she was. I don't know what you did to make her so upset that she had to turn to Quinn. I'll never forgive you for hurting her like you did."

"I'm not here to anger or argue with you, Mrs. Parker. Return the brooch, and I'll leave."

"Well, I guess you're right because she wasn't wearing it when she died. I do know the only reason she held on to life as long as she did was so she could talk to you before she passed. For that, I was thankful because I had her with me that much longer, even though she wouldn't eat and could barely talk. Her father or I sat with her every minute."

Billy nodded. "When I gave Elizabeth the brooch, we were both very much in love. Those are the days I like to remember. I'd like to give Ma's brooch to my brother Steven so he has something to remember her by."

"I remember those happy days, too. All right, Billy, I can see it has sentimental meaning. I'll go fetch it. Wait right here." Returning with tears in her eyes, Mrs. Parker handed Billy a box. "I'm sorry our relationship ended the way it did," she said and closed the door.

Tucking the box into his pocket, he walked to his friend Cain Gibbs' blacksmith shop. Poking his head inside, Cain was working at the forge, so Billy waited until Cain dunked the red-hot piece of metal in water and then stepped forward.

"Billy, it's been months. How are things with you and yours?" Cain asked.

"I'm fine. I see work has you busy. How's the family?"

"Oh, everyone is good. My son is growing tall. Anything new?" Cain asked.

"Well, I'm courting Lydia Hewitt." *If anyone would understand, Cain would*, Billy thought. He was right. He could tell by Cain's grin that his friend was happy for him.

"Bring her around the next time you're in town. I'd like to meet her. I mean, I've seen her before. Oh, you know. You both should come for supper sometime," Cain suggested.

"I sure will. I know you're busy, and I gotta go.

Great seeing you again. I'll bring Lydia by our next trip to town." Billy patted Cain on the shoulder.

Meanwhile, Mark walked to the cattle corral at the end of town and read the beef prices posted outside the door at the Cattlemen's Association Office. *Now might be a good time to sell,* he thought. He picked up a letter for Sarah at the postal office and stopped at the butcher shop to pick up hides as a surprise for Jack. After stowing them on the horses, he met with Billy at Mr. Brooks' Office. Sheriff Sloan was there when they arrived.

"I never thought those men would apologize to a former slave boy," Sloan said, "but they each wrote a page worth."

"I hope you don't mind," Brooks said, "but I've read them. I wanted to make sure they were sincere. They each admitted to wrongful acts, and Quinn mentioned he was sorry for hurting the little girl."

Billy said, "These letters will mean a great deal to Oat. Sheriff, without you showing up when you did that day, everything could have gone terribly wrong. I could have been the one behind bars. And Mr. Brooks, getting those men to agree to our terms must have taken some persuasion. All-in-all, I'm pleased with the outcome."

Mark added, "Speaking for Sarah and myself, we're satisfied with the admissions. The money will be set aside to use later when Johanna and Oat determine what's important in their lives. Thanks again, gentlemen, for everything. Let's go, Billy. We have a few miles ahead of us."

****

"Hey Jack," Billy called. "Come get these smelly things."

"What things? What do you mean?" Jack ran to the

two men and caught a whiff of what was inside the sacks tied to the saddlebags. "You picked up hides. How many did you get?"

"Only eight," Mark said. "Don't worry, I didn't pay but three cents a hide, and these are on me. I figured they'd give you something to do with your free time." Mark snickered.

"Let's get them in the barn," Billy offered. "Then we have news to share."

Once everyone was inside, Abby poured cool drinks and set out molasses biscuits while Mark and Billy recalled the happenings of the day.

"I'm amazed the men agreed to write apologies. Paying restitution for their actions must have cut deep. You know the gossip is probably all over town by now," Jack said. "I hope others heed the warning and leave Oat and other colored folks alone from now on."

The clock chimed, and Mark said, "I want to peek in on my grandchildren before we have to leave. Have they been healthy?"

"Oh yes, and they've grown." Jack opened the door to the bedroom for Mark and Billy to go in.

Whispering, Billy said, "I can't wait for Lydia and me to have our first child."

"You mean it?" Jack said a little louder than he should have. The babies stirred a little and settled back to sleep.

Closing the bedroom door softly, Billy said, "Yes. Ma and Pa gave us their blessing to court. We'll tell the children our good news the next time we're all together."

"Congratulations!" Jack slapped Billy on the back.

Abby added, "Tell Lydia I'm so happy for the both of you."

****

That evening, back at Billy's after Steven was tucked in bed, Mark filled Lydia in on all the news. "The less we say about this to the children, the better," Mark said. "I'll read the letters to Oat and then put them away for safekeeping. He'll know the men now regret what they did, and hopefully, this will give him some confidence when he goes to town again."

"Pa will hold the money until he decides how to best use it," Billy added. Turning to Lydia, Billy said, "Since you'll be leaving with Pa in the morning, would you like to take a walk."

"Oh yes, Billy. We won't be long, Pa. There's still coffee in the pot."

"Thanks, dear," Mark motioned with his hand. "You two go along. I'm fine. But don't stay up all night. I want to get an early start for home."

Lydia took Billy's hand as they walked under a moonlit sky. "You and the boys must come soon so we can tell them our news. I can't wait to hear what they think. I hope they'll be happy for us all." Lydia laid her head on Billy's shoulder.

Billy took her in his arms, and their lips met.

After catching her breath, she said, "I want to kiss you like that forever."

****

When Mark and Lydia arrived home, Oat and Grandma Hewitt took a break from weeding the garden. Oat couldn't wait to tell them everything Gram had taught him.

The house was quiet. "Where are Ma and Johanna?" Lydia asked.

"Mr. Frazer came and got them the day you left.

Mrs. Frazer was having the baby." Grandma explained.

"I pray everything went well," Lydia said.

Oat pulled out a sheet of paper with letters and numbers drawn in every space available, front and back, and said, "I've been practicing, haven't I, Gram?"

"You sure have Oat. And you're getting good." Grandma smiled.

"And I learned how to say some words. I don't say, 'I's a' gonna' anymore. Now I say, 'I'm going to.' And I say please and thank you when I ask for something. Right, Gram?"

"Yes, an—" Grandma started to say.

"And I can say the names of all the letters and write them too. Sometimes I can put new words together on paper and sound them out. I can write my name and everyone's name in the family. Gram says I'm smart. All we have done since you left was work on letters, new words, and numbers."

Lydia smiled. "Maybe we should leave you and Grandma together more often. I'm proud of your progress, Oat. Show me which one is me."

Without hesitation, Oat pointed to Lydia's name, and read the list, and pointed to everyone's name. "See, I can read and write names now. Billy and Steven will be surprised."

Mark patted Oat on the shoulder. "Oat, there's something I want to read to you." He reached into his pocket and removed the letters. "I have four letters from the men who attacked you in town. These men spent five days in jail for what they did to you. They each wrote you a letter, and each is giving you money. They know what they did was wrong. Someday you'll be able to read these for yourself, but until then, have a seat, and I'll share them with you."

John wrote:

Otis,

Please forgive me for trying to run you out of town. If someone tried running my family out of town, I wouldn't be happy either. I'm not proud of what I did and won't do it again. I won't bother you or your family if I see you in town. And I won't join in with anyone else to hurt someone ever again. I know what we did was wrong. Trying to run you out of town wasn't worth spending time in jail and away from my family. I'm sorry you got hurt. I hope you are feeling better.

John

Mark read the other three letters, and when he was done, Oat said, "It sounds like theys sorry and feel bad for scaring me. So theys won't do it again?"

Mark nodded. "That's exactly what that means. You don't have to worry about those men trying anything again. You'll still want to keep close to family while you're in town. You know we all love you, and we'll do anything to keep you safe. Nothing will happen like this again. And if someone ever tries to hurt you, you run to the sheriff's office or scream for help. Someone will help. I pray there will never be a next time."

"Me too!" Oat was quick to say.

Grandma asked, "Well, what did we decide we wanted to eat for dinner, Oat? You better eat soon so you can get on your way to Billy's.

"We decided on vegetable soup with beans, peas, tomatoes, and onion," Oat insisted.

"Why those vegetables?" Lydia asked.

"Because that's what's ready to pick. Right Gram?" Oat smiled.

Grandma nodded. "He's absolutely right. I think that will make a fine soup. And I'll see what I can rustle up for a special dessert."

Chapter Twenty

A week later after an early breakfast, Mark checked on the fields, returned, and announced, "I'm taking a ride over to call on the Frazers and see if Sarah and Johanna are ready to come home. Would anyone like to ride along?"

"I would love to," Ruth said, "if you're taking the wagon."

"Of course, Ma. How about you, Lydia?" Mark asked.

"I'd love to see the new baby, but I better stay here. I'm designing two skirts and want to sketch out the paper patterns for them. I'm thinking one skirt will be gathered with a belt, and the other will have rows of ruffles."

"Please tell everyone that I send my love, and I'll have supper ready when you get back. Do you think Ma and Johanna will be coming home with you?"

"They might. Better cook some extra just in case," Mark suggested. "Be sure to bring your shawl, Ma. The ride home could be chilly. I'll hitch up the horses, so come out when you're ready."

"I hope they had a little girl," Ruth remarked.

"Me too," Lydia replied. She was preoccupied thinking of the skirts she'd stay home and work on to lift her spirits after the disappointment of Billy's response the other day to her big news. *I'll have all day to myself to finish these patterns. My dresses must be successful.*

They just must, or I'll look like a fool to everyone in town—if I ever get there.

****

Hearing the sound of a wagon pulling to a halt, Sarah wiped her hands on her apron and hurried to the door.

Mark helped Ruth from the wagon and turned to see his wife standing nearby.

Sarah hugged Mark tightly and gave him a kiss before she whispered in his ear, "With all the babies born this year, I'm wondering if we shouldn't have one more?"

"Eyes wide, Mark gazed in wonderment. "Really?" was all he could say, not noticing Sarah's wink aimed at Ruth as they went inside.

Johanna and Ethan were playing with the chickens and burst into the house. Johanna jumped into her father's arms, and he twirled her around a few times.

"Well, tell us the big news, Ethan?" Mark asked the young boy. "Did your ma have a baby boy or a little girl?

Johanna crossed her arms, standing tall and proud. "Tell him, Ethan. She's your sister. Tell Pa and Grandma what your ma had."

"Ma had a little girl. I'm a big brother now, and I'll be a big help. Her name is Laura, and she likes to sleep. I know Ma will let you hold her if you want."

"Laura and Emily are napping. I think Seth is in the barn or out at the fields," Sarah added.

"Well, I must say, whatever you have in the oven smells wonderful," Ruth commented.

"I think I'll go find Seth." Mark chuckled. "I'll let you ladies catch up. There's lots to tell."

Sarah took out the muffins and gave the bread pans

a half turn. "Tell me," She said to Ruth as she prepared tea for them. "I'm eager to hear what happened. Did Mark and Billy press charges against Quinn for hurting Johanna? And what happened to the other men who attempted to lynch Oat?"

Ruth looked up from her chair. "Well, they didn't really press charges. The men agreed to pay restitution in exchange for not going before the judge. Quinn is paying one hundred dollars for hurting Johanna, and the other men and Quinn are together paying a hundred dollars to Oat."

Sarah placed her hand over Ruth's and declared, "I can't believe they'd pay that much."

"Oh, they made a deal, Sarah. Quinn accepted to keep the event from going public. But you know everyone is already gossiping. The dastardly men have three months to pay. Oh, and they each wrote an apology to Oat that Mark read to him to help him understand. And the clincher is, if they don't pay in three months, the lawyer is going to publish the apology letters in the newspaper."

Sarah slapped the table. "Oh, I don't doubt they'll all pay with that condition hanging over their heads."

"I don't think the outcome could have been any better. Mark and Billy did a fine job," Ruth finished saying as the men walked in for something cool to drink.

Emily came out of the bedroom, rubbing her eyes. "Oh, it's so good to see everyone. Hello, Mother Hewitt. Hello Mark. Baby Laura is still sleeping, but I'm sure she'll wake up soon."

The children tumbled in from their play, and everyone sat around the table catching up on their busy spring and summer while enjoying the muffins and cool tea.

A tiny cry came from the bedroom. Sarah fetched the new baby and gave her to Ruth, who rocked her back to sleep. "She's so precious," Ruth said, tucking the blanket under Laura's chin.

After a glance at his pocket watch, Mark said, "We'll have to leave soon if we're going to make it home in time for supper. Would you like us to take Johanna home?"

"Well, actually, I think we'll both go with you." Sarah smiled. "Emily and I were just saying how well she is doing, and since I was going to ask Seth to take us home tomorrow, your timing is perfect. Let me gather our things, and we can give Emily and Seth their home back."

"We can't thank you enough for coming on such short notice and staying as long as you have," Emily said. "Thank God there were no complications with the baby, and having you here was comforting."

Seth nodded and said, "Thanks for everything, Sarah. You being here sure made my life easier. And bringing Johanna was a good idea. Ethan liked having her here, and she kept him busy. And thank you too, Mark."

Sarah smiled. "I was glad to help. Did you have a list of supplies you wanted us to pick up for you?"

"Oh, yes. Here." Seth handed the paper to Mark and walked to the cupboard to get money.

"I'm sure we'll be going to town at the end of the month to pick up Lydia's fabric order. Will that be soon enough?" Mark asked as he shook Seth's offered hand.

"Of course. I'll plan on coming to pick things up a week or so after that. Could you get a newspaper for us, too?" Seth picked up Sarah's bag as they all went outside, said their good-byes, and headed for home.

****

Hearing the sound of horses, Lydia looked up from her work, at the Regulator clock. *"Where did the time go?"* She thought.

Johanna flew through the door. "Lydia," she crowed and gave her sister a hug. "I've missed you so much."

"I've missed you too, sweetheart. Did Ma come with you?"

"Yup, and Pa and Grandma too," Johanna held the door open for her grandma.

"I've been busy every minute," Lydia said, "I lost track of time, and I haven't started cooking."

"I know what I'm hungry for," Johanna said. "Let's have creamed eggs on grilled bread with pickles. A whole jar of pickles."

"A *jar* of pickles?" Grandma chuckled.

"I like pickles," Johanna said. "I'll fetch the eggs." She was out the door and back in minutes carrying a full basket.

Lydia hurried to gather her pattern pieces and clear the table. After all her hard work, the last thing she needed was to have anything spilled on them.

"Now I'll get the pickles from the root cellar," Johanna said and scurried out the door.

"Mother," Lydia said as she kissed her mother hello, "How is Mrs. Frazer? Did she have a boy or a girl?"

As Sarah put water on for the eggs to boil, she shared the news of baby Laura.

"The baby is so tiny. Was I that small when I was born?" Johanna asked as she placed the eggs carefully into the water.

Grandma explained, "Yes, dear. All babies are that small when they're born. Just like the twins were small, but you saw how quick they grew. And they'll be even bigger when you see them next time."

Chapter Twenty-One

During the next week, Lydia wrote letters to textile, button, lace, and thread manufacturers that she had located in her Godey and Peterson's lady magazines. Wanting to make sure she got the best items, she contacted additional suppliers for prices and samples. Last fall, she had purchased the Singer Sewing Machine she wanted and was becoming proficient in its use. She finished one of her custom dresses and planned to wear it when she asked the ladies for their decision. All that was needed were fabrics and notions to begin production of her full line of dresses.

"Ma, I'm nervous about spending so much of my hard-earned money. I read in one of my magazines that the war depleted some materials. The letter from New York included sample swatches and a price list. I sure hope these other companies send the same."

"I'm sure if they see you're interested in purchasing, they'll send a price list," Sarah said.

As Lydia laid out pattern pieces, she carefully kept track of how much material went into each of her five designs and had Sarah check her figures. Seeing the costs add up, Lydia said, "Maybe starting with three dress designs and making them in different fabrics is wise. I'll order the material my next trip to town. That should give me time to meet the October deadline."

Sarah put down her pencil. "That's taking a big leap

of faith, Lydia. Don't you think you should wait until you know for certain that the ladies will agree to sell your ready-to-wear dresses?"

"I suppose you're right. But I don't care what it takes. I'll go from store to store if necessary until I find a place to sell them. My business will be a success. My day dress designs may not be as stylish as those coming from Ohio and New York, but they are originals and will be new and exciting to the women in Dead Flats."

Sarah pushed away from the table. "I know how strongly you feel, dear. Take things one step at a time is all I ask."

Lydia's mind drifted. *Someday, women will come from other towns to buy my off-the-rack dresses. There will be so many orders that Grandma and Johanna will have to help Mother cut out the patterns and pin them. All I'll do is design patterns and sew. My dresses will become so popular that the President's wife will write to ask me to send her one of my latest creations.*

Billy and the boys bolted into the house and jarred Lydia back to reality. "You're here. I wasn't expecting you so soon," she said.

Billy winked. "We couldn't wait to get here. We even stopped off at the creek and washed up before we came, didn't we boys?"

Steven grinned. "Yeah, the water was pretty cold to swim, but Oat and I did anyway since Billy said we had to wash our hair. We didn't stay in long, though. Billy sure was in a rush to get here. He said you both want to talk to us."

"What you wanta tell us?" Oat asked.

Lydia sat down, and Johanna settled beside her. "Billy and I have something to share with you."

Grinning from ear to ear, Billy said, "I asked Lydia if I could court her, and she said yes."

"You're joshing," Oat said. "She's your sister. Courtin' means you want to get hitched."

Billy smiled. "You're right. We grew up together as brother and sister. My parents died when Steven was very young, and the Hewitts took us in. It's like your situation, Oat. We took you in to live with us, and we call you our brother."

"It means Lydia, and I want to love one another like a husband and wife, which is different from sister and brother. I know it sounds confusing, and you may not understand everything, and that's all right. Lydia and I will spend time together and someday get married. We'll still love you and everyone else like we do right now."

"You mean when you get married, Lydia will move in and live at our place?"

"Yes, Steven, she'll live with us, and she'll change her last name to Henry," Billy explained.

"You'll still be my brother and sister, won't you?" Johanna asked and crossed her arms, waiting for an answer.

"Yes, but Billy and I will marry and have our own family one day," Lydia explained.

"Why not jist get hitched now? Why court first?" Oat asked.

"I want to start my dress business, and I need Ma's help, so living here is better for now." Lydia slipped her arm around Billy. "So what do you think?

Oat nodded. "It's good with me."

Steven said, "Me, too."

Johanna added, "I guess courting will be all right. You'll still come and visit us when you're married, won't you?"

"Yes, we'll visit often. Pa will still need help with the hay and Ma with the canning and butchering. You'll see us a lot. And you can come visit us, too," Billy said.

"All right, then," Johanna said. "Hey, come on, boys, let's go see the foals."

Giving Billy's waist a squeeze, Lydia pulled him close. Laughing, she said, "I suppose at their age, I'd be more interested in seeing the foals too."

****

Meeting at the creek the following week, Billy and the boys swam while Lydia spread a blanket and unpacked lunch. Grandma got comfortable in a chair and started reading a book. Mark and Sarah stayed home today.

"Time to eat, everyone," Lydia called.

Steven was the first out of the water, followed by Oat. Billy carried Johanna on his shoulders to the blanket piled with food and helped her dry her hair before sitting down to the mid-day meal.

As soon as Steven finished eating, he said, "Can Oat and I go fishing now?"

Johanna protested, "I want to go fishing, too."

"You can come. I don't mind," Oat said, and the threesome got the poles out of the wagon.

Lydia packed away the empty crocks and dishes while Billy helped the boys dig worms.

As the children went off to fish, Billy called, "No horsing around, and no going in the water. Fish from the bank and yell if you need any help. Stick close together and boys, help Johanna bait her hook."

The three youngsters waved and hurried downstream to a favorite fishing spot.

Grandma put down her book and said, "You two run along. I'm going to sit and enjoy the sunshine."

****

Walking upstream together, Billy took Lydia's hand. They came upon a limb from a fallen elm tree to sit on. Gazing into Lydia's eyes, Billy said, "We know each other pretty well, but I don't think I've told you much about my real parents. They were very much in love and loved me with all their heart. I wasn't spoiled, but I didn't want for anything either. You know my father was a lawyer. He was an important man in town. My mother didn't have a job, but she took care of me and did all the housework, cooked our meals, and was active in the community."

"I didn't know all this," Lydia said. I knew you lived in a large town, but you never talked about your family."

"That's because they died young, and your family took me in when I was at a low point in my life. I'm grateful to Mark for bringing me to the farm when he found me."

Lydia tilted her head. "What do you mean when he found you?"

"I was living with an old drunk peddler. We moved from town to town selling elixir, pots and pans, and anything else he could swindle from people to resell at a profit. He didn't treat me well, and Mark got me away from him. I'm still not sure how, but I was thankful at the time and still am. I'd never have met you if I hadn't met Mark."

"Well, I'm glad he got you away from that peddler, too. Ma told us you hadn't had an easy life. Jack wanted you to stay with us right from the start. I worried if you and Jack were friends that, Jack would do things with you instead of me. I was afraid I'd be left out, but the two of you always included me even though I am a few years younger than both of you."

Billy picked a tall blade of wide grass and handed it to Lydia. "Age doesn't mean as much to you now, does it?"

"No, the difference in our ages doesn't matter at all. And I don't feel like your little sister anymore either."

"Good, because you're not my little sister. You'll be my wife one day, and sooner than later, I hope." Billy picked a blade of grass for himself and holding the grass tautly between his two thumbs, put his hands with the blade of grass to his lips and blew. A shrill sound filled the air.

"My turn," Lydia said, and held the blade of grass to her lips, blew, and a whistle tone rang out.

Billy threw his grass away and tried a different piece with the same results. "You always were better at getting sounds from your grass blades. You skip rocks across the water better than me too."

"Then I'm the one who should teach our children how to grow up on a farm and keep themselves amused." Lydia smiled. "You think the boys are done fishing yet?"

"Not if I know my little brother. He likes catching them as much as he likes eating them. Speaking of Steven, when I first brought him home, you and Jack were good with him. He took right to you, even more so than Ma. You never complained about having to put up with him. Why was that?"

"He became part of the family because you were part of our family. And he was so cute and could have gotten into so much trouble if we didn't all keep an eye on him. I can't imagine our family without you and

Steven. And now Oat is part of our family, too. He needed you when he was in a low point in his life. You opened your home to Oat, and now I know why you offered to take him in. You have a kind heart, Billy Henry, and that's one of the reasons I love you." She leaned over to give him a kiss.

Billy reached for Lydia and knelt on the ground, gently pulling her to him. They lay beside each other, she on her back looking toward the brilliant blue sky and him gazing down into her big brown eyes. "I love you, Lydia. Looking back, I believe I've always loved you. First as a friend and now as a lover." Lowering his head, he brushed his lips over hers.

Lydia's body tingled. Touching his face, she wanted more.

Billy's body was resting on hers, his arm bracing his body so he wouldn't crush her. They kissed. He pulled back, but she returned her lips to his. They began exploring each other's mouths again.

Billy pulled back to catch his breath and gazed into her eyes. His arm nearly numb, he rolled onto his back and took her hand.

"You make me feel safe. When we're together, I feel like there isn't anything we couldn't do, Billy."

"I feel the same way. We'll have a good life together, Lydia. I promise we will." Billy gave her hand a squeeze.

Lydia sat up. "Come on, we better get back."

"You're right. I don't want you getting home too late, or Pa won't let you come again."

Walking hand in hand back to the picnic site, they could hear the boy's loud voices and then a shriek from Johanna. Lydia picked up the pace. "They beat us back, and my guess is they're gutting a fish. Johanna's a little squeamish when it comes to blood and guts."

Chapter Twenty-Two

At the end of the month, Mark was ready to go to town. He needed boards from the sawmill, and Lydia was anxious to hear the ladies' decision on her dress proposal. The two of them stopped at Billy's and sent Oat and Steven to the Hewitts' farm to help with the chores until they returned.

Billy gave Lydia a kiss on the forehead. "You look beautiful in your dress. I'm rooting for you, Lydia. I'm sure you're eager to hear if your business plans have all worked out."

"Thanks, Billy. We'll be back in time for supper." Lydia blew him a kiss as the wagon pulled away.

On the way to town, Mark and Lydia stopped at Jack and Abby's.

"We can't stay long," Mark said. "We're headed for Dead Flats and wanted to see the twins, plus get a list if you need us to pick up supplies."

"My, they've grown. They're so cute," Lydia whispered to Abby as she peeked in on Benjamin and Annabelle sleeping in the same cradle, arms intertwined. "I hope to learn if the dress shop ladies will sell my dresses. Keep your fingers crossed, please."

"We will. We know how much this means to you," Abby said as she quietly closed the door.

As they enjoyed a quick cup of tea, Lydia spoke of the latest news. "Billy said he shared with you that we are courting. Ma and Pa gave us their blessing, and we already told the children. They took it pretty well. I couldn't be happier."

"We're happy for both of you," Abby said.

As Jack gave Lydia a hug, he whispered in her ear, "I knew everything would work out. Make sure to tell Billy I can't wait to call him my brother-in-law."

Mark pointed to his pocket watch. "We better get going, Lydia. Oat and Steven should be at the farm soon. I'm sure Grandma will spoil them with special baking today."

"We're all set for supplies, thanks for asking," Jack said as he loaded the latest batch of leather goods for Lydia to sew into the back of the wagon. With final hugs and good-byes, Lydia and Mark set off.

****

In town, Lydia took a deep breath, straightened her shoulders, and entered Creative Fashions, the only dress shop in town. Hearing the sound of the sewing machine come to a stop, she called, "Hello. Are you available?" While waiting for one of the ladies to come from the backroom, she admired a dress that was no doubt waiting for a client's final approval.

The curtain slid to one side, and Violet entered the room.

Lydia's heart pounded. "Violet, so good to see you," she managed to get out. Taking a deep breath, she continued. "I hope you and Josephine have had time to consider my offer and are interested in my proposition."

"Well, dear, we discussed your idea, and we asked our clientele if they would be interested in buying readymade garments. They all assured us they would not. Josephine and I don't think your dresses would be a good fit for our Creative Fashions Shop. We're sorry if that ruins your plans, dear. It seems Dead Flats isn't the town for your readymade dresses."

You're wrong. I know you're wrong! Lydia wanted to yell in protest. Her anger rising, she bit her tongue to keep from crying, smiled, and said, "I think my readymade garments are just what this town needs, and come October, if not sooner, you'll see I'm right. Thank you for your opinions, but I will definitely be pursuing my plans." Turning on her heels, she said, "Good day." And strolled out the door.

At the dry goods store, Lydia sought Mrs. Cooper, who was measuring a length of rope for Mark, who stood within hearing distance. Pasting a smile on her face, Lydia said, "Hello, Mrs. Cooper, I'm starting a ready-to-wear dres—"

Mrs. Cooper cut her short. "I hope you're not thinking of asking me to sell them here. I wouldn't sell as much fabric if I did. Violet told me all about your designs and ideas. I figured you'd come ask me next."

"I understand, Mrs. Cooper. Thank you for your time." *Come hell or high water, I will sell my dresses in this town even if I have to open a storefront of my own,* she thought. "I'll meet you at the wagon when you're finished here, Father." Lydia turned and left.

Determined to find somewhere to sell her dresses, Lydia marched across the street to the harness shop. Jack had suggested early on that Ezra Gray might be inclined to rent her a space.

Weaving her way through harness straps and leather goods hanging from the rafters, she found him bent over a bench working. "Hello, Mr. Gray. I'm Lydia Clark, Jack Clark's sister. I have a business proposition for you."

Mr. Gray raised his brow and straightened. "Well, my dear, how can I help you?"

"Please hear me out before you say anything. I have an idea to make ready-to-wear dresses for the ladies of this town and eventually branch out into other garments. I have designed five different dress styles, have a sewing machine, and I'm buying lovely fabric to make them. They will be ready to sell by the beginning of October."

"Well, young lady, aren't you something. That sounds like an ambitious plan."

"I asked the ladies at the Creative Fashions dress shop and Mrs. Cooper at the dry goods store and they all turned me down. They said their clients didn't like my idea of ready-wear, and that my dresses would take away from their businesses. So you see, I'm without an outlet or a storefront to sell my originals. I'm sure they will sell, and the other women must think so too, or they wouldn't be so against my having them in their stores."

"I see," Ezra Gray said with a furrowed brow. "Are you suggesting you would like to sell them here? And would you be here in person to sell them yourself? I know nothing about women's fashions." He chuckled.

"I thought about that. I'd have to move to town and have a place to stay. I don't have the extra to spend on lodging right now." Lydia sighed.

"Well, there is a storage room in the back we could turn into a place for you to sleep. And there's a stove for heat and cooking. It wouldn't be much, but if you want to try, I'd be glad to help fix it up, and I wouldn't charge you to use it."

"You mean you're willing to let me live here and use your store to sell my dresses? I'll pay you a commission on each dress sold like I offered the other shops. And I can help you sweep and clean, wash the windows, and keep the store tidy." Lydia held her breath, awaiting Mr. Gray's answer.

"Well, come to think of it, Miss, I don't use all the space at the front of the store for my business. There are two nice big windows for people to see inside. Can't imagine what they'd think if they looked in and saw finery on display. In a harness shop? That would be something! I think we should give your dress shop a try and see how it works out."

Lydia spontaneously reached out and hugged Mr. Gray. "I'm so excited. Oh, thank you. Thank you, sir. I can't wait to tell my folks. I don't know if you know Billy Henry, but we are courting, and I can't wait to tell him, too. Could I look at the storage room space?"

"Sure, it's right back here. October, you say, is when you want to open your business?" Mr. Gray asked.

"Yes, the first of October." Lydia nodded as she looked around to make sure there would be enough room for a bed and her sewing machine. As her eyes darted around the small space with its stacks of crates and boxes that would need to find other locations, she said, "This will work fine, Mr. Gray. And I'd need a smaller space to enclose for a dressing room, but I don't see that as a problem. My father or Billy can come up with something. It won't even need a real door, maybe a curtain. Yes, that would do, and I'll have to get a full-length mirror. Yes, yes, fine, I can make this work!"

"I'll have the storage room cleaned up and space ready in the front of the store by October. The back needs cleaned out anyway. Cleaning will give me something to do. Since my wife passed away, my evenings have been long and lonely. Having someone to keep me company during the day will be nice. Talk to your folks and your young man and see what they say. Let me know for certain your next trip to town. You'll show those shopkeeper women you can make it without them. Good for you, young lady. Stop in anytime you're in town."

"Oh, I will, I will. Thank you, Mr. Gray. You have no idea how much I appreciate your offer. Moving to town is a big step, but if it means opening my own shop, I've got to at least try. Thank you again, Mr. Gray," Lydia called over her shoulder as she flew out the door.

"You'll never guess what happened, Pa." Lydia jumped up onto the wagon seat, excitement written all over her face. "I talked to Mr. Gray at the harness shop. He's going to let me use some of his storefront space and fix up a room for me to stay in town so I can sell my dresses. Can you believe it? I got turned down twice, and I didn't give up. Billy will be so proud of me."

"Congratulations, sweetheart. But are you sure you want to move to town? Will you feel safe living on your own?" Mark questioned. "You've never lived by yourself before. This is a big step."

"Oh, Pa. I know it's your job to want to protect me, but I'll be fine. Right there in my own shop, making and selling my own dresses. It's what I've wanted for so long. I have to go to the postal office to see if my samples came. I'm so excited. I know Ma and Grandma will be happy for me too."

At the postal office, the clerk returned with several thick envelopes. Letters from Connecticut had arrived containing samples. Lydia took a minute to look everything over and then decided to order more fabric, lace, and buttons than originally planned. "Oh, Pa, if I order all my supplies today, I should have everything sooner, but I need to withdraw money from the bank."

"Go ahead, dear. I've picked up a letter for your mother. I'll wait for you in the wagon."

Lydia dashed to the bank and returned to fill out order forms and send them on their way.

She felt as light as a feather. Her spirits were high. At the wagon, Mark said, "Lydia, you worked so hard to make this all happen. I'm proud of you for not giving up."

****

Billy waited for Lydia as the wagon pulled to a stop. She hiked up her skirt and ran to his arms.

Twirling her around, he asked, "Did the ladies say yes?"

"No, both the dress shop and Mrs. Cooper turned me down." Lydia's smile grew wider.

"So why are you so excited if they said no?" Billy asked.

"Well...I asked Ezra Gray if he would let me use some space in his harness shop, and guess what?" she blurted out. "He agreed," Lydia went on her tiptoes to give Billy a kiss on the lips.

Excitement brimming, she danced with joy. "He even said I could live in a room in the back of his store for free. I know that changes our plans a little, but we can make everything work. Don't you think?"

"Lydia. What are you thinking? If you move to town, everything changes. Come inside so we can talk about this. You don't mind, do you, Pa? We won't be long." Billy took Lydia's hand.

"No, you two go ahead," Mark said, unhitched the horses, and started the evening chores.

Billy sat down at the table and held his head in both hands. "Ezra Gray? You're saying you want to live in the harness shop? Is this what you really want, Lydia? Did you sign a contract or give him a final answer?"

"No, no contract or anything. But this is the only way I can sell my dresses. I'll pay Mr. Gray a commission on each one, and I can set up my machine and sew when I'm not busy in the store. Ma and Grandma can still help cut out the patterns. I told Mr. Gray I wouldn't be ready until October to move in."

Billy looked away. "Did you ever take my opinion into consideration? I don't like it, I don't like it at all. You've already made up your mind, haven't you? I wish you had discussed this with me first. This is a major decision, and you didn't even think to ask my opinion. Ma and Pa always discuss things that affect both of them and the family before making a final decision. You moving means we'll be apart."

Lydia's excitement drained away, but she soldiered on. "There's a potbelly stove in the back for heat. I'll cook on it. And if I don't go out at night, I'll be safe." Her smile faded, and her whole body went limp. "Don't you understand, Billy, I must try. I have to see if my dresses will sell. I know they will. I only need a chance to prove myself. Please try to put yourself in my shoes. I already ordered fabric today and spent most of my money." Lydia let out a sigh.

"You moving will delay our courting. I'm sure other things will happen, and your business will always keep you from me. Is that what you want? You'll be there all alone. God forbid, what if something happens? I won't be there to take care of you. It's not safe for you living all on your own, that far away." Concern streamed from every word as he shook his head in frustration.

"Moving means I have a place to sell my designs, and I can work on them every minute. By spring, I'll know if my business is successful, and I'll figure out what to do next. I'm sorry I didn't ask your opinion, but I thought you'd be happy for me." Lydia took his face in her hands to give him a kiss.

Billy pulled back. "Of course, I'll be happy for you if you succeed. But we should have discussed things first. Now your mind is made up. What about you living with the boys and me? I thought that was part of what you wanted. I'm not sure you can handle both your dress business and a family. It seems like your dresses are all you care about."

"You're wrong, Billy. I do want to live with you, Steven, and Oat once we're married. I need some time to prove myself. I'm not a town girl. I like farming, but I still believe this is the best arrangement for now. If everything goes as I hope, perhaps I can hire someone to do the selling at the store, and I can design, sew, and keep the books once we're married. I want to make my business a success, and I want a life with you, too. I thought you'd be more supportive. We can work things out. We have to."

Billy pushed back from the table. "I don't see that happening now."

"Don't give up on us. I certainly haven't. I'll figure out a way to succeed and be a good wife." Tears trickled down Lydia's cheeks as her high spirits ebbed.

The young couple looked at one another, each realizing the significance of the moment. Much was hanging in a delicate balance—their future life together,

Lydia's dream, and first steps of independence. They simultaneously reached for each other and embraced.

Chapter Twenty-Three

After an early breakfast the following morning with few words exchanged between Lydia and Billy, Mark and Lydia returned to the Hewitt farm and sent Oat and Steven back to Billy's place. Lydia couldn't wait to tell her mother and grandmother all her news.

"I was disappointed after the ladies in the dress shop turned me down. They said their clients wouldn't buy ready-to-wear clothes although I doubt they ever asked them. I tried to talk to Mrs. Cooper at the dry goods store, but she turned me down too. She worried she'd lose fabric sales if she sold my dresses. I wasn't about to give up. I remembered Jack telling me about Mr. Gray and his harness shop. You know, the man who lent Jack the book on tanning hides that he read cover to cover three or four times? Mr. Gray and I made an agreement that I could use some space in his shop, right up front by the big windows, actually. And he offered me a room in the back of the store where I could live. Billy and I talked. He's not very happy about me living in town, so I don't know what that means for our future. I feel I should try it, living in town, I mean. I have to prove I can make my business successful. I'll show those ladies that I'm no quitter. But Billy is not exactly in agreement, and now I'm torn," Lydia shared, dismay written on her face.

After supper, she laid out the fabric samples to show her family. "These are the materials I choose for my first dresses." Laying the calico, a gingham, and homespun fabrics on the table, she said, "Won't they be beautiful?"

"Yes, dear, just lovely," Sarah said. "Such quality material. I'm so very proud of you. I know you're going to do well with your business. I just wish you didn't have to move so far from home. Are you sure you'll be all right by yourself?"

"Don't worry, Mother, I'll be fine. I'll be so busy, I won't have time to think about anything but working," Lydia assured her mother as she gathered the samples.

"Father," Lydia said, "Don't forget to give Ma the letter from back east. I'm sure she's dying to hear if Aunt Matilda had her baby. I know it's not due until the middle of August, but he or she could come early."

"Read the letter now," Johanna insisted as Mark handed Sarah the envelope. "Read it to all of us."

Sarah tore open the envelope and read:

June 20, 1866

Tidioute, Warren County, Pennsylvania

Dearest Sarah,

I visited your sister the other day, and I'm sure she is having a boy. Even Doc thinks so because of her size and how she is carrying. Matilda and Robert are so excited. Of course, Robert wants a boy, and Matilda would love a little girl. I'll write immediately and let you know all the details once it's here.

Emma is also looking forward to her new arrival in November. With Jack's twins, that makes me a grandmother and great-grandmother all in one year. I could not be prouder.

Mathew and Lynnette are finalizing their plans for the wedding. Please pray for good weather. They decided to try for an outdoor reception at the church.

They can move inside if necessary, but Netty has her heart set on being outside. I so hope all works out the way they are planning. They are so much in love, and it is sweet to watch them together. Mathew found them a house in town on Elm Street. The people will be moving out in September. It is not real big, but there are three bedrooms so they will have plenty of room to start a family. And that is exactly what Netty wants as soon as possible.

With Mathew gone, it will be your father and me in this big old house. I had an idea but wanted to run it by you first. Your father and I would like to ask Mathew and Netty to come live with us until we pass. Afterward, the house would be theirs for taking care of us and would stay in the family. We won't be around forever. I'd love to be able to help with the children as much as possible. There is no sense in them buying a house and then selling this place once Pa and I are gone. Please write and let me know what you think. Your father is in agreement with me. I await your reaction.

It's going to be a busy fall and winter, but I can't wait. Tell everyone all of us back east send our love and miss you all terribly. Kiss the twins for us and tell Ruth the family that bought her home are fixing up the front porch, and they too just had another baby.

All my love,
Mother

Sarah folded the letter and held it close to her heart before placing the neatly folded paper back in the envelope.

"Well, Ma, what do you think about the house?" Lydia asked.

"I don't have any objections. I think Mathew

moving in makes perfect sense. The real question is will Mathew and Netty want to live there? I'm sure Mother and Father would give them their privacy, but they would eat meals and share common areas as well. I'll send a note and give Mother my thoughts. Lydia, why don't you write your grandma and tell her about the changes in your life? I'm sure she'd love to hear all about your news."

"All right, Ma. Certainly, a lot has happened lately, hasn't it? And I don't think all is resolved yet," Lydia responded. "I'll be sure to write."

Chapter Twenty-Four

While the family was gathered for the morning meal, Sarah said, "Today is a good day to do some canning. There are plenty of tomatoes, cucumbers, and green beans. I'm sure Billy's garden is thriving as well. Lydia, you'll probably need to give him a hand, and I'm sure Abby would appreciate help too."

Johanna said, "I want to help. I love canning."

"Good. You can help pick the produce with Lydia while Grandma and I get the jars boiled and the knives sharpened." Sarah smiled. "I wonder how Billy and the boys are doing. I thought they'd come visit this week, but probably they're busy getting the hay in. Your father could use help getting ours in too."

"I thought they'd come visit, as well," Lydia said, thinking about the time away from her work that the day spent canning would steal. To meet her deadline, she needed every moment to work.

"I miss them," Johanna added. "And I'm going to miss you when you leave us, Lydia. I won't have anyone to play with or anything to do."

"Sure you will," Grandma said. "I'll keep you busy. We'll have all kinds of fun. I can teach you how to knit and do needlepoint."

"And with the scraps from Lydia's sewing, I thought we'd make a quilt this winter," Sarah added.

"All right, we'll have a good time," Johanna

admitted.

"You'll also have Momma Kitty and Muzzy to keep you company. Since I won't be here," Lydia said. "You'll have to feed and care for them every day and help Pa gather the eggs and feed the chickens. In fact, you can start taking over those chores right away. I won't have time once my fabric arrives."

"That won't be a chore. I love the cat and chickens, and they like me. I'll start today," Johanna said. "But first, let's go pick the tomatoes.

****

A wagon pulled in as Sarah put the first batch of tomatoes on the stove to cook. "Wonder who that is," she said, heading for the door with Johanna right on her heels.

Billy drove the wagon kicking up dust with Steven and Oat waving their straw hats.

"Lydia, Lydia, Billy's here," Johanna called out.

Not liking the way their last conversation ended, Lydia wanted to talk and make amends with Billy. She caught up to the wagon. "I'm so glad you're here. We thought you might come this week to help Pa with the hay. He's already in the field."

Billy pulled the wagon to a stop and said, "We finished our hay yesterday and picked all the ripe tomatoes last night, but I don't know how to can them. They're in the back."

"Yeah, four bushels. And we brought jars too," Steven said. "Billy said we didn't have time to can. Canning is woman's work."

"You and Ma had the same idea. We're canning our tomatoes today, too," Lydia said. "But if you think canning is only woman's work, you're wrong. You'll have to help at some point."

Jumping to the ground, Billy picked up Lydia and twirled her around. Setting her on the ground, he whispered in her ear, "You look beautiful, even when you're upset with me."

"No, I don't. You just missed me. You need to come visit more often." Lydia kissed his cheek, took his hand, and they headed for the house as if their last conversation never happened.

"Have you eaten yet?" Sarah called.

We had muffins and jam, but I'm still hungry, Ma," Steven said.

"Come in. I'm sure I can manage to fix you something to eat before you help your father."

"We brought this morning's eggs and some milk. Will you cook some?" Oat asked.

"Sure I will," Sarah reached for a frying pan. "Johanna, dear, set three places at the table, and boys, tell us what you've been up to."

"Steven asked, "Ma, is my face red?"

Everyone turned and stared.

"No," Sarah said, "Aren't you feeling well?"

"Oh, I'm all right. I've just eaten so many tomatoes these past few weeks, I feel like one."

Chuckles filled the room.

"We have other vegetables that needs canning too," Oat said, "but we had the most tomatoes."

"Are you able to stay the night?" Lydia asked.

"Yes, I got one of the neighbor boys coming to do the chores tonight and tomorrow morning," Billy took a seat at the table.

Johanna began snapping beans, and Lydia and Grandma washed and cut the cucumbers for pickles. The boys ate before heading out to the fields to help Mark.

Finished for the day, Sarah carried the last tray of jars to the root cellar and gave them homes on the shelves. Doing a quick inventory of food, she thought. *With Lydia moving to town, she'll need a supply of canned goods to take with her as well. We better not waste a single vegetable this year. I'll need to keep an eye on the garden and declare canning days as needed for the rest of the summer.*

That evening, Mark called the family together. "Thanks for your hard work today, everyone. We'll certainly sleep well tonight. Tomorrow Steven will go with Grandma and Lydia to Billy's and get started on the canning while Billy and Oat help me finish the hay."

"Can't I go?" Johanna asked.

"Your Ma will need help to finish canning, and with Lydia gone you promised to do her chores," Mark said. "I'm sure we can find something to keep you busy."

"Oh, you mean like going berry picking and stopping at the swimming hole?" Johanna winked.

"I think that could be arranged." Mark winked back. "Now off to bed." He waited for the children to climb the ladder and called to them, "Sweet dreams."

Billy took Lydia's hand, and they went outside to talk in the warm summer night.

"I didn't like the way we left things last week. I still don't like the idea of you moving to town, and I hope you will reconsider."

"Let's go to the barn so we can talk," Lydia insisted.

Once inside, they sat on the back of the spring wagon as they had done so many times before.

"I'm not going to change my mind, Billy. I can't. I have too much money tied up in fabric and supplies not to follow through. I want to prove to myself and to the people of Dead Flats that my dresses are worth buying and that I am a good designer and dressmaker. Why can't you understand? This is something I must do for me." Lydia took his hand.

"What I'm beginning to think is that your dresses are more important to you than me." Billy turned and looked deeply into her eyes. "We don't need the money you'll make selling dresses to survive on the farm. I still have money from what my parents left me, and once we're married, we can turn the fields into cash crops that will pay enough to keep us happy and raise a family. You do want a family, don't you?"

"Yes, I want you and a family very much. And I want to see through my plans for my ready-wear dress business too." A tear trickled down her cheek.

"All right, All right, don't cry. I can see you aren't going to give up your dream, but I'm not going to give up mine either." Billy pulled her close and kissed the top of her head.

****

As Lydia drove the wagon into the yard at Billy's, she exclaimed, "Look at that garden. It hasn't been kept up! Look at those weeds. They're everywhere. What happened, Steven?" Lydia shook her head in dismay.

"We had to get the hay done. The garden looked better before we started haying. Really it did." Disgraced, Steven hung his head.

Grandma, in disbelief, said, "You know your mother would be disappointed to see this mess of a garden. Look at the size of those beans and cucumbers. They should have been picked and eaten at least a week ago. It's going to take a good three or four days to get everything canned and this messy garden back into shape."

Inside the house, Lydia looked around. The place looked a little run down since her last visit. "We may as well get started. Steven, you unhitch the team and fetch some baskets. I'll get large bowls and start picking."

****

Finally, after days of work, Grandma announced, "I believe we've canned every ripe vegetable in the garden. I hope Billy and Oat arrive soon so we can get to Jack and Abby's."

Tying her hair back, Lydia said, "Until they show up, Steven and I are going to clean a little more. Steven, fetch all the dirty clothes you can find and bring them outside. We can drag those rag rugs out, too, and I'll help you get them on the clothesline. They need a good beating. Once that's done, we're mopping the floors. That will be a good start."

Steven dashed off to obey.

After dragging the rugs outside, Steven said, "When are you going to come live with us, Lydia? When are you and Billy going to get married?" he asked.

"Maybe sometime next year. Why do you ask?" Lydia helped lift the rug over the clothesline and started to beat it with a paddle. Dust flew everywhere.

"We sure could use you around here to keep the house clean and cook some of your good meals. Billy does his best, but he can't keep up with the farming and all the housework. Oat and I help, but Billy says all the time that when you two get married, he'll feel better."

Lydia bent down to Steven's level. The concern on her little brother's face worried her, and she gave him a kiss on the forehead. "I know you love Billy, and so do I. Don't worry. He'll be fine. Now fetch some water so I

174

can put it on to warm, and I'll start on the floors."

Grandma gave Lydia a thoughtful smile. "He's right, you know. These boys need a woman to take care of them. Don't let your whole life be consumed by your business. Remember who loves you and that you love life on the farm. You take such pride in everything you do."

"I know you're right, Grandma. It's just that I've dreamed of designing and selling my dresses for a long time. I must prove that I can make my business happen and be successful."

"You're already successful with Jack and his business. And I'm proud of the way you saved your money and bought your sewing machine. I understand wanting to see your dream through to the end, but then what? What happens when you're successful?"

"I haven't let myself think that far ahead. I have too much to do right now. I'm torn between my business plans and my relationship with Billy. He wasn't in my life like he is now when I dreamt of designing and selling my own dresses. Now I have a chance to make those dreams happen. I have to do this for me. This is my one chance. I must make him understand."

"All I'm saying is, don't let your business dreams take you away from the people you love. If you do that, you're making a trade, and you may never get back the life that has made you who you are. I know Billy is reluctant to let you go and is in turmoil. Where do you see yourself next year at this time?"

"I don't know. Everything depends on my dresses selling. I need to make back the money I have in materials and supplies, and I want to expand into other garments."

Grandma interrupted. "And where does Billy and your family fit into your plans? This sounds like a full-time career. And in order to sell your dresses, you have to live in town and not here with Billy. I've said my piece for now. But I want you to think about what I've said."

As Lydia drifted off to sleep that night, she recalled Grandma's words, *'I understand wanting to see your dream through to the end, but then what? What happens when you're successful?'* And Billy's words after I said I thought he'd be more supportive, and that we could work things out. *'I don't see that happening now.'* Then Steven's words, *'Billy does his best, but he can't keep up with the farming and all the housework.*

Chapter Twenty-Five

Billy and Oat arrived back at Billy's farm in time for the evening meal. Everyone swapped stories, and afterward, Steven took Billy to the root cellar to show him what was accomplished while he and Oat were helping Mark.

"We'll eat real good this winter," Steven boasted. "Grandma and Lydia taught me how to can, and we'll be able to put up the rest of the garden ourselves. Grandma said we'll need more jars, at least four dozen."

"All right, little brother. You're in charge of the garden from now on."

"I sure am. Lydia was mad about the way the garden looked when she arrived. I won't let the weeds take over again. From now on, we'll either eat or can every vegetable."

Once the boys were in bed, Grandma settled into the rocker with her Bible, and Billy took Lydia's hand to take her outside so they could talk.

"Can you drive Grandma and me to Jack's tomorrow and then go into town to check the mail while we help with the canning? If my fabric has arrived, I can get started. Would you go to town for me? Pleeease," Lydia begged.

Billy kissed her forehead. "You know I'm not in favor of you moving to town, but I also know you won't give up. How can I say no to you when you're so darn cute? I'll go to town if it helps. What do you think about Steven and Oat being on their own tomorrow? Oat may not feel comfortable after what happened in town."

"I think they'll be fine. I've done some thinking while I've been here. Once I move in, maybe we could add a small room for me to do my sewing?"

"Do you remember the little one-room structure with the lean-to on the back for the animals that your father Samuel and Uncle Richard built when your family first moved here? Are you thinking something that size or bigger? Planning an extra room seems a bit early when you don't know how things will work out yet."

"Oh, I remember that first winter in that tiny shack. I've never been so cold. Some nights even fully dressed under the blankets, you couldn't keep warm. The wind whistled through the cracks. Pa would patch one, and another one would start up. Ma kept us busy, but in such a small space, that task was difficult. I remember she told us a story every night. She'd reminisce about her childhood and share tales of good times they had with their parents,—birthday parties, and holidays. I always stayed awake to the very end."

Billy knew the mention of that shack would bring to mind good memories. Mark had told him once about the family's meager beginnings in Kansas. "I hope you'll have your own good memories to share with our children someday," Billy said as he put his arm around Lydia. "If you need an extra room added to the house when we get married, I'll be glad to build a room for you if it means you'll be here with us and not in town." He kissed her gently, and they strolled back to the house, arms about the other's waist.

****

"I'm taking Grandma and Lydia to Jack's today and heading into town. I thought you boys could stay home if you want. I'll be back in time for supper, so you'll be alone for the day. Will you be all right by yourselves?

The boys looked at each other, then Steven said, "I'm good with staying home if you are Oat. We could do anything we want all day long."

"I guess it's good," Oat said. "We could clean up the shed and churn some butter."

Lydia nudged Grandma and smiled. "I could leave a list of chores for you to do if you think you'll get bored."

Steven assured her, "No, we don't need a list. We won't get bored."

"And we'll even fix supper for when you get home," Oat added.

****

After taking Lydia and Grandma to Jack and Abby's, Billy arrived in town late morning and pulled the team to a stop in front of the bank before walking across the main street to the postal office. The clerk took Lydia and Sarah's letters and handed him two large boxes addressed to Lydia. "Thank you," Billy said, "This will make Lydia very happy."

Stowing the boxes in the wagon, he walked to the dry goods store and bought canning jars, salt, and vinegar, along with some candy for the boys and Johanna as a surprise.

When the horses stopped at Jack's, no one rushed out to greet him. *That's odd*, he thought. Jumping down and grabbing Lydia's boxes, he set them on the porch and returned for the canning jars. Entering with a box of jars under his arm, he saw why nobody rushed out. Everyone, even Jack, wore aprons. Jack was scrubbing piles of vegetables. Lydia was cutting green beans, and Abby was stirring a steaming pot of tomato sauce while Grandma was filling jars and sealing them. They barely looked up when he walked in.

"I see you're all hard at work, so I'll leave these canning jars for you and be on my way. I don't want to leave the boys alone any longer than necessary."

Lydia looked up. "No mail for me?" she asked.

"Well, let me check." Billy stepped out the door and returned with his arms loaded.

"Boxes! My boxes arrived!" Lydia dropped the knife, ran to Billy, and gave him a hug. "I can't wait to open them! Thanks for picking them up for me, Billy." She wrapped her arms around him and gave him a kiss on the lips. "We should be finished in a day or so. With Jack's help, it's going quickly. I can't wait to get home and start sewing."

"The boys and I will come get you the day after tomorrow. Don't worry. You'll be sewing in no time. I wish I could stay and help, but I've to get home." Billy chuckled, walked over, and patted Jack on the back. "You're doing a fine job. Sorry, I gotta leave." Billy gave Grandma and Abby a kiss on the cheek and attempted to kiss Jack.

Jack ducked just in time.

Billy chuckled on his way out the door.

Oat and Steven had made a pot of soup from the bounty of the garden. Oat lifted the lid and gave the vegetables a stir when Billy walked into the house and said, "That smells pretty good. Is the soup ready to eat?"

"It sure is," Oat said.

"That's good. I'm starving. I'll put the horses away, and then we can eat. I won't be long," Billy said.

"I told you he'd be hungry when he got home," Steven said, setting the table with bowls and spoons. "And I can't wait to try the muffins we made to go with the soup."

"Thanks, boys," Billy said, hearing the tail end of Steven's comments to Oat. "I guess from now on, you can help with the cooking and the baking. And we need to do a better job of keeping the house clean too."

"We's help," Oat said.

"We will help," Billy corrected him.

"I am learning," Oat said, then repeated. "We will help."

"You're doing really well, Oat. We're all proud of you. Oh, and don't let me forget, we have to fetch Lydia and Grandma in a couple of days."

****

Lydia and Grandma's bags were already on the front steps when Billy and the boys arrived.

Steven jumped from the wagon. "I want to go see Benjamin and Annabelle. I bet they've grown since last time. Come on, Oat. I hope they aren't sleeping."

Grandma put her arms out to catch the boys as they flew through the door. "Abby's feeding the babies in the bedroom. She'll bring them out when she's done. Why don't you two go find Jack? I think he's in the barn working on his leather projects."

"All right, Grams," Oat said, and he and Steven ran to the barn.

Billy heard someone behind him. He turned, and Lydia flung her arms around him and gave him a kiss.

"I have enough fabric and notions to get a good start on getting patterns cut and sewing done."

"I'm still not fond of this whole idea," Billy said but

received no response from Lydia.

****

"I'm glad Grandma was willing to put the boys to bed so we can be alone. I was so looking forward to spending time with you," Billy said as they walked, holding hands in the moonlight.

Billy kept the conversation light, explaining, "The boys made soup and muffins to surprise me when I got home."

"It's good spending time with you too, Billy," Lydia shared, then said, "I'm so excited." She gave his hand a squeeze.

Billy smiled as they strolled in silence for a few steps.

Breaking the silence, Lydia said, "Now I have fabric. I can start sewing."

"Sewing. Your business. Your dresses. That's all you want to talk about anymore, Lydia. I'm tired of hearing about it." Billy dropped her hand and picked up the pace heading back to the house.

Lydia rose early the next day and didn't mention anything about dresses the entire three-hour ride home with Billy and the boys.

After briefly chatting with everyone, Steven was ready to leave. "Come on, Billy, we've got to go. I didn't think we were visiting all day," Steven said, pacing between the well and the wagon. "You said Oat and I could stop and fish at the creek on the way home."

"I'll catch four and eat them all myself," Oat boasted.

Steven retorted, "Well if you're catching four, I'm catching five."

Billy said, "Whoa, there. Don't you think we better

see if they're biting before you start counting how many you're going to eat? I thought if we caught extra, we'd salt them for another day."

Steven bobbed his head. "Oh, I guess you're right. Come on, let's get going. I already said good-bye and kissed everyone."

"Well, I haven't," Billy said. "Go climb in the wagon. I'll be along in a minute." He took Lydia's hand, and they walked behind the barn returning shortly, holding hands and both smiling happily.

Lydia gave Billy a kiss on the cheek. "You will come next week, won't you?"

"I'd do anything for you. I'd come even if I was sick with a fever." Billy kissed her forehead.

****

That evening Lydia showed the family the material and supplies that arrived. "There is still more coming, but I can get started tomorrow.

Awakened by anticipation, Lydia was ready to begin her work, and soon fabric was laid out, patterns pinned, and she was ready to cut when Sarah reminded her the table was needed for the mid-day meal.

"Father, do you think a space could be set up in the corner of the sitting room for me to work?" Lydia asked.

"I can make you a makeshift table from the boards we got at the sawmill," Mark said. "Maybe you could help?"

Lydia flung her arms around her father. "I'll help. Can we get started right away?"

"I'll get my tools and show you which boards to bring inside," Mark instructed.

"I'll help too," Johanna offered.

Mark made a trestle table four and a half feet wide

and six feet long. There was room to get around the table easily. Soon the project was finished.

"Now I have a workspace of my own." Lydia hugged her father. "Thank you, Pa, for making this possible." Lydia laid out her fabric and began cutting. She was so intent on her work that the next thing she heard was her mother saying, "Time for bed."

"I can't believe it's so late already," Lydia said as the clock chimed.

"I know you want to get your dresses made, but you must have a good night's rest, or you'll be tired in the morning." Lydia climbed the ladder and lit her candle.

Sarah called after her, "Sweet dreams."

Sarah offered assistance the following day. "I'll pin on a pattern while you're sewing. Oh, dear, she said, I'm running out of straight pins. Do you have more?'

"I never thought about needing more pins. I'll have to get some from Mrs. Cooper the next time I'm in town. Maybe Grandma has some?" Then she remembered she had borrowed Grandma's pins weeks ago. "I'd better start a list."

"You might want to add spools of thread as well. It'd be so inconvenient to run out." Sarah suggested.

"Good idea, Ma. I won't get far without more pins and thread."

Chapter Twenty-Six

As promised, Billy visited within the week carrying a bouquet of flowers.

"Oh, thank you, they're beautiful," Lydia gushed, then immediately rushed him inside the house to show off her new workspace and her partially completed garments. She hoped he'd take more of an interest after seeing her accomplishments.

"This one is waiting for lace. I need buttons to finish this homespun, and I ran out of the right colored thread on the calico," she explained.

Billy threw his hands in the air. "I've told you that I don't like this idea of yours. It's not that I don't think your dresses will sell. They look beautiful. But you're single, and you'll be vulnerable in town. Couldn't you make them during the winter and try selling them next year at the Harness Shop or in a different town?"

"I could, but I wouldn't know the dress shop owners in other towns. And they may have readymade clothing in their store by then. Traveling would take time, and that's time away from sewing. Besides, I have to try locally first, and the Harness Shop is the perfect location. If I don't sell anything before the snow flies, I'll come home and try your suggestions, but I'm confident they'll sell."

Changing Billy's mind was impossible, so Lydia changed the subject and said, "Come on, Billy. Let's take a walk so you can tell me what you and the boys have been doing."

She slipped her hand into his. "Promise that you'll come visit at least every other week. The Harvest Festival is coming up. Maybe we can all go to town and enjoy the festivities. You said you were going to enter the shooting contest this time. I do hope you win."

"Me too. I'd like to give the rifle to Oat. He's a good shot. Maybe he'd like to enter himself? There was a black man entered in the last contest. I'll ask him and see what he says." Billy kissed her cheek.

"What was that for?" Lydia gazed into his eyes.

"Because I love you, and I love the time we spend together."

"I love you too, and we'll be together as man and wife by this time next year."

Billy smiled. "I know what you can do this winter when you have free time."

"What's that?" Lydia asked.

"You can design your wedding dress."

"I'm already ahead of you on that thought, but there is something special that you could do for me."

Billy looked at Lydia quizzically.

"Ma and I were talking. I need a sign to put in the front window of the Harness Shop to let people know a dress shop will be opening soon. I'm trying to come up with a name. I was thinking something simple like Lydia's Ready-Wear Dresses. What do you think?

"I think you're asking the wrong person. If I had my way, there wouldn't be a dress shop that takes you away from me. I'll make you a sign, but you'd better ask Ma and Grandma about a name."

"Can you take me to town next week?" Lydia

pleaded sweetly. "My other fabrics should arrive by then, and we can get the material for the sign."

"Yes, I'll take you. Only if Pa can bring you and picks you up."

"I'll ask him. Why? Are you too busy?"

"The boys and I were going to put up produce next week, and we're still working on the corn crib. If Pa can't bring you, you'll have to wait a week." Billy shrugged his shoulder, then said, "You can wait a week, can't you?"

"Well, if Pa can't bring me, I guess I'll have to." Lydia kicked a small rock down the dirt path.

At dinner, Lydia asked, "Pa can you take me to Billy's one day next week? He'll take me to town if you can get me to his place and pick me up."

Mark swallowed hard. "I guess I could, but Grandma would have to go with you. Why don't the two of you go back with him today?"

"I'd rather give my packages a few more days. They should all arrive by the middle of next week," Lydia said.

Mark shook his head. "All right, if I have to. Ma, can you go along?"

Ruth shook her head. "They're only running into town. I think they know what's expected of them by now. I'd rather stay here."

"All right. You know Ma, and I trust you. I'll take you."

"Thanks, Pa. I'll make you your favorite dessert for taking me." Lydia smiled.

"And what do I get," Billy said.

"You get the pleasure of my company for the whole ride to town and back."

Steven finished a bite of food and said, "We'd rather

have dessert."

After their meal, Billy and the boys headed home, and Lydia returned to sewing.

****

See you in three days," Mark said, dropping Lydia off at Billy's and quickly turned the wagon around and headed back.

"Three days!" Lydia called out, then bit her tongue, seeing the produce hanging on the vines. "All right, I'll see you in three days, and I'll make sure to get all the supplies."

Billy and Lydia dropped the boys at Jack and Abby's and arrived in town early afternoon, parking the wagon in front of the dry goods store.

"I want to check for mail first," Lydia said, then rushed across the street to the postal office while Billy got down and stretched his legs.

"Anything for me today?" she asked the clerk.

"Why yes, you have several boxes and a couple large envelopes. I don't think you can manage everything in one trip."

An unfamiliar voice in back of her said, "I'll help you if you need a hand."

Looking over her shoulder, there stood a young man about her age. She had never seen him before and was taken aback by his clean and mannerly appearance and his willingness to help.

Lydia gazed at him and said, "Oh, thank you, but that won't be necessary. I can make two trips. The wagon is at the dry goods store, and my brother can help me." She knew the second she said the words 'my brother' she should correct herself and tell him they were courting, but how would she explain without going into a lot of detail? And did the truth really matter? She'd probably never see him again.

"No, I insist," the polite man said.

"Here you go, Johnathan." The clerk handed the young man the large parcels, and Lydia gathered the envelopes bulging with supplies and samples and led the way to the wagon.

From the middle of the street, Lydia called, "Billy, can you come give us a hand?"

Billy immediately headed to help, meeting them as they stepped up onto the wooden walkway on his side. "Here, I'll take those. Thanks for your help."

"My pleasure. She would have had to make two trips, and I had free hands," the young man said. "And, by the way, my name is Johnathan Bellows. My mother and I moved to Dead Flats a few months ago from Ohio. I've never seen you in town before."

"No, we live west of here. This is Lydia, and I'm Billy Henry. Thanks for your help. I'll take the packages from here."

"Yes, thank you," Lydia said, dismissing Johnathan Bellows and turning her attention to Billy. "Come. We must get supplies, and then I want to show you my new dress shop. I can't wait to open my packages, but I'll wait until we get back to your place."

Johnathan Bellows walked back across the street.

Lydia and Billy dropped the boxes at the wagon.

Hurrying into the dry goods store ahead of Billy to find the things on her list, Lydia said, "Here, Billy, we need everything on these two lists, and don't let me forget to pick up two newspapers."

After loading the supplies into the wagon, Lydia bought the newspapers and tucked them under the seat.

Next, they stopped at the hardware store, bought two boards and some paint for the sign, and added them to the wagon.

"Come along," Lydia said, "One last stop before we go home," and rushed Billy up the street to talk to Ezra Gray at the Harness Shop.

"Why hello, young lady." Mr. Gray smiled as he greeted her. "Have you made a decision on opening your shop with me, or did you find a better spot?"

Lydia reached to shake his hand. "I'd like to take you up on your offer, Mr. Gray. I think this will be a great location. I also want you to meet Billy Henry. We are courting, and he'll help me move everything in."

The two men shook hands.

"We want to look around and see what I might need to get started," Lydia said.

"Go ahead. If you need me, I'll be in the back," Ezra said and disappeared out of sight.

"I want to remind you, I'm here under protest. I still don't like the thought of you living all by yourself. You living in town alone doesn't feel right to me." Billy took her hand and pulled her toward him. "Please change your mind now before Mr. Gray is involved."

"I can't, Billy. I know the timing isn't great. But even if I stayed home, I wouldn't get to see you over the winter. At least, if I'm here, I can work on my dresses and start selling them. I'm not forgetting our commitment to each other. I love you. And I want a family with you one day. But I need this chance first."

Billy grimaced at the thought. "What if this is our last chance. I'm afraid if your business is successful, you won't have time for me. You'll want to stay in town, and sewing will mean more to you than I do."

"I'll never let that happen. I promise." Lydia wanted to kiss Billy, but the door opened, and a man walked in, calling Ezra's name.

Before their lips touched, Lydia pulled back and called out, "Back here, Sir. I'll get Mr. Gray for you."

Billy released her, and Lydia made her way to the back of the shop to fetch Mr. Gray.

While the two gentlemen talked, Lydia excitedly took Billy's hand and began showing him the storage area that would be her room. Then, she pulled him to the front of the store where her dresses would be on display.

"Aren't these windows great? People will be able to look right in. I could use clotheslines strung on poles to hang my dresses. I'll also need a place for women to try things on if they want. The older women probably won't, but the gals my age will want to make sure they fit. This corner would work nicely, don't you think? Could you build two more sides? I'll make a curtain to cover the opening. I can even help you if you like. I'll check with Mr. Gray to make sure he doesn't mind. The walls don't have to go to the ceiling. Just high enough that the men can't see in."

Billy took in a deep breath and exhaled slowly. Raising his hands in surrender, he said. "I'll help because I love you, and I know you can't build things yourself. But I must say, helping goes against my better judgment."

****

That evening, the boys played a game of checkers. "King me," Oat crowed. "You won't win now, Steven. I get to play Billy next."

Lydia dried the last dish. While Billy stepped outside to empty the pan of dishwater, Lydia began going

191

through her boxes and doing a quick inventory of items.

"Everything I ordered has arrived. I can't wait to get started." Her hands floated over the fabric. "This color is nicer than I imagined. And look, this lace will work wonderfully with this homespun material."

Billy interrupted. "Lydia, why don't you and Grandma come visit us for a few days? Or we could meet for a picnic?"

"I'd lose at least two days of sewing if we visited. I think you really want me to do your canning and cleaning. I simply do not have the time to waste."

"Waste?" Billy raised his voice. "It would be a waste of your time to come and be with me here on the farm that we're planning to someday share? What do you think you're going to do once we're married? You won't be sewing every minute. Not even every day. Sewing can't take up all your time. You'll have responsibilities. When we have children, are you planning to have time for them? Your family should come first."

Lydia turned and looked Billy squarely in the face. "I'm sorry, Billy. I didn't mean to upset you. I didn't really mean visiting you would be a waste. I guess my mind is focused on getting my dresses done by October. I don't have a lot of time. If they aren't made, I can't sell them. If I can't sell them, I can't reinvest my money in my business. Everything depends on my having the dresses ready to sell when I open. There must be a good selection for people to choose from. If not, they may not buy again. I need to make a good first impression, Billy. I thought you'd understand…if you cared."

"Sweetheart, I have resigned myself to the fact that you have to try to make your business work. I'm trying to see your side of things. But you must promise me that come spring, no matter what, you'll move back home."

"I can't promise you anything right now," Lydia said, rushing out of the room.

Steven and Oat looked at each other, then at Billy.

Billy shook his head. "Who's winning?"

Chapter Twenty-Seven

Canning jars filled with garden produce covered the table. After putting her things by the door, Lydia gazed out the window and said, "We got a lot done. This food will fill your stomachs this winter."

"Tell Grandma she was right," Steven said. "I'm glad we got more canning jars, and by the looks of the garden, we might need even more."

A wagon approached. Pa coming to pick her up, no doubt. She turned to Billy to ask, "What day next week would you like to meet at the creek for a picnic?"

A smile lit Billy's face. "How about Wednesday? Maybe everyone can come this time."

"All right, Wednesday it is." Lydia gave Billy and the boys' kisses on their cheeks and smiled. Handing her Pa packages to carry, she gathered the rest of her things as Billy picked up her carpetbag. Waving good-bye, from the wagon seat, she said, "Come on, Pa. I want to get home so I can start sewing."

After a hearty meal of beef stew and savory biscuits, Lydia spent most of the night sewing on buttons and lace to finish some of her dresses. Now that she had all of her supplies, she planned to work late every evening and take advantage of her mother's help as much as possible.

By mid-week, she had completed five dresses, and three more were in various stages of completion. With Johanna doing her chores and the help of her mother and grandma, she was sure she could reach her goal of fifteen dresses by the time she moved to town. *If everything goes as planned, the next time Billy comes to visit, I hope he sees my dedication and effort and shows more support.*

****

"I'm so glad we decided on a picnic. I can't remember the last time we all got in the water and had so much fun," Lydia said, dripping wet and grabbing a towel to dry off. I'll help Grandma and Ma set out the food and we'll call you when we're ready."

"Pa, with all of us swimming around, those fish are probably miles away by now," Steven said. "We won't have a chance to catch them."

Billy skimmed the palm of his hand across the surface of the water to splash Steven's face, then said, "That's all right, little brother. We'll stop and fish on our way to visit the family next week."

"Good that you're coming," Mark said with a chuckle. "I'm going to put you to work sharpening the sickles. We'll need them again in a few weeks."

"Come and get it," Sarah called.

Everyone got out, dried off, and headed to the quilt, where a feast of fried chicken, cabbage salad, pickled eggs, and freshly made rolls looked inviting.

Before everyone was done eating their pie, Lydia started packing the picnic dishes and loading baskets in the wagon.

"Pa, we could at least try dropping a line in the water and see if they're biting, couldn't we? We brought our fishing poles. Oat and I will even dig the bait. Right, Oat?" Steven grinned.

"Sure will. I got a real taste for fish. Billy cooks

them up real good," Oat added.

Mark said, "All right, we'll try. Grab your poles, shovel, and the worm can."

"I'm coming too," Johanna shouted.

"Then you must be quiet," Steven reminded her.

"Well, I don't feel like being quiet today, so I guess I'll stay here." Looking around, Johanna asked, "Where are Lydia and Billy?"

****

"We should make this our spot," Billy said, coming upon the fallen limb they sat on during the first picnic they shared.

Kneeling on the ground, Billy gently pulled Lydia toward him. They lay together, Billy on his back and Lydia curled up beside him with her head on his chest.

"What do you think life will be like when we get married?" Lydia asked.

"It'll be great," Billy said. "We'll do everything together. We'll raise Steven and Oat and have children of our own. As many as you want. We aren't that far away from Jack and Abby or our folks. We can visit one or the other every week. Living at my farm, you'll be closer to town. We can expand our fields and raise cash crops, plant a bigger garden as our family grows, and raise enough beef cows to butcher every year for meat. Pa has taught us well. We won't always have an easy life, but as long as we're together, we'll do fine. I can't wait to have you beside me always."

"It sounds like our life will be wonderful, Billy. I know you'll be a good father. You're more like a father to Steven and Oat than a brother. You take real good care of them. I know cooking, keeping the house, and canning is women's work, but you've done well. No one is wasting away to nothing. I want to make a family with you, care for you, and be your wife. I really do, but I can't tell you a date right now. Farming is in my blood too. I'm going to ask Pa if we can butcher early this year so I can help." Lydia was being careful not to say anything about her moving to town, and Billy hadn't mentioned her move either.

They lay together, Billy's arm resting on Lydia's leg that was draped across him. Moving his fingers softly along her thigh, he imagined her next to him in bed on their wedding night.

Lydia, too, was thinking of the future they would have as husband and wife. She wanted to make him proud of her and start a family right away, but she pictured her dress shop as part of their life too. Somehow, someway, she would get him to see her side of things where her business was concerned. *One step at a time*, she reminded herself as she turned her body and took his face in her hands.

"Oh, please kiss me, Billy," Lydia said.

Without hesitation, Billy raised his head, and their lips touched. He embraced her, pulling her close to his awakened body. Their mouths joyously explored each other's in passionate entanglement. Suddenly Lydia sat up. "Wait, Billy, wait. You're going so fast. I have to catch my breath."

Billy slid his hand along her back and caressed her neck before burying his fingers in her hair. "I love the way you feel. You're beautiful, Lydia. You'll be a beautiful bride."

"I can't wait until you're my husband. When we're close like this, you stir feelings in me that I've never felt before." Her heart pounded, her body tingled with a warmth that made parts of her throb. She wanted to feel this pleasure all the time and knew Billy was the only one that could make her feel this way. After taking a few deep breathes her breathing returned to normal

"Billy. Lydia. Where are you?" A sing-song voice rang out not far away.

Springing to his feet, Billy called, "Over here." He helped Lydia off the ground. "I guess we lost track of time."

Steven, Oat, and Johanna ran to them.

Steven arrived first. "Pa says, we gotta get home. Hurry up. He wants to get back to do chores."

Billy picked up Johanna and put her on his shoulders. Lydia took the boys' hands and asked, "How many fish did you catch?"

"Only two each. Pa caught two, too, and he gave his to us, so we have enough for supper," Steven boasted.

Oat shook his head and chuckled. "Pa don't want to clean them, is all."

Chapter Twenty-Eight

Deep in thought about the dresses she had laid out to review, Lydia struggled with deciding what to charge. *I may have used the same pattern, but each is a little different than the other, depending on if I used lace or not or if I added a button. Every dress will have a different price*, she finally decided. *But how do I charge for my time?* Before she knew it, her mother's voice interrupted.

"Come help fix the noonday meal," Sarah called.

I'm not sure what to charge for these," Lydia said as she cleared them from the table. I can calculate the cost of materials, but how much should I charge for my time?"

"I'll tell you the same thing I told Jack when he was trying to decide his prices," Mark said. "Don't price them too low. Your time is worth far more than you realize, and you've put a lot of time and effort into designing as well as making them. It's finding the perfect price that people will pay. You can always run a sale if they aren't selling. But if you start out too low, you may sell out in a month without making enough profit to reinvest."

"Your father is right, sweetheart," Sarah added. "Yes, they are day dresses, but they are your design, and they are beautiful. I can see girls your age as well as church ladies wearing them."

To help, Grandma drew fancy paper tags, and Johanna cut them out. Lydia attached the tags to the size labels she had sewn into the collars. Looking at the prices in her magazines, taking the commission she would pay Mr. Gray, the cost of materials, and her time all into consideration, she priced her dresses in the range of two and a half to five dollars. *Will everyone be able to afford to buy one?* No, she decided. *But there were plenty of women in town that could. Jack has done well with his leather business, and I hope to do the same. Oh, no. I haven't stitched the last batch of items that Jack gave me, and I know he wants them in the store in time for the Harvest Festival.* Glancing at the wall calendar, she noted September was only two weeks away. *I better get started.*

Putting her things aside, she opened the bundle of items. "Ma, look at all this work Jack sent me. There's a good four or five days of work here. Can you cut dress patterns for me while I work on this project?"

"Sure, I'll help. You lay them out. I'll pin and cut them. Now that we have more pins, the job will be easier," Sarah suggested, "If you ask Grandma, I'm sure she'd sew buttons on that homespun dress that's almost finished."

Grandma overheard the conversation and said, "If you thread the needles, I'll help."

"Oh, thank you both for all your help. What will I ever do without you?" Lydia gave them each a hug and threaded a needle for Grandma, and one with heaver waxed thread that she used on the leather.

"What can I do to help?" Johanna asked.

"Well, I'm going to need a lot more tags," Lydia said. "Can you trace around the ones Grandma drew and make more?"

"Sure I can," Johanna offered.

As everyone worked on a project, Lydia mused aloud, "I haven't come up with a name for my shop yet. Any ideas? Billy said he'd make a sign for me to put in the store window that says 'Opening Soon,' but I think I should have the name of the store on the sign too. I don't like the obvious name…Lydia's Dress Shop. How about something catchy with ready-wear in the title?"

"How about Lydia's Custom Designed, Ready-Wear, Dress Shop," Grandma suggested. "Written on three lines."

"That's what they are, but don't you think that's a mouth full?" Lydia sighed.

"I think they're fancy," Johanna said. "What about Lydia's Fancy Dresses."

"I'm glad you like them, sweetheart," Lydia said, "But I was thinking Lydia's Ready-Wear Dress Shop.

"I like that name," Sarah said, "it says what they are, and you can explain that you designed them when you speak with customers. Word of mouth will spread fast if the women like what's for sale and there is nothing not to like. I'll bet you sell out before Christmas. Some women may want you to make custom gowns for them for the holidays. That will take more of your time, so be careful before you make any promises. You may not be able to get fabric shipped to make them in time. I think I'd stick to your plan of ready-wear if I were you."

"You're right. Mother. I will stick to my plan and branch out into my skirt patterns if I have the fabric and time. I know I have to sell ten dresses before I have enough money to order additional fabric. I already have a new design in mind."

****

Billy had reluctantly cut the boards he bought in town and jointed them together to make a sign to announce Lydia's dress shop opening. Every time he thought of Lydia, his mind would wander, and the project took him all morning to finish.

By the time the boys finally arrived at the Hewitts, the sun was high in the sky, mid-afternoon.

Lydia ran out to greet them.

Pulling the sign from the back of the wagon, he handed it to Lydia and said, "Here, I made this for you. Did you come up with a name for your dress shop?"

"I decided on Lydia's Ready-Wear Dress Shop. It's short and says everything. Did you bring the paint?"

Billy reached in the back of the wagon and handed her the paint. "You'll have to do the painting yourself," he said, turned, and went inside to talk to his father, and Lydia lugged the sign and paint to the barn.

"Pa, is Mr. Frazer coming over to take care of the animals so everyone can go to the festival this year?" Billy asked.

Mark raked his fingers through his hair, "He has to stop by to pick up his supplies this week or next. I'll ask him then. I'm sure he won't mind, but I can't say for certain. If he can't come, your ma and I will stay home, and the rest of you can go to town. Lydia can drive the wagon to your place, and you can all go together."

"I'll fix enough food for you to take so you can all enjoy the town picnic whether your pa and I come or not," Sarah added, but you'll have to keep an eye on the children."

Grandma grinned, "I'll help watch them in the evening so you and Lydia can go to the dance. That's all

Lydia's been talking about. She wants to wear a dress she made to show off one of her designs."

Billy shook his head. "I don't know how much I'll feel like dancing if that's all she wants to show off. The boys and I won't be over next week. We'll wait and hopefully see everyone when you come for the festival. I wonder if Jack and Abby will go."

Lydia walked in and only heard the part about not coming next week and Jack and Abby. "They might go to town if they haven't gone yet," Lydia said. "I know Abby is eager for her folks to meet the twins, and I'll be taking Jack's leather goods to the hardware. He already has them priced."

"We can drop by and see if they're home on our way to town. They may need supplies if they aren't able to attend," Sarah said.

"I know!" Lydia said abruptly. "We could go a day early, and that way, I could get the leather goods to the hardware and my opening soon sign in the window of the harness shop."

Mark pursed his lips. "I don't feel right asking Seth to come an extra day. With the new baby, he shouldn't be away from his family that long."

"You're right, Pa," Lydia agreed. "I understand."

"We aren't staying for supper today, Ma," Billy announced. "We have leftovers we have to eat up, and since we got a late start, we'll head home in a little while. The boys wanted to come see Johanna, and I wanted to know the plans for the festival."

"I'll send this pumpkin pie home with you to enjoy for dessert," Grandma winked at Billy.

Billy winked back. "Thanks, Grandma."

"Billy," Lydia said, "Do you have time to take a

walk before you leave?"

"If we go now, I guess I do." Billy headed for the door.

Once out of earshot, Lydia asked, "What's wrong with you today?"

"Oh, nothing. Why do you ask?"

"You don't seem yourself is all? Are you feeling all right?"

"I'm fine. Maybe a little tired."

"Are you excited about the shooting contest? Have you been practicing? Is Oat signing up?"

"I've decided I wasn't going to shoot, and Oat shouldn't either. With what happened in town back in July, talk will still be circulating about what happened and about the four men who did it. I think maybe the boys and I should stay home this year."

"No! You must go to the festival!" Lydia exclaimed. "I mean, I really want us all to go as a family. Going as a family will show we are united."

"Don't you really mean, going as a family you can show off your new dress and even show off me as your new beau? Isn't that really why you want to go? Oh, and to put your new sign in the window. We can't forget that."

"Of course, I want to introduce you to my friends as my beau, but I also want to spend time with you, dance with you, and enjoy the time with you and our family."

"Well, I'm going to talk to Pa and see what he thinks. If he says it's a good idea to stay home, that's what I'm going to do."

Billy walked in the house and said, "Pa, I was thinking it might be a good idea if the boys and I not go to the Harvest Festival. You know…because of what happened in town earlier this year." Billy took a seat at the table. "What do you think?"

"Well, there will probably be some talk, some stares, and plenty of gossip, but I don't think that's enough reason for us to miss the festival. The boys and Johanna need to go back in town surrounded by family so they'll feel safe and not afraid. Are you sure Oat is the reason you don't want to go?"

"No, not the only reason, I guess. I don't know how to get Lydia to understand me once and for all."

Mark patted him on the back. "We all do things we don't want to do sometimes, Son. You and Lydia are going to have to work this out between yourselves."

Chapter Twenty-Nine

"Mr. Frazer is caring for the livestock, so we all came," Johanna was quick to say as she jumped into Billy's arms.

Mark moved Ruth's chair to the back of Billy's wagon and helped her get comfortable.

"Ma and I will stop off at Jack and Abby's," he said. "The rest of you can head to town. We'll catch up with you this evening. We'll arrive before dark. Save us a spot."

Lydia grabbed the sign she painted and returned for the bundle of leather goods.

Once everyone was settled, Billy called to the horses, and they were off. Mark and Sarah followed, turning off to visit the twins.

In town, Lydia got off in front of the hardware with the heavy bundle of leather goods. "I won't be long." She waved. "I'll find the wagon. Try to park in the church grove where we usually do."

Entering the store, she spotted the owner and called out, "Hello, Mr. Hovis, I brought items for you, and I wrote out the item list and prices. Do you have time to check them off now, or should I come back?"

"Now is a good time. I'm glad you brought more. You can see I ran low." Picking up one of the new belts from the pile, Mr. Hovis looked it over. "You and your brother sure do nice work. Everyone that buys your items says so, and lots of people come back and buy other items you make as well."

"Thank you for telling me. I'll pass that compliment on to Jack. I'm sure he'll be pleased. Take your time. I'm going to look around."

Lydia walked up and down the aisles, and a hundred things ran through her mind that she might need to live in town alone, but she refrained from buying anything. Money would be tight, and she knew it. Strolling back to the counter, she said, "I see you're finished. Was everything in order?"

"Quite in order, young lady. And here are the profits from the items that sold." He handed her the money.

After counting the tidy sum, she signed the receipt, thanked Mr. Hovis, and put the money in her pocket. She kept one hand on the wad of cash at all times until she arrived at the wagon and quickly tucked the money away in a safe place.

"Steven, Johanna, and I are gonna walk Grams to Doc Glasgow's office," Oat said. "You wanna come along, Lydia?"

"Sure," she said, "Let me fetch my sign to put in the window of the harness shop on the way. Isn't Billy coming?"

Steven took Grandma's hand. "He said he'll catch up after he feeds and waters the horses."

Lydia struggled a little but proudly carried the sign that would announce her dress shop opening. When they arrived at the edge of town, Johnathan Bellows spotted her struggling.

"That looks heavy. Let me carry that for you," Johnathan offered. "Where are you headed?"

Lydia set the end of the sign on the ground and

rested for a moment. "No, thank you. I can manage."

"We're heading for the Harness Shop," Steven said.

Not asking this time, Johnathan picked up the sign and read aloud, "'Opening Soon, Lydia's Ready-Wear Dress Shop.' Why that's you. You're opening a dress shop here in town?"

"Yes," Lydia said, "And I can carry the sign myself."

"No harm in letting the young man help, dear," Grandma interrupted. "I'm Lydia's Grandmother, and these are her brothers, Steven and Otis, and her sister Johanna."

"Hello, I'm Johnathan Bellows. You have another brother, too, right? I think his name is Billy." Johnathan tucked the sign under his arm and invited Lydia to take his other.

Grandma nudged Lydia, and she obliged.

"Yes, his name is Billy," Lydia reluctantly said.

When they arrived at the shop, Lydia took the sign from Johnathan, ran in, and placed the sign in the center of the window. She found Mr. Gray in the back of the store, working.

"Hello, Mr. Gray," Lydia greeted him. "I put my sign announcing the grand opening in the window. Here are the answers to some questions you might get as people inquire." She read each important point she had written down for him. "The dresses are designed and made by Lydia Clark. Dresses will come in three different sizes and different fabrics. The grand opening is October first." She handed him the paper.

"All right, young lady. You sure have thought of everything." Mr. Gray wiped his brow. "If I get inquiries, I'll tell them the information. I'm sure your dresses will be a big success."

"Oh, and I plan to move in and get set-up the week before. I see you have most of the things out of the storage room. Don't worry, I'll help you when I arrive. I must go now, my family is waiting, but I'll stop in again tomorrow. I want to show my Ma the shop."

"All right," Mr. Gray said. "Come by anytime."

Flying out the door, she asked, "Does the sign look all right? She had centered the sign in the middle of the window.

"The sign looks fine, dear." Grandma Hewitt took Lydia's hand.

Johnathan backed up to look. "Perfect," he said.

Lydia smiled and said, "Thank you for carrying the sign for me, but we must keep going. We have errands to run."

"You're welcome anytime. I live down the street from Mr. Gray. If you need a hand, let him know. He knows where I live." Johnathan turned and walked away.

"Lydia's Ready-Wear Dresses," Grandma said as they continued down the street. "They'll be the talk of the town before the night is over. You wait and see."

The window shade was still open when they reached Doc Glasgow's office. "Good, he's still here," Grandma Hewitt said cheerfully as she opened the door.

Hearing the bell on the door, James stepped out from the inner office, exclaiming his delight to see Ruth and the family. "I hoped you'd come to town. Ruth, can I take you to supper tonight? And tomorrow, we can go to supper, take chairs to the dance, and listen to the music."

Ruth blushed. "I'd love that. I'll meet you here. What time?"

"How about 6 o'clock. I have a standing reservation

for that time at the restaurant. Don't worry, children, I'll return her to your wagon afterward."

Just then, the door opened, and Billy walked in asking, "What don't I have to worry about?"

"I just explained that I'll take good care of Ruth tonight at dinner and walk her back to your wagon after the dance." Doc shook Billy's hand, and the family left to stroll through town.

"My stomach's growling," Steven said. We didn't eat any dinner today. What's for supper?"

"Remember we brought vegetable soup from the garden," Billy reminded him. "And I thought we'd make skillet biscuits. Boys, you're in charge of getting a fire started while I mix up the biscuits."

"What about me?" Lydia asked.

"Well, I guess you can help if you want. We've gotten used to fending for ourselves." Billy pulled the sack of cooking gear from the back of the wagon.

The boys returned with kindling and a few larger limbs and got to work.

"Let me make those biscuits," Lydia demanded. "Once the boys get the fire going, why don't you take Johanna and the boys to town with the pumpkins they brought to sell? I remember when we couldn't wait to sell the pumpkins that you and Jack grew so we could go to the store and buy candy with the money we earned. Go on, but be back in an hour to eat."

Each of the boys carried a burlap sack, and Johanna carried an armful of little pie pumpkins to spread out on a blanket. Billy looked on from a distance.

In a half-hour, they sold out and had collected fifty cents.

Dividing the money as agreed. Oat insisted, "We

needs to bring more next year. That's twenty cents for Steven and me 'cause we planted them and hauled them to town, and ten cents for Johanna's help sellin 'em."

"Yeah, we need to bring a whole wagon load so we can get rich," Steven said, holding out his share of the take in the palm of his hand.

"Thanks for letting me help," Johanna said. "I want to go get candy with my nickels."

Billy walked over and interrupted. "I'll tell you what Pa always told Jack and me after we sold pumpkins. He'd say, 'It's always best to save some money for a rainy day.'"

"What's that mean?" Johanna asked.

Oat answered, "I think he's saying, don't spend all the money today."

"That's exactly what I'm saying." Billy smiled and tousled Oat's hair. "I'll let you go get candy, but save some of your money for later. Remember, Lydia's fixin' supper."

****

"Don't you want a bowl of soup," Steven asked Grandma Hewitt as he took a muffin from the skillet.

"No, you go ahead. I don't want to spoil my meal with Doctor Glasgow tonight. Besides, your folks should be rolling in soon, and they'll be hungry."

Steven took a seat and asked, "Are we all going to the dance tomorrow night, Billy?

"I'm sure we'll go as a family, and we're going to the picnic tomorrow, too. I know you've been looking forward to all the food and desserts. That will be fun."

"Have you made a final decision yet? Are you going to shoot this year, Billy?" Lydia asked as she ladled a bowl of soup and handed it to him.

211

He replied, "I haven't decided yet. If Pa shoots, I might."

"He took the gun when he went for a walk the other day, and I heard a few shots. He didn't come home with a rabbit or anything, so he might have been practicing." Lydia dished up her soup and sat beside Billy.

"When will I be old enough to shoot in the contest?" Steven asked.

Lydia chuckled, remembering. "I think Pa let Jack shoot when he was sixteen, so you have a few years to wait. But I remember Jack asking the same thing every year, trying to convince Pa he was old enough."

Johanna pointed. Look, it's Ma and Pa. They made it."

Mark pulled the wagon up beside Billy's in the church grove, and Lydia dished them up some food as they joined the family.

Grandma asked first. "How are the children and the twins?"

"Everyone is doing fine, and they send their love," Sarah said. "They would have loved to join us but felt keeping the babies out of town a while longer would be best. They did say they'd be coming in next month to Abby's parents to stay a few days and asked if we'd stop in to see her folks while we're here."

"We can do that in the morning, Ma," Lydia said. "I'll go with you, then we can walk to the Harness Shop. I want to show you my sign and the space."

"All right, sweetheart," Sarah agreed.

Finishing with supper, Mark and the boys tended to the horses while Grandma primped and put on her shawl.

"Come along, Billy. You can walk me to Mr. Glasgow's house," Grandma requested.

"Can I come too?" Johanna asked.

"No, dear, you better stay and help Lydia." Grandma took Billy's arm as they strolled.

"Once out of earshot, Grandma said, "Billy, I know you and Lydia are not seeing eye-to-eye about her business. I wish you would have seen the joy on her face when she walked out of the Harness Shop after putting the sign you made her in the window. I really do feel this endeavor is something you must agree to let her try."

Billy jammed his hands in his pockets and grumbled, "You know there is no stopping her, don't you." His voice rose. "I've tried and got nowhere. She doesn't even listen to me when I talk about her business. I don't want her to resent me for keeping her from her dream, but what if her dream becomes her whole life?"

"There, there. We don't know how she'll make out, but you must let her try. She's taking on a lot, and you worry about her and what this could mean to your relationship. I truly believe she loves you and wants a life with you and the boys. You'll work this out."

"You know Grandma, I've been thinking that maybe we should call off the courting for now if her business means more to her than I do."

"I don't think that's the case at all," Granma insisted.

Billy stopped right in front of the Harness Shop to read the sign, then countered, "Maybe if I break things off and she thinks she might lose me for good, maybe then she'd see my side."

"Well, suit yourself. You're going to do what you feel is best. I suspect that calling things off now would break her heart."

Arriving at the doctor's house, Grandma paused

before knocking.

"Maybe you should talk to your Pa about your feelings before you take an action you might regret," Grandma said, then knocked.

Returning to the church grove, Billy found himself going past Elizabeth's house and thinking, *I don't want to make a mistake with Lydia like I did with Elizabeth. I loved her and thought she loved me, only to learn her heart was never truly mine. No, that couldn't be the case with Lydia.*

Chapter Thirty

There was excitement the following day. Joseph and Martha Spencer had come to visit a spell last night, and the family agreed to join them for the community picnic.

Lydia and Sarah left to visit Abby's parents and planned to stop at the shop on their way back. Billy and Mark decided not to shoot in the contest. Grandma was reading a story to Johanna. The boys were dressed and antsy waiting around for the women to return.

"I'm taking the boys to the creek to skip rocks," Billy called to Mark, who was watering the horses.

"Hold up a minute. I'll go with you."

Arriving at the creek, Mark said to Steven and Oat, "Don't get your good clothes too wet. Go and have fun."

The boys nodded and took off to the water's edge looking for flat rocks, and began the competition to see which boy could skip a rock the most times with each throw.

"I'm glad you came along, Pa. I want to talk to you about Lydia. It's no secret I don't like her plans to move to town and sell dresses. I let that be known right from the start, but she's determined. Now, she put her sign in the window, and she's going through with opening her store. I attempted to talk her out of this whole idea several times, but she won't even discuss her business with me anymore."

"I see you're upset. I have reservations about her

moving too, but Lydia worked hard for years to make this happen. Her business plans didn't just come overnight. Ever since she and Jack went into business together, she's been saving her money with this goal in mind. I'm actually proud of her for following through, and so is her mother." Mark rubbed his chin. "We understand her opportunity is happening at a bad time for you, but I think you need to give her some space to see what happens."

"That's the problem. Her dresses will be a huge success, and then what? She still won't have time for me. Her business will come first. Grandma says she feels Lydia really does love me. But if she loves me, wouldn't she want to stay home with me?"

"What's wrong with you, Son? Didn't you learn anything with Elizabeth? Lydia's young and has big dreams. You must give her a chance to prove herself. The timing isn't perfect, but if you keep making demands and acting selfish, you might regret your actions later."

"Pa, I'm thinking of breaking off our courting while Lydia's living in town. Maybe if she thought she could lose me forever, she might think twice about this dream of hers and consider if it's worth the risk," Billy said, confusion and hurt evident in his voice.

"Billy, I won't tell you what to do. You must follow your heart. But do you think breaking things off is really the answer? Perhaps if you put your plans on hold for six months, maybe the two of you could work this out in a mutual way."

Six months. That's half a year. A half-year without Lydia. I don't want to wait that long. When we're together and not talking about her business, we're happy. That's what I want. Billy wrestled with his thoughts until he heard Steven's voice.

"Six skips. That's my all-time record!" Let's go, Billy. I can't wait to tell Lydia." Steven grabbed Billy's hand and pulled his big brother back to reality.

****

The children spread the blanket by the Spencers' quilt in time for the picnic to start. The families enjoyed catching up on news.

Sarah shared, "Mrs. Proctor, Abby's mother, was dressed and able to sit at the table while we had a lovely chat. She says she's feeling much better. And after touring the inside of the harness shop, meeting Mr. Gray, and seeing Lydia's sign in the window, my nervousness about her living in town is calmed."

Steven asked, "Why didn't you and Pa shoot in the contest this year, Billy?"

Billy answered, "I had other things on my mind today and wouldn't have been able to focus."

Mark used the excuse, "I didn't practice enough."

Steven asked his ma, "Did you bring a pie to enter in the pie contest?"

"No, not this year. It's time to give the younger girls the opportunity to win the blue ribbons. I know my family loves my pies, and that's all that matters at my age. You'll be eating my would-be entry for dessert."

Grandma chuckled to herself and said, "Wait until you're my age. You won't care what people think of you or your pie."

Katy and Hannah Spencer hadn't seen Lydia in a couple years and had many stories to share. The girls knew Billy and Lydia and were surprised when she introduced him as her beau.

"We've been courting for three months now," Lydia

shared.

The sisters squealed in delight at the news.

"Girls," Martha Spencer called, "Will you carry the dishes to the tables? And don't forget to take large spoons."

The four girls, including Johanna, each took a dish to share with the community and then returned to carry pies and pudding to the dessert table.

During the meal, Mark, Billy, and Joseph talked farming, Sarah and Martha caught up on family matters while Grandma entertained the younger children with a story of a picnic she attended in her younger years.

Lydia told her friends the details of courting. "We had to ask for our parents' blessing, and now we can hold hands and kiss. Billy is a good kisser," Lydia whispered. After that subject was thoroughly exhausted, she shared her dress shop and grand opening plans. "I'll have punch and cookies and invite the newspaper to do an interview to promote my custom-designed dresses. I pray there is a good turnout, and I sell a few dresses." Lydia beamed with pride. "I will have at least ten dresses in stock at all times, and they will come in different sizes and a variety of fabrics."

Billy overheard the conversation and took note of the pure joy on Lydia's face as she shared with her friends. At that moment, he was proud of her.

Steven nudged Billy to get his attention. "I'm ready for dessert."

"Me too," Oat agreed.

"Go ahead. I'm going to wait a few minutes so my food settles, and I'll have more room." Billy observed their actions and the reactions of people around them as they loaded their plates with wedges of pie and other sweets. No one bothered them or even spoke to them, which was fine with Billy. He noted there were a few other colored folk at the picnic, mainly staying to themselves, but Oat seemed content being with the family.

As the picnic ended, the girls collected their serving dishes while Sarah and Martha packed the baskets. Grace, Martha's oldest girl, stopped by with her daughter for a few minutes to chat.

"Boys, why don't you fold the quilt and blanket, and we'll let the men talk until we're ready to leave," Sarah said.

Before returning to the wagon, Billy asked, "Can you watch the boys for a while, Ma? I want a photo of Lydia in her beautiful dress, so I have a remembrance of her this winter while she's away."

"Of course," Sarah said. "Take your time."

They found the photographer set up in his usual place at the end of town.

Billy asked, "Do you have time to take a photo of this beautiful woman?"

Lydia blushed.

"If she can sit right this minute, I do. Otherwise, you'll have to come back in an hour," the photographer said.

"She's ready." Billy turned and gave Lydia a kiss on the cheek.

"Billy, I want you in the photo, too. Let's have two made. That way, I'll have one, and you'll have one," Lydia insisted.

"All right, whatever she says goes," Billy said to the photographer and turned to Lydia, "Do I look good enough for a picture with you?"

"You look very nice." She brushed her fingers through his hair, smoothed his shirt, and fixed his collar. Don't look so serious. I'm going to smile in the picture like I smile all the time. That's how I want you to see me."

"Hold still until I say you can move," the photographer said.

The thought of Lydia's sweet smile made Billy smile as well.

"You can pick these up tomorrow and pay me then," the man said.

"Thank you, we'll see you before twelve." Billy nodded.

"I wish Jack's family were here," Lydia said. "We could take a new family photo to send east."

"Maybe next year," Billy took Lydia's hand. "And maybe you'll be carrying our child by then. Wouldn't that be something?"

"It sure would." Lydia squeezed Billy's hand as they walked to the wagon.

****

That evening, Steven and Oat accompanied Billy and Lydia to the dance while Grandma dined with James Glasgow. Sarah and Mark, with Johanna in tow, joined the Spencers to enjoy the evening with their special friends.

"Can Oat and I get punch and cookies?" Steven asked.

"Sure," Billy said. "I'll go with you."

Lydia pointed in the directions of her friends. "I see Katy and Hannah. I'll be back in a few minutes. Please bring me a cookie, too." She hurried off to visit.

The music began, and Lydia's friends wanted to

dance. They all knew the song, a square dance that didn't require a partner. The three girls joined in, as did Johnathan Bellows.

Looking on, Steven pointed out Bellows to Billy. "Hey, that's the man who helped Lydia with her sign the other day."

What do you mean he helped her with her sign?" Billy asked, an emotion rising in him that put him on sudden alert.

"He carried the sign you made to the harness shop for her. He said the sign was too heavy for her, and Grandma told Lydia to let him help. That's all."

"Oh, that's all? He only carried her sign?" Billy remarked sarcastically, his thoughts filled with images of Quinn and Elizabeth. *But Lydia isn't Elizabeth.* Still, he felt it…unwelcome flashes of anger, suspicion, and jealousy.

"Yeah. He mentioned your name, but I wasn't paying attention," Steven said.

Billy became quiet, watching to see if the young man made any overtures to Lydia. He remembered seeing him helping Lydia once before carrying her large packages from the postal office. Billy would keep his eye on him tonight.

When the song ended, Lydia said good-bye to the girls and headed Billy's way. Johnathan swept her back onto the dance floor as the band started another tune.

"Would you care to dance?" Bellows asked.

"No, actually, I wouldn't. I want to spend time with my family." Lydia stopped in the middle of the crowd, turned, and walked away, leaving Johnathan standing by himself.

When she reached the boys, she asked, "Where's my

cookie?"

"Well, you were dancing, so I ate it," Steven said. "We can get you another one. There's lots more."

"One more for each of us, and pick one to take to Johanna," Lydia told the boys. Aware of Billy's shift in mood, she decided to ignore it. She hadn't danced with Johnathan of her own accord. She was sure Billy saw the whole incident, or at least the end when she left Johnathan Bellows standing alone on the dance floor.

Billy was an excellent dancer. She'd seen him dance with Elizabeth and wished she was the one going through the steps with Billy. Tonight, her wish would come true.

As Billy took her hand, they melted easily into each other's arms and glided around the dance floor in perfect step and rhythm. To others, they looked as though they had danced together for years. Even if practiced, the dance was not easy to perform so effortlessly. Actually, Billy and Lydia had danced before but not in public and only when they were teaching Jack to dance. Lydia's dress flowed, and Billy was so attentive that those watching might easily conclude they were married.

It wasn't only the slow songs they danced to. The couple danced to every song the band played. They didn't tire, and they didn't care what others thought. For that time, they were in each other's arms, and nothing could come between them. Billy's dark mood lightened with every turn.

When the musicians took a break, the young couple went for punch and joined their family.

"You two turned a lot of heads dancing like you did. I'm sure you didn't notice the looks you were getting, but I thought you'd like to hear about it." Mark chuckled.

"Good, I made my point, then. Lydia is my girl, and

I don't want any other guy thinking he can move in on her," Billy said, puffing his chest out a little as he took Lydia's hand.

"I don't want to dance with anyone but you, anyway, Billy. You're the best dancer I know. And, I don't want other girls thinking they can dance with you, either." Lydia stood close by Billy, remembering how she felt when he held her.

Soon a group of girls dropped by. Lydia didn't know their names but had seen them in town before.

One said, "You're Lydia Clark, aren't you? We saw your sign in the window of the harness shop. When will you be opening your dress shop?"

"The big day is the first Monday in October," Lydia said.

"And is the dress you're wearing one of your own designs?" asked another.

"Yes, and I have other originals, too," she said, going on to answer all their questions. "Be sure to tell your friends," Lydia called out as the girls walked away, and Billy looked on.

"Well, that was exciting. They can't wait to see my other designs and promised to come to the opening." A smile lit Lydia's face.

The fiddles started up again. "You and Pa go dance a few songs, Ma. We'll stay with the children," Lydia said, then spotted Grandma and Doc Glasgow sitting on the other side of the crowd. "Look, there's Grandma," she said, "Let's go say hello."

After a couple of songs, Sarah and Mark joined them.

Johanna yawned, and Mark happened to catch her with her mouth wide open. "It looks like it's time to take the children back to the wagon and get them to bed," he said. "Let's go. It's been a long day, and I'm tired too."

"Lydia and I'll be back when the dance is over. We'll try not to wake you. Same arrangement? The boys under the wagon and the girls inside?" Billy asked.

"Since we brought two wagons this trip, the girls will sleep in our wagon and the men in yours, Billy," Mark announced.

"Ruth," James Glasgow suggested. "Why don't you stay at my house in the spare room? I'm sure you'd be more comfortable there than in the back of the wagon. We can get your things now if you'd like. I've had enough of this night air for one evening."

"Yes, Mother," Mark said. "Please take Doc up on his offer. I'll feel better knowing you're in a real bed and not on a blanket in the back of the wagon."

"All right, dear, I'll see you in the morning." Arm in arm, Grandma and the doctor strolled off.

Billy and Lydia danced until the last song, their attention on each other and taking only an occasional break to catch their breath and enjoy some punch. Walking back to the wagon, Billy slipped his arm around her waist and pulled her close.

"This was the best night ever. I want to hold you in my arms for the rest of our lives," he said. In the shadows of the church grove, he turned her toward him, and they kissed deeply.

After catching her breath, Lydia said, "I want us together, too, Billy. You'll see. We'll be together forever.

****

The next morning with the wagons packed, Sarah pulled a letter from her pocket and read aloud to the family.

August 18, 1867
Tidioute, Warren County, Pennsylvania
Dearest Sarah,

Your sister Matilda had a baby boy, six pounds, two ounces, and they named him Robert Martin Junior. He is a happy little boy and perfect in every way. Robert wants to call him RJ. We will have to wait to see if that happens. He was born August 16th, about seven-thirty at night. I could not be happier for Matilda and Robert. They prayed for a boy, and the good Lord saw fit to answer their prayers.

We were horrified to hear what happened to Otis and Johanna. Please be careful when you are in town. Gossip and stories can be so hurtful. That unthinkable attack will stay with your children the rest of their lives. The monetary compensation will not take away Johanna's scar or Otis's memories. Be there for them and comfort them. Your love will help them heal.

Matthew and Lynnette are ready for their big day on September 22nd. It is hard to believe all my children will be married. Your father and I talked to them about living here at the house and taking it over when we pass. Everyone is in agreement with the arrangement, which makes us all very excited. This house will stay in the family. You know you will always be welcome here if you ever come home to visit.

Emma and Abel are excited for their new arrival in November. As long as the baby is healthy, they do not care if it is a boy or a girl. So much has happened this year.

I could not be more delighted for Lydia and Billy. I received Lydia's letter and must say we were surprised about their decision to court and Lydia's announcement of starting a business. We wish them much happiness and success.

Your father and I are in good health, and we hope this finds everyone in Kansas well and in good spirits. I better close for now. I will write again after the wedding.

Love always, Mother

"I'm so glad they had a little boy," Lydia said. "It sounds like they'll have a busy next few months with the wedding and babies."

Sarah added, "And I'm glad Matthew and Netty decided to stay in the house. I'm sure knowing they'll be there is a relief to Mother and Father."

"That reminds me," Billy said. "Lydia and I have to fetch the photos from the photographer."

The photographer handed Lydia the tintypes as Billy dug in his pocket for the money to pay.

"Oh, good. We're both smiling, and we look happy," Lydia announced.

"We are happy when we're together," Billy said and looked at the photo. "You look beautiful, but the photo will be a sore substitute for holding you in my arms."

"I've never had a photo of you, Billy. Now I can look at you whenever I want, and you'll be with me always," Lydia said. "I can't wait to show everyone."

Chapter Thirty-One

Time flew by after the Harvest Festival. Lydia waited until the last minute to go through her clothes and decide what to take to town. She thought of Billy and all the arguments they'd had about her leaving. She had put her foot down, and she wasn't changing her mind now.

I'll take all of my better clothes. If I'm dealing with the public, I must look my best, she thought, as she added nightgowns and other necessities to the carpetbag. When she couldn't squeeze in one more thing, she packed personal items like her comb, hairpins, ribbons, clips, a new bar of soap, shoes, and boots in crates. She threw in a shawl, the first scarf she ever knitted, and a warm winter coat. Looking around one last time, she packed the photo of her and Billy and the quilt her mother had made her.

She also used crates Mark built for other items like a few dishes and silverware, a skillet, and a small soup pot—items Grandma brought with her from Pennsylvania. Everything, including her sewing machine, her ready-wear dresses, and sewing supplies were packed and lined up against the front wall in the sitting room, waiting for Billy to take her to town.

When the wagon pulled in front of the door, the boys ran into the house.

"Ma, Pa, Grandma, guess what," Steven shouted.

Johanna ran to hear the announcement.

"Billy, Oat, and I talked, and we decided to spend the winter here, with you—if you'll have us, that is. We thought with Lydia gone, you might want some company to keep you busy. Can we stay?"

A huge grin covered Sarah's face.

"Of course, you can," Sarah said. "In fact, Pa and I were going to suggest you stay. There's no sense you three living alone this winter. You're welcome here anytime. You should know that by now."

Steven grinned. "That's good because we brought the cows and milk cow with us and some of our other things already."

"Let's get this wagon unloaded and the cows to the pasture, boys," Billy said. "And Ma, can the boys stay here while I take Lydia to town. I figured we'd stay at Jack's tonight and get an early start in the morning. I'll return here with another load of things from the house and the root cellar."

"That's fine, Billy," Mark said. "I'll give you a hand."

Johanna jumped with joy. "See, Grandma, I'll have someone to play with this winter after all."

Loading the wagon didn't take as much time as Lydia thought, and the moment of departure was suddenly upon her. She tried not to get emotional, but tears started to pool in her eyes. She brushed the moisture away.

Johanna gave her a hug. "I'll take good care of Muzzy and Momma Kitty. Don't worry, I'll feed them and the chickens every day. I love you, Lydia."

Lydia bent down and gave her sister a hug and kiss. "I love you, too, Johanna, and you be good for Ma, Pa, and Grandma."

Steven approached with a smile on his face. "I'll miss you. You sell all your dresses real quick, Lydia, so you can come home, and you and Billy can get married."

"I sure will try, little brother. You and Oat take care of Billy for me while I'm away. Make him smile every day. I'll be home before you know it.

Oat stepped forward and gave Lydia a big hug, and kissed her on the cheek. "You be careful in town. Don't take no chances, especially at night. We all want you to come home real soon."

Grandma held out her arms for a hug and then handed Lydia a small box. I thought you might wear this and think of me," she said.

Lydia unwrapped the box and found a small brooch with dainty flowers that Grandma thought would go nicely with the necklace Lydia always wore. "Thank you, Grandma, it's beautiful. I promise I'll wear your brooch and think of you every day." She kissed Grandma's cheek.

Sarah stood beside Mark, struggling to hold back the tears.

"Ma, if you start crying, I will too. This really isn't a good-bye, but rather until I see you again, so no tears, all right?"

"All right. No tears. I know this is a big step for you and one you've dreamt about for a long time. It's an exciting opportunity. Be safe and keep your wits about you. You'll be making a lot of decisions on your own over the next few months. They may not all be right but learn from your mistakes and do better not to make them again. I love you, sweetheart."

"I love you too, Ma. Thanks for all your help and all your good advice. I'll take your advice to heart and do my best."

Mark wrapped his burly arms around his daughter and held her close. "I'm sure you will, Lydia. Your Ma and I are proud of you. Remember, if you ever need anything, you can go to Sheriff Sloan, Doc Glasgow, or to the Proctor's house. I have no doubt there's good things in store for you. Stick to your plan and make good things happen. We're all rooting for you." He slipped her two twenty-dollar gold double eagle coins and whispered in her ear, "Here, in case you need them."

Lydia tucked them into her pocket. "Thank you, thank you, Pa. Spring really isn't that far off. I know by this time next year, Billy and I will still be together."

Taking a step back and looking around the house one last time, she said, "I can't wait to see all your smiling faces again. Come on, Billy, let's go.

****

After spending the night at Jack and Abby's, seeing the twins, and another round of good-byes, Billy and Lydia arrived in town. He pulled the wagon to the back door of the Harness Shop and started to unload.

Mr. Gray had the storage room emptied and clean when she arrived.

Lydia placed her bed and nightstand, and the room was complete; a tight fit, but she didn't complain.

After all her things were unloaded, Billy brought in six upright wooden posts with jointed bases to string rope on for displaying the dresses in the window.

"Oh, Billy, they're perfect. I didn't know you made these for me." Lydia kissed his cheek.

"I'm glad you like them. And there is one more thing I hope will work." He walked to the wagon and returned with two hinged board and batten walls and put them in the corner to use for the dressing room. I'll let you and Mr. Gray set them up, and all you need is a curtain."

Billy tousled her already disheveled hair and said, "Why don't you clean up a little, and I'll go get rope, so I know everything is ready for your opening. When I return, we can get a bite to eat, and then I need to get home."

They strung the rope on the poles like a wash line, and Billy showed her how to shorten them, if necessary, by pulling the rope through the holes and tying them off. "Now let's go eat. My stomach is growling."

The town clock struck twice as the couple entered the roadhouse at the end of the street.

"You're all moved in now," Billy said as he pulled out Lydia's chair.

He added, "Don't let me forget. The boys sent along pumpkins for pudding, bread, muffins, or whatever you want."

"That was sweet of them. Please thank them for me. I really am going to miss everyone, but most of all, I'll miss you." A tear welled at the corner of her eye, and she brushed the droplet away.

"I know what you mean. The house won't be the same without you there. I'll miss talking to you and seeing your beautiful smile."

"At least we have our photos," Lydia's lip quivered, "I'll be looking at your picture a lot. Every morning and every night, for sure."

The waitress asked, "Do you know what you'd like. The specials are on the board."

"No, we're sorry. We'll need a minute, but could you bring us two glasses of water, please?"

"Sure thing," The waitress said, "I'll be back in bit."

"I'm going to have chicken and biscuits," Lydia said, "And if I know you, you'll get meatloaf, mashed potatoes, the vegetable, and gravy."

"You know me pretty well. That's exactly what I'm ordering." Billy caught the waitress's eye and motioned they were ready. They ordered, and before long, steaming plates of food were placed before them.

"You know if you need anything, my friend Cain, the blacksmith, would be glad to help you. His wife, Jillian, is real nice too. They invited us to come visit sometime, but when we're in town, there are always other things to do. They're good people, and I know they'd do anything for you. And like Pa said, Sheriff, Doc, and Abby's parents can be trusted as well."

"Don't worry. If I need help, I'll ask one of them. But I'm hoping I'll be so busy, I won't have time to get in trouble. Mr. Gray will be there too, and since he's widowed and has no family, I think he'll be happy to have me around for company."

As Billy paid the bill, Lydia heard her name called from across the room.

Lydia saw three of the girls she met at the dance. "Hello, it's so good to see you again."

"We can't wait to come to your opening," one girl said.

"Yes, next week. Not long now," Lydia answered.

"We'll be there," the girls said.

Refreshed by the meal, the couple walked back hand in hand to the shop.

The day had been perfect. Not one argument, no negative comments. Billy bit his tongue more than a few times trying not to mention his pent-up concerns or let his anger get the best of him. Then suddenly, without forethought, a question forced its way to the surface, and he said, "Are you sure you want to stay, Lydia? We can load the wagon right now and go back home if you want."

"I hope you're joking, Billy. All my things are here, and I'm excited about what happens next. I'll truly miss you, but it's here I belong for now. Maybe you'll get to town before the snow flies. Or if we have an easy winter, you can visit more often. But don't take any chances. I don't want anything to happen to you because of me. I'd never forgive myself."

Brought to his senses, Billy responded, "I should be able to come in November if the weather holds. Here, Lydia, take this and enjoy a few good meals at the roadhouse on me. I worry you won't eat well, having only the potbelly stove to cook on." He gave her a ten-dollar gold eagle coin.

Lydia slipped the coin into her pocket. "Thanks, Billy, but don't worry. I'll be fine."

As Billy looked around the space that Lydia would be calling home, frustration rose and again overtook reason. *She'd be living here instead of at home, where she belongs. If she was home, she wouldn't be spending time with the likes of Johnathan Bellows. I didn't like him the first time I met him. I'd have her all to myself if she'd only come home now instead of waiting until all this dress business is over. What if she turns into a town girl like Elizabeth and decides not to come back to the farm? Or she could become so successful selling her dresses that she'll think the farm isn't good enough for her.*

Billy's cheeks flushed. He wanted to bite his tongue, to keep from saying something he might regret later, but before he could stop himself, he blurted out, "I think maybe we should call off our courtship until you come to your senses or you come home this spring."

Heart-struck, shocked to the core, and speechless, Lydia turned, went into her room, and closed the door. She sat on her bed. Fury at war with a sense of profound loss tore her in two directions. *If, after all the time we spent talking about my business plan, he now wants to break things off, that's fine with me. I'll prove him wrong.* Lydia thought, wiping away a tear. *If Billy can't accept me as I am, then maybe he doesn't truly love me. Maybe we aren't supposed to be together. I'll be fine here by myself.* Lydia wrapped herself in her quilt, resolving to live out her dream on her own without Billy if things came to that.

Burying her face in her quilt to muffle cries, Lydia vowed, *I'll start my business and become successful. I'll show him.*

Left only to guess at her reaction and what she was thinking, Billy heaved a sigh and slowly turned to leave. He thought he heard her crying, but what could he do?

What have I done? Grandma and Pa told me not to mention breaking off our courtship. But I had to try one last time. I thought if she knew I was willing to call things off, she might see how much I love her. Billy slammed his fist on the counter, hung his head, and walked outside, defeated in his efforts to make Lydia understand his side of their relationship.

Mr. Gray caught up to him on the wooden walkway.

"I'm sorry, Son. I overheard your conversation. I can tell you're regretful, but you better let her cool down tonight. Let her sleep on what you said. She may have a different outlook in the morning. Any chance you can stay and come back tomorrow?"

"You're right. I can't leave knowing Lydia's upset with me. I must make things right between us. I love her, but she drives me crazy. I'm afraid she'll want to live in town permanently when her business takes off and not want to get married. What if the farm life that I offer her isn't enough?"

Mr. Gray patted him on the back. "You have some thinking to do, young man. Come back in the morning and tell her you love her. You being here will go a long ways to mending fences. Trust me. After forty-five years with my Missus, I know the power of those three little words."

"Thank you for that and for everything you're doing for Lydia. I'll be back in the morning."

Billy pulled the wagon onto a side street so he could see the back door of the harness shop. He always kept an extra blanket in the wagon. He'd be fine tonight. While he unhitched the horses, Johnathan Bellows walked past the alley on the wooden walkway. He was dressed up wearing a nice waistcoat and trousers, while Billy was in work clothes. The door to the shop opened, then closed. *Was Bellows going to the harness shop to see Lydia or Mr. Gray?* Billy didn't dare look in the window. After stabling the horses, he walked to the church grove to calm down.

Later, returning to the wagon by the dim lamplight on the streets, he quietly tried the back door of the shop. Locked, that was a relief. He could imagine Lydia inside unpacking her things, excited about the future that lay ahead for her.

That night, he wrestled with the possibility of her rejection in the morning. *I was a fool to mention breaking things off. What if she won't forgive me? What if she won't even talk to me? Worst still, what if she thinks it's a good idea to separate?* He searched desperately to find the right words to tell her his true feelings and concerns.

In the middle of the night, shouts echoed from the street. A few shots were fired, more hoots and hollers, and then everything settled down. *Lydia must have heard the shouts and shots, too,* Billy thought. He attempted to go back to sleep, but his worries gave him no rest.

Inside, Lydia heard the commotion. She was pulled from a deep sleep by noises that never woke her while living on the farm. Gunshots. Men yelling. She pulled the quilt tightly around her like protective armor to ward off danger and opened the door of her room. The shop was faintly illuminated by lamplight filtering through the large front windows. Shapes looked ghostly. Lydia felt unsure, unsettled. The angry, disappointed feelings she had when Billy suggested they break off their courtship were replaced by wishing his strong arms were around her. Had she made the right decision? She had been so sure.

Chapter Thirty-Two

Sleeping fitfully after the nighttime ruckus, Billy awoke as Dead Flats sprung alive with people. He walked to the creek to wash, still unsure what the future might hold after his outburst with Lydia. He had searched desperately all night to find the right words. The same line kept repeating in his head. *I've been a fool. A real fool. I love Lydia and want her in my life regardless of her future plans. She needs to know I love her even though I acted rashly, and I pray she'll forgive me.*

Returning from the stable, he started to hitch the horses to the wagon when Mr. Gray unlocked the back door and walked to Billy's wagon. "I might have a solution for part of your worries," he said.

"I'm listening," Billy nodded.

"After much consideration, I thought, what if Lydia stayed with me for a while?" Mr. Gray proposed. "Actually, she'd be doing me a favor. I'm afraid I don't take good care of myself since my wife passed. When I get home, I don't feel much like cooking. I have a spare room, all furnished. We could walk home after work together. If she fixed the meals and did a little cleaning, I wouldn't charge her for the space she's using in the shop. Do you think she'd agree? I can speak with her about it. Maybe after having her first night alone in a new place, she'll feel different.

"I think that's a great idea, Mr. Gray, and thank you. You'd put to rest the concerns of everyone in the family, knowing Lydia won't be staying alone in the shop at night. And Lydia is an excellent cook. I know firsthand." Billy finished strapping the horses to the wagon. "I better talk first to apologize and say those three little words. Then I may need your help to persuade her to move in with you. I'll be in as soon as I finish here," Billy said.

Noting Lydia already at work setting up the window display, Mr. Gray greeted her, "Good morning, Lydia. How'd you sleep?"

"Actually, I'm afraid I didn't get much sleep. It's much quieter at the farm than here in town. Please remind me to pick up a rat trap. I heard the pitter-patter of little feet scurrying across the floor. And would you mind if I put a lock on my door? I think I would feel safer." Lydia unfolded a dress to place on the clothesline Billy had built her.

"That's fine with me, dear. I supposed you'd want to have your dresses in the front window a few days early so people would take note, so I cleared space for you. If you need more, let me know. Now I'll leave you to your work and if you need anything, call me." Mr. Gray busied himself until Billy walked through the back door, then he stayed within earshot.

"Billy, what are you doing here? I thought you left yesterday," Lydia said, straightening her stance.

The distance between the couple was like a chasm. Billy finally managed to blurt out, "I couldn't leave without telling you I love you, Lydia. I truly do. I'm here to ask you to forgive me. I should never have spoken to you the way I did, threatening to end our courtship. I hope you know that's not what I really want. If we're apart, I'm afraid you'll forget me, or worse yet, find someone you like better. All I can offer you is farm life. What I'm trying to say is, if you'll still have me, I still want a life with you when you come home." Billy waited for Lydia's response.

After a long pause, Lydia said, "I thought I knew you, Billy Henry. Your words hurt me terribly to think you would consider ending our courtship. I need some time to think. I feel you don't want me to succeed and that you don't trust me." She turned to walk away.

"I do trust you, Lydia, really I do. You've been steadfast throughout all this, and I'm the one who caused the problems. I've been so worried about you being here alone that I guess I couldn't see things clearly and thought if we weren't courting, I wouldn't worry about you so much. But that wouldn't happen, because I love you too much. Mr. Gray talked a little sense into me and made a suggestion that I hope you might consider."

Mr. Gray walked around the corner and offered, "Let me explain, Billy."

Puzzled by the request, Lydia gazed quizzically from one man to the other.

"My dear girl, I might have a solution where you won't need to put that lock on your door."

Lydia leaned in to listen.

"Why don't you come live at my house in my sparc room? You'd be doing me a huge favor, and in return, I won't charge you for using the space here. Billy told me your cooking is the best, so what do you say? Would you at least come look at the house before you say no?"

"It's the perfect compromise, Lydia, don't you think?" Billy smiled tentatively.

"You're right. How can I refuse? But I think I'll still

pick up a rat trap," Lydia gave Mr. Gray a hug. "You're being so nice to me, and you don't even know me, Mr. Gray."

"Well, I know if I ever had a daughter, I'd want her to have your determination and be like you. We'll get along fine, Lydia."

"Ma and Pa will be relieved too. You know they will. Is there anything you want me to move to the house before I leave?" Billy asked.

"Yes, thank you. If you'd take the crates of food, I'll pack my carpetbag again."

Billy picked up a crate and carried it to the wagon.

After loading everything that Lydia wanted to bring to her new lodging, she called, "I'm ready, Mr. Gray."

Turning the sign to *Closed* and locking the doors, Mr. Gray joined the couple.

With the settling in completed, Billy stepped closer and gave Lydia a tender kiss on the lips, but she stiffened. As he said good-bye, her coolness toward him was evidence that she hadn't accepted his apology. "I'll try to come see you before the snow flies, maybe the first week of November. You can tell me all about your business adventures then." One last kiss on a cool cheek, and he drove out of town.

****

Lydia looked around Mr. Gray's two-story residence with a staircase to an upper floor instead of a ladder to a loft. Each room had a window. There was even a hand pump and sink inside the kitchen for water. In the living room, a painted portrait of Ezra and his wife was prominently displayed. They both had little smiles like the photo of herself and Billy. "Mr. Gray, Lydia said, "Your wife was pretty. How long were you married?"

"Forty-five years, three months, and five days," Mr. Gray replied, "And if you're going to live here now, please call me Ezra."

"All right, Ezra." Lydia smiled.

****

As he rode away from Dead Flats, Billy wrestled with thoughts of going back to straighten out the situation, then thought better of his decision and continued on to Jack and Abby's.

I've attempted to put up roadblocks along the way to stop Lydia, but she's determined. She's been that way her whole life. If I keep trying to hold her back, she'll resent me for not trusting her. I attempted to explain my reason for wanting to break things off, but I doubt she was even listening. Everything was great until I made that stupid, last-minute mistake.

I was so gosh-darn dumb. Now she'll think she's free to see whoever she wants.

Billy arrived at Jack and Abby's in time for supper. "Do you have enough for one more?" he asked, happy to see a friendly face.

"Of course there's enough," Abby said. "You're always welcome here, Billy."

Jack raised his brow. "We expected you last night. What happened?"

Billy slouched and explained, "Before leaving to come back yesterday, I suggested we break off our courtship while Lydia's living in town."

Abby gasped.

"I guess I hoped to shock her back into her senses and make her give up her business idea, but all I did was make her angry."

"Oh, Billy, how could you." Abby sighed.

"I wasn't thinking straight, so I stayed the night instead of heading out. Lydia and I spoke this morning. She's really upset with me."

Jack and Abby looked at each.

"I know I hurt her feelings, and I'll never do that again as long as I live. One good thing happened, though. Mr. Gray invited her to come live with him, so at least I know she's safe," Billy said.

Jack shook his head. "William Henry, if I find out that you hurt my sister, I'll kick your butt." He passed the potatoes and changed the subject. "Are you and the boys going to harvest your corn soon? I think I'll give mine a couple weeks to dry on the stalk and pray we don't get an early snow. I won't need any help since I don't have as much planted as you and Pa."

Billy took a gulp of milk and said, "I'll give ours another week, then help Pa with his fields. With Lydia gone, the boys and I are going to stay with the family this winter. I'm planning on going to town the first week of November to see how she's doing and apologize. Hopefully, she'll listen to me. Do you want help butchering this year?" Billy asked, taking a bite of bread. "I could help you after I see Lydia."

"All right, I'll put that on the calendar," Jack said.

Abby asked, "Did your ma see my parents during the Harvest Festival?"

Billy's face brightened a little. "Yes, Ma and Lydia visited your folks and said your ma was doing well enough to sit at the kitchen table to chat and that she was feeling better. I'm sorry, Abby. I should have told you that as soon as I walked in. I know how concerned you are for your parents."

"That's all right, Billy. That's good news. Jack and

I are going to Dead Flats to visit them soon and show them their grandbabies. Seeing the twins should perk up her spirits. We'll check in on Lydia and make sure she's all right."

After a leisurely meal, Jack got up to do the chores, and Billy offered to help, asking, "Do you mind if I spend the night, Abby? I'm too tired to go the rest of the way home tonight."

"What have I told you? You're always welcome here. When the twins get old enough to go to Uncle Billy and Aunt Lydia's house for stay-over visits, you'll understand why." Abby grinned and began the dishes.

****

After picking up some crocks and canned goods from the root cellar at his farm, Billy drove to the Hewitts in silence. Only one thing on his mind…Lydia. *Now Jack and Abby are mad at me too. I can't tell anyone else what I've done. I don't want the whole family upset with me. Jack was right. I almost wish he had taken a swing at me. I didn't mean to hurt Lydia, but how could she tell from the stupid way I behaved? I wish I could talk to her right now. No, I must get home, but I'm going to Dead Flats in November, whether it's snowing or not.*

I'll apologize and pray she'll talk to me. I only hope it's not too late and that someone else won't sweep her off her feet.

Pulling into the yard, the first words out of Steven's mouth when Billy's wagon came to a stop at the Hewitt's were, "What took you so long?"

"Spent the night at Jack and Abby's and then stopped by the farm and packed up part of the root cellar. No need to worry, Little Brother. You know I can take care of myself. Now it's time to unload all those canned goods. I hope nothing broke getting them here."

"So how's our girl doing," Sarah asked.

Billy mouthed the words, 'I'll tell you later."

Sarah nodded and went back to preparing supper.

When the boys returned, Steven announced, "Not one broken jar, but I don't know where we'll put any more food. The root cellar is packed."

"We never had this much food where I grew up." Oat said, in awe. "We'll eat good this winter."

Oat's comment gave Billy pause to remember the past spring when he brought Otis into the family. *Not even a year, and look at everything that's happened since then.* As his mind drifted, he was reminded how thankful he was to Mark and Sarah for taking him and Steven into their home so many years before. *I want to offer Oat the same opportunity to have a good life, and I'll do my darnedest to help him along. Not only food and shelter but knowing he's safe and loved.* Billy suddenly remembered, *This will be Oat's first Christmas as a free person. With Lydia away, I'll have to help the boys and Johanna make gifts. I want to make this a special Christmas for everyone.*

When the children walked out to do their evening chores, Billy shared Ezra Gray's offer with his folks. "In the end, Lydia agreed to stay at Ezra's home. She seemed happy with the new arrangement."

"I knew the Lord would work everything out for the best," Grandma said. "I turned to God for answers, and he worked a miracle, in my opinion."

Billy struggled to pretend everything was all right. His heart ached with constant twinges of guilt for his blunder with Lydia.

Chapter Thirty-Three

Lydia's stomach was tied in knots, her heart was pounding, and she was frozen in place. The time had come for the grand opening of Lydia's Ready-Wear Dress Shop. There was nothing left to do but open the door. Her dresses, with their attention to detail and innovative designs, were awaiting the approval of the women of Dead Flats. The punchbowl and glasses she'd borrowed from Mr. Gray graced a table laden with plates of raisin-filled and molasses cookies. Thoughts raced through Lydia's head of what her mother and grandma would say at this moment as a group of women gathered outside waiting to come in. Breathing was difficult. She stood motionless. This was the moment she had worked toward for many years.

"You'll do fine, dear. Now you better turn that sign to *Open*. You don't want to keep your customers waiting," Ezra Gray encouraged. "And if you need a hand, I'm here to help."

"Thank you, Thank you for everything, Ezra. None of this would be possible without you." Calmly she walked to the door, reversed the sign, and opened the door to the next chapter in her life.

She greeted the ladies as they flowed into the store. "Welcome to Lydia's Ready-Wear," she said. "I'm Lydia Clark, and I'm delighted to meet you. As you can see, there are different dress designs in a variety of sizes and fabrics with prices attached. There are cookies and punch in the corner by the dressing room. Feel free to try on the dresses before you buy. Take your time and browse. If you have questions, I'll be happy to assist you."

Two women tried on dresses that fit perfectly. Her first two sales.

Another woman liked a dress and decided she would add lace at the bottom.

"This one fits pretty well," one customer said, "but needs a tuck here and there. I can do that. Not having to order the pattern, pick out material, and do all the work myself is nice."

One woman asked, "I like this design, but not in this material. Can you make this pattern in a different fabric?"

Another lady said, "This design is beautiful, but the color isn't to my taste."

Lydia shared, "These are original designs, shown in a variety of fabrics which may not please everyone's taste. The cost of the clothing reflects this new approach. Some adjustments may be required. Usually ones you can make yourselves. I'll be ordering different fabrics on a regular schedule, so there will be a good selection at all times. In fact, I'm hoping to have two skirt designs on display next week."

Some women liked the idea of trying on the clothes before purchasing. Many appreciated the novel idea of only needing to make small adjustments such as a hem length. Some thought the prices were a bargain, and others had different opinions. Lydia soon learned responses were as varied as the customers.

A newspaper reporter stopped by to ask her

questions about the new business in town. *Great! Free publicity,* she thought. Halfway through his list of questions, Lydia could tell the young man had no experience writing about women's fashion. She was able to direct the interview to the information she thought would attract customers. The man couldn't write fast enough. *Original designs in different fabrics....*

"Could you repeat that last sentence?" he asked, then wrote feverishly to get every word down on paper. "You can read my article in print tomorrow. Make sure to buy a newspaper," he said before leaving.

By the time the man left, Lydia was sure his article would say what she wanted.

As promised, the girls from the festival arrived with their friends. Two bought dresses, and, as they walked out, one girl spoke for them all. "We'll be back. We can't wait to see the skirts."

A heavy-set woman approached, holding a dress, and said, "I like this design very much, but there isn't one in my size. Would you be willing to make me one of your designs?"

"I certainly would. If you stop by tomorrow, I could take measurements then," Lydia offered. "And I'll add your size to my collection.

"Is ten o'clock all right?" The woman asked.

Lydia smiled. "Yes, let me write that down. Your name, please."

"Mrs. Baccus," The woman said. "You'll get to know my name quite well if I like what you make."

"You can pick out the design tomorrow, Mrs. Baccus," Lydia said, trying to contain her excitement. Repeating the name, she realized the woman had clout in this town. She was the mayor's wife.

Lydia had to fill the punch bowl three times, and there wasn't a cookie left at the end of the day. She counted at least twenty-five women who attended the opening and either browsed or bought a dress.

When the last person left a little after five, Lydia let out a huge sigh of relief and turned the sign to *Closed*. She sank into a chair, weary after being on her feet all day. Eight of her fifteen dresses had sold. In her wildest dreams, she never thought she'd sell that many on the first day. *I need to reorder fabric right away, or I'll be out of dresses and, without dresses, I'll be out of business.*

Lydia caught a glimpse of Ezra in the back of the shop and walked back to talk to him. "What a day!" She said.

"Are you ready to go home? You didn't take a break to eat during the day, and I bet you're starving." Ezra began putting his tools away.

"I did sneak a couple cookies when no one was watching," Lydia said, "but I am hungry, and I can't wait to tell you all about my day. I want to do a quick inventory before we leave."

After counting the dresses on each rack, Lydia calculated she had sold two large, three medium, and three small-sized dresses. She collected the money from the cash register, locked the door, and walked home with Ezra thinking, *My first day was a huge success. I wish I could tell my family.*

That evening, Lydia worked on a fabric order that included everything she needed to replenish the inventory. This time, she chose a red and black plaid, a green calico with a half bolt of solid green fabric to match, a brown and red homespun, and a black on ivory print. In addition to the fabric, she bought lace, buttons, and thread. Adding up the order, the total came to twelve dollars more than she took in. *Pa gave me money, and this is how I'll use some,* she thought. *I could be out of dresses until the order arrives. Perhaps I can buy fabric from Mrs. Cooper, so there are garments in the shop to sell. Hopefully, the other dresses sell. I'll need that money to buy more fabric.*

She heard Ezra call, "Lydia, come join me for tea and a cookie."

"But I thought I took all the cookies to the shop this morning," Lydia said.

"I figured those women didn't need to eat all of them, so I put a few back to enjoy tonight." Ezra chuckled.

"I'm glad you did." Lydia smiled. "I still can't believe I sold so many dresses today. I wish Ma and Grandma were here."

"I'm sure they were thinking about you, dear. They know how much this day meant to you." Ezra dunked a cookie into his teacup and took a bite.

****

Dressed and ready to leave for the shop the following morning, she called out, "I'll see you as soon as I can, Ezra. I meet with Mrs. Baccus today."

She hurried to the postal office to get her order out on the first stage. Then, hiking up her skirt, ran to the dry goods store and bought four yards each of four different fabrics to make skirts. She arrived at the shop with only minutes to spare before opening time.

Mrs. Baccus was prompt. The taking of measurements and planning took nearly an hour. As the women chatted, Lydia showed the mayor's wife her five designs.

"I ordered new fabric this morning." Lydia described the choices, and the mayor's wife decided on the brown and red homespun. "You've chosen the most expensive fabric, Mrs. Baccus, a testament to your good taste. As a result, the cost of the dress will come to more than the other dresses, and I won't have a final price for you until it's made. Would you be amenable if I asked for a guaranteed sale on this dress?" Lydia held her breath, awaiting a reply.

"Well, I guess that's fair. You did give me a chance to pick my fabric, and I know my measurements aren't your typical ready-wear size. All right, young lady, to help you out, I'll make a payment now, knowing the finished dress will cost more. I appreciate you taking the time to see me today, and I hope you do well with this idea about ready-wear clothing. This town needs your shop, and you will see more of me if I like the dress." With that, Lydia's potentially influential client moved the ready-wear business forward in Dead Flats. Lydia knew she had passed some sort of test and that the mayor's wife's influence in town could mean significant sales for Lydia's Ready-Wear in the future.

Chapter Thirty-Four

Come in, come in," Harold Proctor said and called to his wife, "Betsy, come see who's here."

Moving slowly into the room, Betsy's eyes brightened, and a smile appeared as she held the back of a nearby chair for support. "Sweethearts! What a surprise! It's so good to see you. And you brought the babies."

Handing the twin she was holding to Jack, Abby helped her mother to the settee and, once they were both comfortable, motioned for Jack to bring her Annabelle and Benjamin.

Meet your grandbabies, Grandma. This is little Annabelle, named after your mother, and this is Benjamin, named after Jack's Grandfather. Although they're only six months old, I can already tell they will be close when they grow up. When one does something, the other does the same. They're so cute to watch when we lay them down together. It's like they talk back and forth and actually understand each other."

Harold, looked down on the babies from behind the settee. "They're beautiful, Abby, just beautiful. When the doctor told us both babies were perfect, and you survived through labor, we cried in happiness."

"They're perfect," Betsy said, a tear trickling down her cheek. "Thank you for bringing them to meet us. I'll remember this moment always. My daughter with her own family."

"We would have come sooner, but we wanted to wait until we felt they were strong enough to make the journey," Jack said. "They did fine. Slept most of the way and fussed only a little."

"Well, they're wide awake now," Abby said, "And probably a little hungry. Jack, why don't you and Pa go talk in the kitchen, and Ma and I'll come join you in a while."

Once Abby started feeding Annabelle, Benjamin let out a noise as if in protest that his sister got to nurse first.

"Oh my, what a loud voice you have, little one. You must wait your turn," Betsy said, rubbing his belly to comfort him.

"It wouldn't have mattered which one I fed first. The other always lets me know they're waiting their turn. But they are eating well. We'll take them over and let Doc look at them while we're here, probably tomorrow. We also want to see Jack's sister and her new dress shop."

"Your Pa cut out a newspaper write-up about the shop opening for you," Betsy called, "Harold. Where is that clipping about Lydia's dress shop? Let Jack read it."

"It's here somewhere. I'll find it," Harold called back.

"It seems that Annabelle is done. I'll trade you babies, Ma, and you can burp her for me."

Holding Annabelle to her chest, Betsy gently rubbed and patted the baby's back. "There, there, little one. You're fine, just fine. Grandma has you, and she loves you very much."

When Benjamin was finished, Abby burped him and called to Jack, "Come help with the twins so Ma and I can join you in the kitchen."

"Let me run out and get the cradle first. Maybe they'll take a nap since they ate." Returning, Jack set the cradle in the kitchen near the warm cookstove, then helped his mother-in-law stand and assisted her to a chair in the kitchen.

Abby brought the babies and handed Benjamin to her father. "What do you think, Pa? Should we keep them?" she joked.

"I'd keep them both. And if I know you and Jack, you're already thinking about having another one for them to play with," Harold said, rocking the baby in his arms.

"I'm not thinking about that until next year. These two are a handful. They keep us both quite busy." Jack looked at Abby as she placed Annabelle in her mother's arms.

"Was I a good baby, Ma? Or did I give you a hard time?" Abby asked.

"As I recall, you were quite good. I do remember that you didn't like to eat peas." Betsy turned to see Abby's reaction.

"And I still don't eat peas. Don't tell the twins. I'm going to make them eat peas because you made me eat mine." Abby laughed and looked at Jack.

"I like peas," Jack quietly said. "Let me read you the article about Lydia's shop," he began, "'Lydia Clark, a resident of Riley County for twelve years, opened Lydia's Ready-Wear Dress Shop with her originally designed dresses and plans to expand her fashions into other garments for the fine ladies of Dead Flats.' The article closes with, 'Miss Clark will feature new fabrics and designs frequently, thus attracting a discerning clientele that appreciates a quality product at a reasonable price.'" Jack commented, "This is sure to bring her business. Ma and Pa will be so proud. I hope she got copies for them."

"Here, you can have this cutting. I'm sure Lydia thought to get extras to share with the family. For a girl so young to have a promising business in a town like Dead Flats is a real accomplishment," Betsy noted.

Both babies were nodding in their grandparents' arms, and Abby placed them in the cradle.

Jack headed for the door. "While they nap, I think I'll go see Lydia. I won't stay long."

Abby called after him, "Tell her I'll come visit tomorrow."

****

"Hello, young lady. I need help picking out a dress," Jack said in a deep voice. Lydia looked up from her sewing. "Jack! How wonderful to see you! How are Abby and the twins?"

"They're fine. We brought them to see Abby's parents for the first time and put them down for a nap, so I rushed over to see how you're doing. I read the article in the newspaper. Your grand opening must have really been a hit with the ladies."

"Oh, yes! I sold eight dresses, and I've already ordered additional fabric, which I hope will arrive soon. Stock is down to three dresses and a couple skirts. I can't keep a shop open if I don't have merchandise to sell."

Jack nodded. "I'm going to the hardware to check on sales there. I'll bring you your share of the profits, and maybe that will help."

"Good idea, Jack. I never thought to check with Mr. Hovis. At least that will be a little extra. You know, if you hadn't started your business, I don't think I would have realized I could start mine. In a way, you're a part of the reason my dream is coming true."

"I remember when I started my business. We worked hard to get our first items ready for sale. We both know what it's like needing enough product to not lose shelf space. You've put a lot of time and effort into both of our businesses, and I want you to succeed. I'll be right back." He smiled.

Mr. Gray walked from the back of the shop. "I heard a male voice and thought I might have a customer."

"My brother Jack stopped in," Lydia said. "He's in town visiting his in-laws and dropped by to say hello."

"I wish I'd have had the pleasure of seeing him again," Ezra said. "How's his business coming along?"

"Oh, he'll be right back. You can ask him yourself. He walked over to the hardware store to check on his leather sales. I'm sure he wouldn't leave without saying hello. I'll call you when he gets here."

Within ten minutes, Jack was back. "How much money do you need to order your fabric?" he inquired.

"About eight dollars," Lydia said, knowing she hadn't earned that much.

"Here," Jack counted out eight dollars. "This is your earnings plus enough to make it eight. Now, get that fabric order on the evening stage."

Lydia threw her arms around her brother. "Are you sure, Jack?"

Picking her up, Jack spun her around. "I'm sure."

Lydia grabbed her shawl. "I must run to the house to get the information. How long are you staying in town?"

"We're leaving the day after tomorrow. Abby said she'd come visit, probably in the morning. You go. I'm going to talk to Mr. Gray, and I'll let him know you left for a while."

"Please tell him I ran home, but I'll be right back. Thanks again, Jack. I owe you." Lydia said as she flew out the door.

"Mr. Gray?" Jack called.

Ezra came from the back room. "Jack, boy, it's good to see you. I've seen men come into my shop wearing your work. I can tell it's yours. You take the time to do fine tooling, and the stitching is even. All quality."

"Thank you, Mr. Gray," Jack said, "I learned a lot about the art of leatherwork from the book you lent me."

Mr. Gray and Jack chatted. "Good seeing you, Mr. Gray. I always enjoy our talks and learn something new each time. But if I don't get back, my wife will skin me alive for leaving her alone with the twins for too long."

"Stop back anytime. You're always welcome," Ezra said and shook Jack's hand. Lydia hadn't returned yet, so Ezra sat at the counter to keep an eye on the shop. She walked in a few minutes later, quite excited.

"Can you believe I'm ordering more fabric, Mr. Gray? My dresses are selling faster than I anticipated."

****

The morning sun shone through the window of Lydia's Ready-Wear Dress Shop. "I'm so glad you like the skirt. The color looks lovely on you." Lydia was saying to a customer as Abby walked in. "I'll be right with you," she called out.

After the lady left with her purchase, Lydia gave Abby a hug. "Boy, am I glad to see you, Abby. I need your opinion."

"Sure, anytime," Abby offered.

The girls sat at the counter, and Lydia began. "I love

meeting people and helping them select a dress. I feel a real sense of pride and accomplishment when someone purchases a dress and leaves the shop, but I can't keep up with the demand. I had to order fabric the day after my grand opening because over half the dresses in inventory sold that first day. I had to buy fabric from Mrs. Cooper to make skirts, so I would have garments to sell. The fabric that I ordered should arrive any day now, but I don't have Ma and Grandma to help me. I'm realizing I can't do everything myself and must confess, I'm feeling a little overwhelmed."

Abby took Lydia's hand. "Jack told me he gave you some money to order more fabric, so soon you'll have plenty. If you keep your turnover up each month and invest your money back into your business like you are now, your only problem is production. You can't do everything yourself. You need to hire someone to take Ma's place, cutting out patterns and maybe helping with customers. That way, you can run the sewing machine, or you'll never get caught up."

Lydia tucked a stray hair behind her ear. "I thought of that, but who?"

"What about your friend Grace?" The girl we always see at the picnics. She lives in town. Maybe she could help. Or what about Billy's friend Cain? Maybe his wife would like part-time work. And I'll write down two of my friends' names. I'm sure you could trust them."

"But I could only pay them a small amount to work for me," Lydia said, shaking her head.

"Don't be discouraged. You won't know until you ask. Maybe they would welcome working two or three days a week for a few hours. How much time do you spend cutting out a dress? How many could a person cut out in a day? Could they work from home? You'll figure everything out. I know you can make this work, so you better get out there and find someone soon." Abby smiled with encouragement giving Lydia new hope.

Lydia gave her sister-in-law another hug. "Thanks for listening, Abby, and thanks for the names. I know I talked your ear off, and you've got to get going, but if you see Billy before I do, please tell him I'm doing fine…if he asks.

"Yes, I'll tell him," Abby promised. "Did Jack tell you when Billy stopped on his way home, he told us he stupidly said you two should break off courting? He was upset with himself for saying such a thing. He didn't really mean it, you know."

Lydia responded, "Billy sounded as though he meant every word at the time. His words hurt me deeply, and I'm still in shock from his suggestion. He might have changed his mind, but now I'm having serious doubts."

"You have to remember all the good times you've had together," Abby said.

"I'm trying. I really am. Before, I was sure I loved Billy and deep in my heart believe I still do, but he's broken my trust with his abrupt turnaround. There is nothing he can say or do that will make me give up my dress shop. I've invested too much time and money into this business to fail now."

Looking around, Abby said, "You've fixed this area of the harness shop real nice."

"Thank you, Abby. This place keeps me so busy that I hardly have time to think about Billy. I need to prove my business will work and be successful. I'll work every minute of every day to prove myself. At this point, I'm not sure what will happen with Billy and me. When we started courting, we agreed to take things slow and work things out together, but apparently, he forgot."

Abby stroked her sister-in-law's arm in loving support. "Don't worry, Lydia, I won't say anything to Billy. It's between the two of you, and I'm sure you'll solve all your problems. Meanwhile, take care of yourself, and good luck with your business and finding help."

Chapter Thirty-Five

The following day, Lydia reached out to Grace only to learn she had a full-time job in town.

She walked to Cain's blacksmith shop. "Do you think your wife would be interested in a part-time job at my shop helping with customers and cutting out dress patterns?" she asked.

"I'll mention the job tonight, and she can let you know," Cain offered.

"I'm expecting an arrival of fabric any day, so I might need her immediately."

"I'll pass that information along and have her get back to you," Cain added.

Lydia reached out and shook his hand. "Thanks, Cain, and thanks for being such a good friend to Billy."

She had to open the shop and would speak with the women on Abby's list soon.

A few hours later, a woman came through the door. "Are you Lydia Clark?" she asked, as her eyes glanced around the shop.

"Yes, may I help you?" Lydia replied.

"You talked to my husband this morning about part-time work in your shop. I'm Jillian Gibbs, Cain's wife, and I'd like to hear about the position you told him about."

"It's lovely to finally meet you, Jillian. Billy always talks so highly about you and Cain. And thank you for coming today. I'm really in need of someone to help cut out my dress pieces so I can spend my time sewing. There may be some hand sewing as well, like adding buttons and lace, and you'd need to assist customers." Standing before Lydia was a slender, attractive woman with golden wavy hair, and she was interested in hearing more.

"I sew all my family's clothes. Cutting out patterns and hand sewing wouldn't be a problem." Jillian lowered her head. "But I've never assisted customers before."

"Don't worry about that. You can watch me and see what I say and do. It's easy. You'll catch on. I'm sure you will. You probably know most of the ladies in town. All you do is have a conversation with them to see what size they think they are and what style best suits their taste in clothing. They'll let you know if they like something or not, but we don't offer alterations. The garments are purchased as is, and the buyer is responsible for making any adjustments. This is ready-wear. We offer a finished dress, and if they need a tuck here or there, that would be up to them. This policy allows us to keep the price down."

Nodding an understanding, Jillian asked. "What about the days and hours?"

"They're flexible. I will need help at least three days a week, a few hours a day. You pick the days and times. There may be periods I don't need help, like between fabric orders. I can't promise steady work."

"That's all right. Being able to set my own hours sounds perfect. When would you like me to start?" Jillian inquired.

"An order of fabric should arrive any day. I'd like to go over my designs and patterns with you first. Would you be able to come for an hour or two tomorrow morning?" There was a moment of silence before either spoke. Lydia held her breath, then laughed, "I'm so sorry, Jillian. I never said what the pay would be. I was so excited that you were interested, wages slipped my mind. I can only pay thirteen cents an hour, plus give you a dress of your choice. I know it's not much, but my business is only getting started."

Lydia barely got the word 'started' out of her mouth, and Jillian said, "Yes."

"Yes," she said, "Yes, I think I'll love working with you, Lydia. And perhaps in time, I can learn how to run the sewing machine."

"I'd love to teach you. I think we'll do well working together."

Lydia's fabric arrived on the morning stage. She had hired Jillian in the nick of time. Within a week, there were new dresses on the clotheslines, and the shop was bustling with customers once again. Lydia upped the price of each dress by five cents to help defray the cost of her new part-time assistant, and the dresses were still flying out the door. Mrs. Baccus loved her new dress and vowed to return.

By listening to the likes and dislikes of her customers regarding colors and fabrics, Lydia ordered as much material as she could afford. With a return clientele and word-of-mouth promotion, business flourished, and Lydia was ordering additional fabric every other week.

In the midst of her success, Lydia wondered why Billy hadn't come to town at the beginning of November. Was his absence because of the weather, or couldn't he accept her starting her own business? She'd find out the next time she saw him, but for now, her shop came first.

****

Billy and the boys picked their own corn and then began helping at the Hewitts' farm. He worked at a hard pace, hoping to become so weary he'd fall asleep from exhaustion. Still, he had plenty of time to think.

Lydia was his first thought in the morning and the last when he closed his eyes at the end of a long day. This night was no different. He'd lain on his back, eyes closed, remembering the two of them dancing. His words came back to haunt him, "Maybe we…" Punching his pillow, he lay on his left side, then his right, each toss making him realize what his outburst may have cost him. *I love her so much. Why do I hate the idea of her starting a business and wanting to prove herself? Is it because I want her to depend on me for everything? We could be so happy living on the farm. I can provide for her. We don't need her dress shop money to survive. I don't understand why she won't let me take care of her.*

"Billy," Sarah said, knowing nothing of the agonizing battle raging within him. "You haven't been eating, and I can tell you're not getting enough sleep. I know you've been working hard in the fields, but are you feeling all right?"

"I'm fine, but I'll feel better after I see Lydia. I'll get the corn done, then I'll take off for town. I can't wait any longer to see her."

That night, desperate for sleep to overtake him, he fantasized about his and Lydia's future, torturing himself with questions. Would she say yes when he asked her to marry him? Would they take a short trip together? How many children might Lydia want? *No! I can't think of our future until I'm sure we'll have one together.* Abby's words, "Oh, Billy, how could you?" brought him to reality. *She's probably already successful. I'll do whatever it takes to show her I'm sorry. I'll show her how much she means to me.* Welcome sleep finally came, and his conscience eased once he assured himself his actions were without ulterior motives.

****

The next afternoon as Mark unhitched the team of horses, the reins got tangled. As Mark reached for the harness, a horse jerked, pulling him to the ground and injuring his back. Billy, Oat, and Steven never finished harvesting the stalks on the Hewitt farm until the middle of November. He couldn't leave Mark shorthanded. The boys couldn't do the work by themselves. He had to stay. Finally finished with the crops, Billy was determined to leave for town the next day.

That evening, the wind howled as gale-force gusts buffeted the farmhouse. By daybreak, there was knee-deep snow on the ground and inches piling up by the hour as the storm continued unabated.

Mark spoke up and said, "You better not chance leaving today, Son."

Billy knew Mark was right. Not being able to see Lydia was a hard pill to swallow. He was afraid that every day he didn't get to town was a day she could be seeing someone else or making future plans that would keep her there longer. These thoughts haunted him. He'd wait out the storm and leave the first safe opportunity that came his way.

Nature had other plans. A second record blizzard blanketed the plains. The additional feet of snow blew into formidable drifts making travel impossible. All the efforts, putting up the garden vegetables, butchering two cows, cutting and gathering wood, and harvesting the fields for food for the animals were lifesaving. At the homestead, they hunkered down to wait out the brutal forces of Nature.

Every day, Billy hoped the sun would come out to warm the ground. Then a hard cold spell hit and stayed until the middle of December. The snow melted enough to freeze the paths of packed snow. Taking the horses on ice wasn't safe, and Billy hoped Lydia would understand."

"Face facts, Billy, you're not going to get to town again until spring," Mark said. "With the holidays coming, your ma will want you to stay here. January and February are no time to make that length of a trip either. It looks like you'll have to wait until the thaw to see Lydia. I know you're disappointed, but I'm sure Lydia will understand. If something happened to you, she'd never forgive herself."

"I know you're right, Pa, but the waiting isn't easy. I hope Lydia's all right." Billy hung his head and started to walk away.

Mark reached out and put his hand on Billy's shoulder to reassure him. "Lydia knows if she needs help, there are people she can count on. I'm sure Mr. Gray is looking out for her, too. That was a generous offer by Ezra. I'm so pleased she agreed to stay with him."

"Yes, he's a good man and cares about Lydia. He'll watch out for her, and he knows I love her." Billy felt a little better remembering Ezra's advice about the three little words, *I love you.*

Chapter Thirty-Six

Lydia—December 1866

With the holidays around the corner, several customers approached Lydia asking, "Would you make this pattern for me?" Or "I have this fabric. Would you make this material into one of your designs?"

"I'm sorry, I must decline," Lydia would politely reply. "This shop features ready-to-wear fashions in my original designs. Perhaps in the future, we may be able to accommodate your wishes, but for now, it's as you see it. Thank you for the compliment."

With Jillian's help, there was now an ample selection of dresses to choose from. In honor of the upcoming town festivities, Lydia introduced another original that was a big hit with the women of Dead Flats. Because she used a variety of fabrics and notions in her designs, there was little chance one happily clad customer would encounter another woman wearing the same combination.

One morning, while Lydia struggled to carry a heavy box of fabric and some envelopes across the street, Johnathan Bellows appeared.

"Here, let me carry that. You need a cart to handle these large parcels. If you hurt yourself, you won't be able to sew. And if you can't sew, there goes your business. I see the dresses in the window changing every time I walk past. Things must be going well."

"This is my fourth order of fabric since I opened," Lydia said proudly. "And I hired an assistant. We'll be busy today, so I really must hurry to work."

"Then you better let me carry this for you." Johnathan smiled.

"Thank you. If you take this to the shop, Jillian can manage from there, and I'll return to the postal office to pick up the rest of the packages."

When Lydia arrived at the shop, Johnathan was still there. "Thanks for your help, Johnathan. I'd like to visit, but we have a busy day ahead."

Johnathan took a step closer. "Do you ever take a break?" He grinned. "I wondered if you were going to the Christmas party at the church the week after next and if you'd like to go with me."

"I wasn't planning on going to the party. I told you I don't have time," Lydia said, wondering why she was hesitating to accept Johnathan's invitation. *I'm not sure if Billy and I have broken our courtship or not. He sounded as though he wanted to, but would going with Johnathan be proper? She wouldn't make a commitment.*

"I've seen you in church with Mr. Gray a few times, and I've seen you walking to and from his house. I'm only four houses down," Johnathan said and slid his hands into his pockets.

Lydia caught Jillian's expression from the corner of her eye and said, "I must politely decline your invitation. Thank you for your help with the packages. I'll consider your suggestion on getting a cart. Something with wheels would make toting those heavy boxes easier."

"Good seeing you again, Lydia," Johnathan said. "I'm sure we'll run into each other soon.

After he left, Jillian joked, "Why, I think that young man is smitten with you. But you can't be serious that you're not going to the Church Christmas Party? It's one of the biggest holiday events in town. For the sake of business, you should reconsider. And I know Mr. Gray attends every year, so you could accompany him."

"It does sound wonderful. I haven't been to a party like that since we came west when I was eight."

"Then you're going," Jillian said.

"But what would I wear? Who would I talk to?"

"What would you wear? My goodness, make yourself a special dress. You have time and think of what an excellent advertising opportunity wearing a new design would be for Lydia's Ready-Wear. You're going, and that's that!" Jillian turned and walked away.

Lydia opened her mouth to protest as Mr. Gray walked up and said, "I'm finished for the day. You'll have to lock up tonight. If anyone wants me, tell them to come back tomorrow."

"Are you feeling all right, Ezra," Lydia inquired.

"Yes, dear, I'm fine. I'm going to find a tree for the holiday. I thought we could decorate one tonight. I'll see you at home."

Lydia paused, wondering if the family had gotten a tree yet. *I won't be there to help string popcorn or watch the children exchange their presents. I'm missing so much.* Lydia promised herself, *I'll never miss another holiday with my family ever again. Presents! I better get a present for Ezra and one for Jillian, but what?*

****

Jillian was right. Ezra always attended the church Christmas Party and expected Lydia to go along. For Jillian's Christmas present, Lydia made her a dress in the design and fabric of her choice. She chose the black on ivory. Tonight she wore the dress with a red shawl and a red belt.

When Lydia and Ezra walked into the church, she immediately spotted Jillian and Cain with their son by the punch bowl. Christmas carols were to start at seven sharp, and as she and Ezra made their way across the room to sit with Jillian's family, the pianist struck the first chord of the classic "Joy to the World." Carols rang out for an hour, with everyone joining in. Then attendees mingled and enjoyed punch and cookies.

Lydia noticed Ezra tiring and suggested, "I've had enough. Are you ready to head home?"

Ezra nodded, and Lydia went for their coats.

Johnathan went for his and his mother's coat at the same time. The two of them bumped into each other in the tight space of the cloakroom, causing Lydia to lose her balance and land on the floor.

"Oh, I'm so sorry," Johnathan said as he reached down to help her stand. "I didn't see you there."

Ready to give whoever knocked her down a piece of her mind, Lydia looked up at Johnathan, swallowed hard, and said, "And I didn't see you, either, Johnathan." Lydia smiled, then laughed out loud. "We do keep running into each other, don't we?"

"Yes," Johnathan said, reluctantly releasing her hand. "I wish we could be friends. Word around town is you might have a beau, but men and woman can also be friends, you know."

"I know, and I'd like that," Lydia agreed with a twinkle in her eye, "as long as we keep bumping into each other." Now on her feet, she said. "We were leaving, and since we're going the same direction, maybe we could start over, and you can tell me about where you used to live."

As snow started falling, the two of them talked all the way home as Johnathan's mother, Mary, and Ezra chatted.

"Enjoy your evening. I hope Saint Nicholas finds you," Johnathan called as Ezra unlocked the door to the house.

"I hope he finds you, too!" Lydia called back.

Once inside, Lydia heated milk to make hot chocolate and looked at the clock. "The children back home are all in bed by now. I'm sure Ma made fudge for tomorrow, and the stockings are ready by the hearth. I wonder what everyone made as exchange presents this year." She sat at the table with Ezra as the milk warmed. "Ever since I can remember, our family has made gifts to exchange. This year, poor Billy got stuck helping all the children make their gifts. I'm sure he had his hands full since I wasn't there to help."

"What else do you do as a family for Christmas?" Ezra asked.

"We sing carols, pop popcorn, and decorate the tree with ornaments that we make and add to every year. Jack, Billy, or I always read the story of Jesus's birth from the Bible before going to bed." Lydia made the chocolate treat and set a steaming mug in front of Ezra.

The two enjoyed a few sips, and Ezra handed his family Bible to Lydia. "Would you read the Christmas story to me?" he asked.

Lydia turned to the page and began.

****

The smell of fresh perked coffee filled the air the following morning as Lydia fixed flapjacks and sausage with a stewed dried fruit compote for breakfast. Looking out the kitchen window, fresh snow on the ground showed what looked like deep wagon wheel tracks and footprints that led to and from the front door. "Ezra, time for breakfast, she called.

"Sure smells good. Much better than what I'd have made if I were here by myself." He poured coffee for them and carried the cups to the table where they enjoyed Lydia's sumptuous Christmas breakfast.

Sated, Ezra leaned back in his chair and said, Thank you, dear. That was a lovely beginning to Christmas day. I've not enjoyed any meal like this since my beloved wife was here."

"You're so welcome, Ezra. My pleasure. This is the meal my family is probably enjoying right now. Sharing this meal with you makes me feel closer to them." Changing the tender subject, she asked, "Ezra, have you been outside this morning?"

"Why no, but I see we did get a couple inches of snow. Why do you ask?"

"Come look at these tracks. I haven't gone out yet this morning, either. Whose tracks could they be?"

"Well, maybe we should investigate. There are footprints showing someone coming and going, but only one set of wheel marks. We better have a look," Ezra suggested.

Opening the front door, they found a cart with tall sides, sturdy wheels, and a pull handle. There was a card tied to the handle with a sprig of greenery and a red ribbon. Lydia suspected she knew who delivered the surprise.

She brushed a few flakes of snow away and wheeled the cart inside. Opening the envelope, she read, "Now you won't need anyone's help with your large packages." And it was signed, *Johnathan Bellows.*

"Well, it's obviously for you, dear. What does the card say?"

"It's from Johnathan Bellows. He's helped me carry my heavy packages from the postal office a few times and suggested a cart would be handy for when he wasn't around to help. I can't believe he made this for me. That was so thoughtful of him. Do you know him well, Ezra?"

"Only that he and his mother arrived in town earlier this year and that they live down the street. I must say, I enjoyed talking with Mrs. Bellows on the walk home last night."

Lydia suggested, "Would you mind if I invited them to the house this evening? I'll make some suet pudding and pumpkin bread with the raisins I have left over. I'd like to thank him properly for the time he must have put into making this lovely cart."

"That would be fine and neighborly of us, Lydia."

Lydia brought out Ezra's gifts—a reversible vest that she made from homespun fabrics and a pouch of tobacco. She saw him outside a few times after supper enjoying his pipe and knew tobacco was a luxury he only indulged in once in a while.

"Oh, my dear. The vest is quite lovely, and the tobacco much appreciated. The Missus wouldn't let me smoke in the house, and I only have a pipe full occasionally," Ezra shared.

Lydia beamed at the thought of Ezra's appreciation. "Try the vest on. I want to make sure the shoulders fit right."

He slipped on the vest, buttoned it up, and tugged on the front and sides. "Perfect!" He said. "I'll save this one to wear to church."

"You don't need to save it. I'll make you another if you like."

"All right, if you say so. I'll wear it to church for the New Year's Eve service and for every day. Now let me fetch your present, Lydia." He returned, walking carefully, holding an object that was hidden under a towel.

Lydia lifted the cloth to find a beautiful door decoration she had once admired in his shop. Made of three leather straps attached to a leather hoop, with three jingle bells attached to each strap, the ornament hanging on a door would jingle when the door opened or closed.

"I make these every year for Christmas," Ezra said. "People like to hang them on their doors as a decoration. I sold quite a few this year and thought you might like one for your door when you finally have your own home. Just a little something to remember me by."

Lydia gave Ezra a hug. "I love your present. It's very thoughtful! Thank you so much, Ezra. I'll always cherish it and for now, let's hang it on your front door. I noticed a nail."

****

Later that same afternoon, Lydia walked to Johnathan Bellows' house to invite him and his mother to Ezra's for the evening.

Mrs. Bellows answered the door, "Hello, Lydia, and Merry Christmas. How may I help you?"

"Is Johnathan here? I want to thank him for the surprise he left on my doorstep this morning." Lydia smiled and added. "And Mr. Gray and I would like to invite you both to come visit tonight if you don't have prior plans."

"Johnathan isn't home right now. He does odd jobs for people, and he's out shoveling snow, but I'm sure he would be happy for us to join you this evening. What is a good time?"

"Seven o'clock is perfect. I hope you like suet pudding and pumpkin bread. Or I could make rice pudding if you prefer."

"It's been a long while since I've had the pleasure of a suet pudding, but Johnathan loves rice pudding."

The women chuckled.

"What was I thinking? My brothers would prefer rice pudding too. "All right, then. We'll see you at seven."

Lydia walked home, assembled ingredients and mixing bowls, and began baking. The house was soon filled with the fragrance of spices, and after what seemed a short while, a knock on the front door heralded the arrival of their guests.

"Ezra, can you answer the door. I'm going to run upstairs and change. I'll only be a few minutes." Lydia scampered up the steps and returned to greet her company in the living room.

"I'm so glad you could both come. And Johnathan, I want to thank you for the cart you made me. That was very thoughtful and much unexpected. I'll use your cart on my next trip to the postal office and every trip thereafter." Lydia took a seat next to him, and they began talking about his interest in carpentry and working with his hands.

"I've always enjoyed making things." Ezra overheard Johnathan say, and his words made him think of something he'd been thinking about a lot lately. Who would take over his business when he couldn't manage anymore? What would he do with his shop? Selling his life's endeavors didn't appeal to him, but if he could teach someone to take over, he'd enjoy knowing his legacy would continue. *Maybe Johnathan would be interested. I'll give this more thought.*

Ezra and Johnathan's mother, Mary, discussed the town's politics and if the New Year would bring any concerns. The town was growing, and crime was up. The war had left many poor and struggling.

"My husband died fighting the war," Mary said. "When he didn't come home, Johnathan and I decided we should start over. We sold almost everything we had and came west on a wagon train from Ohio. Dead Flats seemed like a good place to begin, so here we are."

"I do odd jobs, and we make out all right," Johnathan added. I see your carriage house out back is in need of repair. I could fix it for you."

"I sold the horse after my wife passed," Ezra mused aloud. "I guess I should have sold the carriage too, but I couldn't force myself to part with it. My wife and I used to enjoy taking a ride on Sundays after church. She'd pack a meal, and we'd have a picnic. I haven't done that for some time. I don't even know what work is needed, but I wouldn't want the barn to fall down, so I guess it should be fixed."

"You mean you don't have a milk cow or chickens out there? Wouldn't fresh milk and eggs taste good every day?" Johnathan questioned.

"Being alone, I couldn't manage the feed and the extra work to keep animals, so I got rid of the cow and the chickens. Lydia won't be staying long, so it doesn't make sense to replace them now." Ezra looked at Mary. "Do you have a cow and chickens?"

Mary shook her head. "No, we don't have a place for them, but I sure do miss fresh eggs and milk in the mornings."

"Would you like coffee or tea Mrs. Bellows?" Lydia asked.

"Coffee would be wonderful. I grow my own mint and herbs for tea, but a good cup of coffee is a real treat." Mary smiled and said, "Can I help you in the kitchen?"

Johnathan sprung to his feet. "No, you sit and talk to Mr. Gray, Ma. I'll help Lydia."

In the kitchen, Lydia warmed the prepared pot of coffee and cut the pumpkin bread. "I hope you like rice pudding?"

"Yes, of course. I'm sure it will be delicious. Thank you for inviting us tonight. My mother doesn't get out much. She hasn't made many friends in town. I try to get her to do things, but she says it's not the same without Pa."

Taking the plates from the cupboard, Lydia said, "My pa fought in the war, too. My family was fortunate. He came home."

"You look real nice tonight," Johnathan said, in a quick change of subject.

"Why, thank you. I was admiring your mother's dress. Does she sew?"

"Yes, and she made my pants and my vest, as well. She's a good seamstress and enjoys sewing. She used to work at a dry goods store and kept the books."

Lydia tucked that bit of information away with a thought she'd consider further if the need arose. "Could you reach the cups and saucers for me?" she asked.

Placing everything on a tray, Johnathan carried the tray into the living room and placed it on the serving table.

"Help yourselves," Lydia said, delighted to have company to entertain.

The conversation was light, interesting, and informative as they covered a vast variety of topics and events happening across the country.

The topic of slavery came up, and Lydia was glad to hear Mary and Johnathan were behind the Union war effort to free slaves and unify the country.

After their company left, Lydia was in the kitchen washing dishes when Ezra walked in.

"I enjoyed talking with Mary and Johnathan. I haven't entertained at home since my wife passed. I had a pleasant evening, and your bread and pudding were very tasty. We should have them again."

Lydia blushed from the compliment and mused about this Christmas day that she was afraid would make her longing for home. *What a lovely day,* she thought as Ezra grabbed the towel and dried the last few dishes.

Chapter Thirty-Seven

Lydia—January and February 1867

After the holidays, Lydia noticed sales dropped off. "Jillian, with fewer customers, now's my chance to design for spring, and I'm sorry, but I won't need your help until business picks up."

"I understand," Jillian said, "let me know when you need me again. New designs always sell well. Come April and May, people will be arriving in town to pick up seed, and the town will be active again. You already have a good sense of what the women of Dead Flats want. I can't wait to see your new designs. I was wondering," Jillian twirled a piece of her golden hair around her finger, "I've been saving money to buy a sewing machine. Could you teach me how to run the machine before you get too busy sketching? Hopefully, I could sew a few skirts of my own while you're designing."

"I'd be glad to, Jillian. Come in tomorrow. There are plenty of scraps you can use for practice. I'll walk you through the mechanics. It's not hard. I'm sure you'll catch on."

Jillian arrived the following day with scraps of fabric folded neatly in a pillowcase and two full spools of thread.

"Sit next to me at the machine, Jillian. I'll show you

how to wind a bobbin, set the tension, and determine the stitch length. Then we'll go on to thread the needle, use the pressure foot, guide the fabric, and make the machine sew in reverse. This sounds like a lot to learn, but with a little practice, you'll be sewing in no time. First, you need to learn how to use the treadle."

Catching on quickly, soon, a beautiful crazy quilt materialized before Jillian's eyes. "Can I come back tomorrow?" Jillian asked before leaving for the day.

"Of course. I'll be sketching for the next few days, then I have to lay out the pattern pieces. I won't be sewing for a while. You're welcome to come every day if you like. I have lots of scraps. You know me, I don't throw anything away big enough to go into a quilt."

Soon Jillian mastered everything about the sewing machine Lydia could teach her. She then went on to learn some tips on how to lay out pattern pieces for the best fabric usage.

"Jillian, you've come a long ways in the last few weeks. You're a natural, I'd say." Lydia decided now was the time to ask Jillian the question she had been dying to ask. While pinning on a new design pattern, Lydia inquired, "Jillian, now that you know my side of the business and how to work the machine, might you be interested in running the shop for me?" In the silence that followed her proposal, Lydia waited with batcd breath for Jillian's reaction.

Jillian gasped, forcing out the words, "You mean it?"

"Yes. I'm quite sure I've taught you everything you need to know. As much as I love being here, I've decided that moving home has definite benefits. I'll have time to design dresses and plot patterns. The time I take running the shop limits me. If I were home and you were taking care of Lydia's Ready-Wear, I could design and keep the styles changing. And, I miss my family and the helping hands of my mother and grandma." Lydia's thoughts strayed, *and then there's Billy. We have so much to sort out, and perhaps being closer will give us that opportunity. I think I still love him, but does he love me in a way that works for both of us?* Coming back to the moment, she realized, *There, I've asked Jillian about taking over, so I guess I'm serious. And about more than just the shop.* She continued with her explanation to a dumbfounded Jillian, who was still trying to grasp what Lydia was proposing.

"If you take over sewing and making sure the dresses are ready for display, I'll have so much more time. After all, designing is what I love to do the best. I would come to town once a month, bring new design patterns, order new fabric, and check on how things are going. I wasn't thinking of returning home until spring, so that would give us time to practice the new arrangement and adjust anything that needs to be changed. If you're interested, we'll need to find someone to help you and do the bookwork and banking. I'm thinking of asking Mary Bellows, Johnathan's mother. I'm sure you two would get along." Lydia smiled at the thought of asking Mary.

"I know you need to talk to Cain about this big decision, and I'm hoping your answer will be yes. I need to come up with a salary proposal for you, the hours can change if necessary. Customers don't typically shop in the evening, so you can be home with your family." Lydia took Jillian's hands and said, "You've been a good friend, Jillian, and I'll respect you regardless of your answer. Take the weekend and think over my proposal. We'll talk again next week."

Jillian hugged Lydia and said, "I can't tell you what this means, that you put such trust in me. I've seen how hard you've worked to make this business a success. I'll talk to Cain and have an answer for you on Monday." She hugged Lydia again before dashing out the door.

****

That evening during supper, Lydia shared her plans with Ezra. "I've decided to return home if I can find the right people to take my place. I'll start paying you a commission on each dress for allowing me to use your shop space. After all, that was the original deal. I've asked Jillian to consider running the shop. She knows how to use the sewing machine and is quite proficient now. She's talking over my proposal with Cain. If she's willing, I need someone to take her place part-time. I thought about asking Johnathan's mother, Mary. She used to work at a dry goods store and kept the books. I think she'd be perfect, and she and Jillian would get along wonderfully. What do you think?"

"I think I'll miss you something terrible when you leave. I've gotten used to us coming home and having each other to talk to and eat with," Ezra's voice cracked. "I knew this arrangement wasn't permanent, but I've grown to enjoy your company, here and at the shop."

Tears flowed as Lydia gave Ezra a hug.

He whispered, "I'm very proud of you. I knew you'd be successful from the first day you came in and told me of your plans," Ezra pulled out his handkerchief. "I'll miss you."

"I'll miss you too," Lydia whispered and gave him a squeeze. "If you hadn't believed in me and given me the space in your front windows, I wouldn't have been able to open a store in Dead Flats. Who would have thought in such a short time my dreams could come true?"

"When do you plan to ask Mary if she'd be interested in part-time work?" Ezra inquired.

Lydia placed her napkin back on her lap. "I'll wait until I hear from Jillian. She has to agree to run the business, then I'll ask Mary."

"Well, I have news of my own," Ezra announced. "I'm thinking about asking Johnathan to apprentice with me. I know he likes working with his hands, and I'm not getting any younger. Someone will have to take over for me when it's my time. Johnathan would be perfect, and I need to start teaching him now, so he learns the trade and gains respect in town as a businessman."

Lydia said enthusiastically, "Oh, Ezra, that's a wonderful idea. I think Johnathan will leap at the offer."

"He's been coming in a lot lately." A grin crept over Ezra's face. "At first, I thought he was there to check up on you. Lately, though, the questions he's been asking me about tanning leather, the tools, and the projects I've been working on showed his interest. Wouldn't that be something, both of them working at the same place?" Ezra chuckled.

"Is it our turn to have them as guests or their turn to have us? No matter, I think we should invite them for supper so we can talk," Lydia said. "I'm pretty sure Jillian will say yes. I trust her, and you can, too. She and Cain are well respected in town. Mary can watch their son when necessary. Or he can go to work with Cain. I pray Jillian says yes. Now all I have to do is come up with a fair salary to pay her and still have money left to keep new fabric coming in."

****

Lydia was busily drawing a new pattern when Jillian walked in. "Spill the beans. Come on, tell me. What did you and Cain decide?" Lydia asked, her excitement uncontainable.

Jillian nervously twirled her hair around her finger. "Well, both Cain and I were curious if you decided the monthly pay I'd be earning," she said, shifting anxiously from one foot to the other.

"Yes, and I hope you'll both think it's reasonable. I've decided to close on Wednesdays, the slowest day of the week. So you'd work Saturdays, or you could take turns with another person I'll hire to help if you have family plans. I can offer fifteen dollars a month, April through December. We'll have to reduce store hours for the winter, and your pay would be eleven dollars a month. The shop still has to stay open. Profits after salaries will go toward buying additional fabric. I'm hoping sales will be good enough to keep us open."

Jillian breathed a sigh of relief and announced, "I'll do it!"

The women embraced.

"You've made me the happiest woman in the world!" Lydia exclaimed. *I'll ask Mary this week, and hopefully, she'll agree. I can train her before I leave.*

****

"Come in before the wind blows you away, child," Mary said, hurrying to close the door after Lydia entered the Bellow's home.

Lydia brushed the snow from her coat. "I'm here to invite you and Johnathan for supper tomorrow. I'm fixing ham, green beans, and potatoes."

283

"That would be lovely, but only if you let me bring rolls and a jar of apple butter. I know Ezra likes apple butter," Mary offered. "And let me make somethin' to go with our coffee as dessert," she added

"That sounds lovely, Mary. Is Johnathan home?" Lydia inquired.

"No," Mary said. "He's out working somewhere. He cleans the church once a week, but that's his only steady job. I don't know how he does it, but he always manages to bring home enough money and food for us to get by."

"Well, tell him to come hungry tomorrow. We'll see you then." After chatting a few minutes, Lydia went home and shared the news with Ezra.

The following evening, after a delicious meal and small talk, Lydia brewed coffee, Mary plated the oatmeal spice cake she brought, and Ezra and Johnathan retreated to the living room.

While alone, Lydia took the opportunity to talk to Mary. "I understand you used to work at a dry goods store and did the books as well as wait on customers."

"Why yes, I did. I worked there for eight years before we moved here. I looked for a position when we first arrived, but there was nothing available. Why do you ask?" Mary paused, interested in Lydia's response.

"How would you like to work at Lydia's Ready-Wear a few days a week as needed, helping cut pattern pieces, waiting on customers, and keeping the books?"

"But you already have a girl helping you. She didn't leave, did she?"

"No, Jillian's still there. She's going to take my place sewing and getting the dresses ready for sale, plus running the shop while I'm away. You see, I'm seriously considering returning home this spring. I'll still design the dresses, which is what I really enjoy doing, and you and Jillian will run the shop. That is if you think you would like to work again."

"Really? You'd hire me?"

"Yes, I can't think of anyone I'd trust more than you to keep the books. I haven't been much good at keeping things straight myself. I try to write things down and keep up with everything else, but Jillian and I think you'd be great at all aspects of the job. That is, if you're interested, of course." In her eagerness, Lydia rushed on, "You could set your own hours and days unless a fabric order comes in and the work picks up. And there may be days Jillian won't need you. The two of you can work that out between yourselves. Jillian would teach you what she does now. I'm sure you would be a lovely sales clerk, and you already know how to keep the books and make deposits at the bank."

Mary put the knife down and took a seat at the kitchen table while Lydia continued.

"I can only pay ten and a half cents an hour. After the Christmas rush, the hours will be reduced considerably. We're finding women aren't buying as much after spending for the holidays, and there aren't as many people in town right now. I expect business to pick up when the weather warms." Having stated her case to the best of her ability, Lydia sat down beside Mary.

"My dear, your offer is generous," Mary sighed. "But are you sure you want an old woman like me working in your shop?"

"I figure you're about my mother's age, maybe a little younger. I so look forward to the two of you meeting sometime. My mother helped me at the beginning. Besides, what does age have to do with anything? I have women of all ages buying my designs. Even the mayor's wife is a customer. Of course, you'll want to discuss this with Johnathan. I'll look forward to your answer. I don't know who I'll ask if you're not interested."

"Oh, I am interested. And yes, I will confer with Johnathan." Mary beamed with pleasure.

At the same time, the women were talking in the kitchen, Ezra brought up the subject of the future of his business to Johnathan. "This past year, I'm taking in more business than I can handle by myself, and I'm not getting any younger. It's time to find someone to train to take over. I've noticed you seem drawn to this type of work, Johnathan. Might you be interested in such an opportunity? Would you be willing to put time and effort into learning the leather and harness trade? Apprenticing would require serious training" Ezra leaned back, interested in Johnathan's answer.

"I sure would be interested, Mr. Gray. I find what you do very interesting, and I know I could learn and do a good job. With your training and help, I'd be honored to carry on your legacy. Are you really offering me an apprenticeship with you?" Johnathan questioned, the offer still reeling in his mind.

"Yes, Johnathan. I believe we could do well together. You've shown me you are a fine, hardworking young man. And if you're willing to learn, I feel you'd be an asset and one day could take over for me. The apprenticeship would be Monday through Saturday for a six-month period, during which time you'll receive modest payment for your work. After six months, we'll evaluate the progress you've made." Ezra tilted his head and awaited Johnathan's response.

"Yes. Yes, I understand the work involved and the time needed. This is a once-in-a-lifetime opportunity for me." Johnathan shook Mr. Gray's hand. "When can I start?"

"The shop opens at nine o'clock each day, and we close at five or six, depending on how busy we are. I'll see you tomorrow morning." Just then, Lydia and Mary came into the room carrying the dessert.

Lydia smiled at Ezra, who returned the grin. "I think we should leave these two alone to talk for a few minutes," Lydia said as she gave Ezra a hand up from his chair, and they retreated to the kitchen.

Within minutes, Johnathan came to ask them to return to the living room.

Pouring coffee, Mary said, "We don't know how to thank you both for the opportunities you've offered us. Lydia, let me know when you want me to start, and I'll be there."

"And I'll be there tomorrow, ready to learn, Mr. Gray," Johnathan said and grinned broadly.

"If you're both going to be working at the shop, you need to call me Ezra," he said. "I think we'll all get along nicely."

Chapter Thirty-Eight

Early March 1867

It had snowed during the night. A few inches covered the ground as Lydia came out of the postal office, her cart filled with packages. She started to cross the street when suddenly, shots rang out from the hotel saloon. *I better get to the shop quickly*, she thought, and frantically pulled the heavily laden cart into the street. Halfway across, pulling hard to force the bulky cart through piled-up mud and snow, the wheels became stuck in a wagon rut. Tugging to free it, she heard people from the sidewalk calling out.

"Hurry, lady! Get out of the way," a man yelled.

A rumbling noise made Lydia turn to see a driverless wagon pulled by two spooked horses heading straight toward her. In horror, she froze, riveted to the spot, unable to move.

Suddenly, she was thrown to one side, mud gagging her, the pounding of horses' hooves and the creaking of wagon wheels so close she couldn't believe she was still in one piece. There was a loud thud. Taking a deep breath, she sat up covered with snow and dirt, her hair, hands, and face showing the violence of the fall. Her dress was ruined.

People came running from both sides of the street. "Get the doctor!" someone called out.

"If that man hadn't shoved you out of the way, lady, you could have been killed," a man said as he helped her to stand. "Are you all right, miss?" he asked.

Lydia attempted to get a glimpse of the person being carried off the street but wasn't able to see his face. Whoever he was, he saved her life.

"Yes, I think I'm all right. Shaken, but no broken bones. Will you help me, please?" Lydia noted the sturdy cart was intact, but the packages were scattered. She had to make sure that whoever rescued her was safe. She made her way through the crowd of people gathering around the lifeless body to see his face. "Oh no," she cried out when she recognized Johnathan lying motionless on the boardwalk.

Lydia collapsed beside him and took his hand. He was alive, but his breathing was shallow. "Where is Doc Glasgow?" she called out desperately. Stroking his hair and wiping mud from his face, she whispered, "Johnathan, Johnathan, it's Lydia. You saved my life." She sobbed. "If anything happens to you, I'll never forgive myself."

"Make way for Doc Glasgow," a man shouted.

"Did anyone see what happened?" Doc asked as he began his examination.

A bystander called out, "This woman was crossing the street when shots were fired. Then this runaway wagon came toward her full tilt. She was pulling a cart and wasn't going to get across in time. This young man ran from this side of the street and pushed her out of the way. I don't think the wagon ran over him, but he hasn't moved since the men picked him up and carried him here."

Lydia, focused on Johnathan, raised her head and

said, "Doc, you've got to help him. He saved my life. His name is Johnathan Bellows."

Doc hadn't recognized that the young woman, muddy and breathless from sobbing, sitting beside the injured form was Lydia Clark until she spoke.

Doc made sure Johnathan's airways were clear. "I'll need help carrying this man to my office," he said.

Men volunteered for the task.

"I'll go get his mother and bring her to your office, Doc," Lydia offered, glad to do something to help. "Do everything you can for him, Doc." Lydia turned to one of the women standing behind her and asked, "Will you please take my things to the dress shop and let Mr. Gray know what happened?"

"Of course, dear," the woman said.

Lydia ran to fetch Mary and told her about the accident. The two women supported each other as they hurried to Doc Glasgow's office.

Mary went into the inner office while Lydia anxiously stayed in the waiting room.

Johnathan groaned as he sat up on his own and let his legs dangle off the table. His shirt was off, and Mary could see the redness and bruises that would pain him in the days to come.

"I'm fine, Ma. Doc said I'm lucky. Nothings broken, only bruised." Johnathan attempted to put his shirt on by himself and winced in pain.

Mary helped her son get his arms in his shirt and button the front. "You're lucky all right, Son, but the one who was really lucky is Lydia. Thank goodness you acted so quickly to push her out of the way. She said you saved her life."

Johnathan shook his head. "She was caught in the

street with the cart I gave her. She would have crossed safely if the cart hadn't got stuck in a rut. She is all right, isn't she?"

Mary answered, "Yes, dear, she's fine but concerned about you. She's outside in the waiting room."

"Let me walk out on my own, so she knows I'm okay." Johnathan slid off the table and shuffled his way to the outer room, followed by his mother and Doc Glasgow.

"You got the wind knocked out of you, young fella. You'll be sore and black and blue for a week or so, but other than that, you're fine," Doc announced, loudly enough for Lydia to hear.

"See, Lydia, no broken bones. The bruises will be gone soon," Johnathan said. "Are you sure you're all right? I shoved you pretty hard. Maybe Doc should check you over too."

"I'm good now that I know you're safe and nothing's broken. Oh, Johnathan, you gave me such a scare. You weren't moving when they carried you to the sidewalk after you saved my life."

Johnathan swallowed hard. Then, to lighten the conversation said, "Saved your life? I was trying to save the cart I made you. I don't have any spare lumber for patches, so I couldn't let that wagon run you over."

Lydia paused. Once the words sank in, her jaw dropped. Johnathan's teasing sounded so much like her brother Jack that her hands instinctively went up as if to pound the daylights out of him.

Johnathan blocked them and held them firmly. "Come on, Lydia. I'm already sore. You don't need to add more bruises."

She looked at him, and he grinned. She gave him a

hug instead and started to chuckle. Doc joined in the laughter.

Mary chimed in, too, "Well, looks like laughter is the best medicine."

****

Mid-March, the grass peeking through the snow signaled warmer days were ahead. "I can't wait any longer. I'm leaving in the morning for Dead Flats," Billy told the family. "I have to see Lydia and find out if she's all right. I'll bring her home, I promise." Billy had tormented himself all winter. He was ashamed of his outburst during that dreadful conversation when he told Lydia they should stop courting. Would she still be his gal? Would the dreams he had for the two of them come true? All he wanted now was to get her home.

He lit out before dawn to ensure he'd arrive in town well before the shop closed. Riding along, he prayed, *Please, Lord, please let Lydia have forgiven me. I pray she hasn't given her heart to anyone else while I've been gone. I'll bring her home, and everything will be fine again.* The closer he got to Dead Flats, the more his stomach ached, and his head throbbed.

Under his warm clothing, he was wearing his best shirt and vest. He wouldn't let anyone show him up in Lydia's eyes ever again.

Chapter Thirty-Nine

In town, Billy made for the alley behind the shop to park the wagon. After shedding his outer clothing, he finger-combed his hair and headed for the front door of Lydia's Ready-Wear.

When he walked in, Jillian was busily laying out fabric in preparation to pin on a pattern. Billy heard the rhythm of a sewing machine coming from the back room. Jillian saw him and started to say something, but he held his index finger to his lips.

She smiled encouragingly.

He rounded the corner, and the sight of Lydia took his breath away. She looked sophisticated with her hair styled in a braid wound around her head like a coronet. She wore a beautiful dress, no doubt one of her designs. The space had been transformed into a workroom. Bolts of fabric leaned against the wall and cut pieces were stacked in neatly organized piles. Billy waited until the machine stopped, then said, "Lydia, it's so good to see you. You look beautiful. Can we talk?"

"Billy," Lydia said, startled by his sudden appearance. She rose but didn't move forward. "So you finally made it to town. Yes, we can talk. How is everyone? Did you stop at Jack and Abby's?"

"Whoa. One question at a time." Billy stepped closer. "Everyone is doing well. Grandma even sent along a pie. No, I haven't seen Jack and Abby, but we can stop and see them on our way home if you like. And yes, of course, this is my first stop. I couldn't wait to see you." He paused in awkward silence. "I see Jillian is helping. I'm glad you two finally got to meet. Do you have time to talk? There's something I've been waiting to tell you all winter, and I can't wait any longer."

"Everyone's all right, aren't they? No one's sick?" Lydia asked anxiously.

"Everyone is fine. They all send their love and can't wait to see you. I want to tell you something, Lydia, and I need you to listen. Can Jillian watch the shop for a while, so we can take a walk?"

"We do need to talk. Let me get my coat."

"You two go ahead," Jillian offered. "I'll let Ezra and Johnathan know you've stepped out if they ask."

Billy gasped at Jillian's words. Ushering Lydia quickly outside into the alley, he looked her squarely in the face. "You mean Johnathan Bellows is here in the shop?" His heart pounded out of control. His nightmare had come true. His voice rose along with his concern. "Why, Lydia? Why? I apologized! I told you I didn't mean what I said about breaking off our courtship. You must not have heard me right, or didn't you care?"

"You didn't give me much reason to care," Lydia countered.

"I said I wanted you and your business to be successful. And I meant that. I am proud of you. So why did you get involved with Johnathan? I know that's why he's here. He's the one that forced the issue, isn't he? He weaseled his way into your life, and now he's probably the reason why you'll want to stay here." Billy paused, his indignation mounting. He was enraged. His worst fears had come true, and he struck out like a wounded animal.

"Slow down, Billy, you're not seeing things straight," Lydia insisted, put off by Billy's tirade.

"No, I see everything just fine," Billy said, and then took a deep breath to calm himself. "I love you. I've always loved you. We made plans to be together, and now everything's ruined because you had to start your business and stay in town. I'll admit that at first, I didn't want you to succeed. But you were so determined you had to try no matter what. You had to prove to everyone that you could survive on your own, even though I already have the means to provide for you and a family. I thought as long as we had each other, that's all we needed. But apparently not."

"Hold on, Billy, you're wrong, dead wrong. You don't understand." Lydia stomped her foot in frustration.

"No, you're the one who doesn't understand. You don't understand how I feel!" Billy retorted, frustrated and jealous. "Where is this Johnathan Bellows? I want to give him a piece of my mind. How dare he take my girl away from me! I've been worried sick about you seeing other men. Had we not finished the corn later than planned and had the early snowstorm, I would have come in November. We could have talked then, and maybe none of this would have happened. I worried you might start seeing someone else. Now to find out you turned to Johnathan. I'm spitting mad! Where is he?" Billy turned and started pacing when suddenly, Lydia lunged toward him, slapped his face, and stopped him in his tracks.

"Billy Henry, how dare you accuse me of being unfaithful? And how dare you accuse Johnathan! You're wrong, and you need to settle down. You don't know the whole story, and yet here you are jumping to wild conclusions. You have no reason to be upset, no reason at all. In fact, you should be thankful Johnathan came into my life, or I wouldn't be standing here talking to you right now." Hot tears rolled down her flushed face.

"Yes, you heard correctly. Johnathan saved my life. That's the truth. He put himself in harm's way to save me."

Billy took a step back, his cheek stinging from her slap and his head reeling from her words.

"Well…I'm certainly thankful for that, but that doesn't give him the right to take you away from me." *Quinn took Elizabeth from me, and now Johnathan is doing the same thing.* Unresolved pain from his marriage to Elizabeth colored his thinking. "I mean, of course you were grateful. Grateful at the time, but you didn't have to start seeing him because he saved you." Billy threw his hands up and stopped talking, his face red from his unabated suffering.

"Do you hear yourself, Billy Henry? Do you hear what you're saying? Jonathan Bellows, at risk to himself, saved my life. A wagon with runaway horses and no driver was about to run me over. Johnathan ran into the street and, putting his life in danger, pushed me out of the way. Ask anyone. The whole town knows about it. Yes, I'm fine, not that you care, but I thought when you heard, you'd at least be grateful enough to shake his hand."

"I…I am grateful. Very grateful. I'm glad you're all right." Then her words *He saved my life* finally registered in Billy's consciousness. Coming to his senses, he said, "Johnathan saved you? You must have been terrified when this happened…you could have died. Good Lord, I could have lost you."

Shaking his head, barely able to come to terms with what Johnathan did for Lydia, Billy dropped to his knees and pressed Lydia's hands to his face. "Oh, sweetheart, thank God you're safe. Without missing a beat, he raced to another thought, concluding that all was lost. "I don't know what I'll do without you in my life. My days will be so lonely. All the hopes we had of getting married, living on our farm, and raising our family will never happen all on account of me. If you've made your decision, I'll have to live with it, but I'm begging you to reconsider. I lost Elizabeth to Quinn and this town. I don't want to lose you too. I'll change my ways. I love you with all my heart."

"Stop, Billy. You don't know what I've dealt with over the past months. All I've done was try to set everything in order so I could come home. You say you love me, but your accusations say the opposite. With no evidence except your suspicions, you accuse me of being unfaithful."

"Oh, Lydia, I'm so sorry. You're right. I understand now. I've been selfish. While we've been apart, all I've done is think of you and how much you mean to me, how much I want a future with you. I do love you, Lydia, and I'll do anything if you'll tell me that you feel the same about me and that your heart is not pledged to Johnathan Bellows."

"Billy! You still don't understand. I've been trying to tell you, and you kept interrupting. Johnathan's not here in the store because of me," Lydia explained.

"You mean the two of you aren't together? When Jillian said he was in the back, I assumed you were and that he was helping you around the store."

"No," Lydia said. "Johnathan is here because he's

apprenticing with Ezra to take over the harness shop."

"So you aren't in love with him?" Billy asked, relieved but still in the throes of jealousy.

"No! I am not in love with Johnathan Bellows. That's what I've been trying to tell you, but you don't listen," Lydia said as she wiped away tears of frustration.

Billy hung his head in shame. "Lydia, I'm so sorry. I've jumped to conclusions. Apparently, the wrong conclusions.

"I've been out of my mind with worry about you and what you might think of me. The thought of you turning to someone else in a time of need weighed heavy on my mind. And when I heard Johnathan was here, I assumed the worst. I'm sorry. I'm really sorry," Billy said.

"I promise never to jump to conclusions again. I can see success becomes you. You look beautiful. I'll build that room onto the house that you asked for. If you need money for fabric or a new sewing machine, it's yours. I'll bring you to town whenever you want to come. You mean more to me than anything, Lydia. Please, please forgive me. I've acted like a complete fool. Please tell me you still want to come home and continue courting."

"Billy Henry, you make me so furious. There were times when I thought about your strong arms around me, holding me close and making me feel safe. I'm not sure how I feel now. When you left in October, I was deeply hurt. I vowed to succeed at any cost, and, as you can see, I have. You've misjudged me, and you jumped to irrational conclusions about Johnathan. You made assumptions that had no basis except your jealousy. I said that I'd work out a way to come home when the time was right, and I've done that. Jillian is going to run the shop with help from Johnathan's mother, Mary. Ezra and

I have gotten to know Mary and Johnathan quite well, and they are good friends. But after your irrational outburst, I wonder if I really know you at all." Flushed with the outpouring of her long-held feelings, Lydia watched as their true significance finally sank into Billy's sensibility.

He fell back as though pushed, staggering with the realization of how badly he had bungled his way through the past months, his thoughts fueled only by what he wanted.

At that moment, Johnathan came out the back door.

"Hello, Billy. Good to see you. I know Lydia's been waiting for you.

Gathering his wits about him, Billy gave Johnathan a firm handshake and grasped his shoulder. "Thank you…thank you for saving Lydia's life, Johnathan. I owe you a huge debt of gratitude. If there's ever anything I can do for you, please let me know. I mean it. Lydia means the world to me."

"You're welcome, but I only pushed her out of the way. Nothing you wouldn't have done if you were there," Johnathan said and turned to look at Lydia. "We're good friends, Lydia and I. But only friends."

Hearing Johnathan's admission of friendship made Billy realize the truth in Lydia's words. *They were only friends, nothing more.* With a flash of insight, he finally realized he had no right to control Lydia or her feelings toward another person. He couldn't own her. She had a mind of her own and would always make her own decisions. A wave of relief washed over his body and mind. With newfound clarity, he understood how close he had come to losing his true love. He would never put his feelings ahead of Lydia's again. Love and respect were what she deserved and what he would give her from now on. Above all else, Lydia and her wants and needs would always come first.

He vowed he would change and that he would strive from that moment on to be worthy of Lydia Clark.

Changing the subject to break the drama of the moment, Lydia said, "Billy, I have something at the house I'd like you to take home to share with everyone. It's the article the newspaper wrote about my grand opening. Why don't you come and have dinner with Ezra and I tonight, and I'll give you the clipping? Grandma's pie would make a lovely dessert, and we can talk then."

****

That evening, enjoying a slice of Grandma's pie with steaming mugs of coffee, Billy said, "Ezra, I can't thank you enough for inviting Lydia into your home and everything you've done for her and her business. I'm sure she'll miss you."

"Lydia brought much joy back into my life, and I know I'll miss her, too. Johnathan and I have been talking about fixing up the carriage house and getting a milk cow and chickens when the snow is gone. I would never have met him and his mother, Mary, if it weren't for her." Ezra gazed at Lydia with deep appreciation.

The young couple moved into the parlor to talk. Ezra, discerning there was much to be settled, discreetly excused himself. "It's been a busy day and I'm going to turn in early. I'll see you at the shop in the morning."

Reading the clipping Lydia handed him, Billy commented. "Everyone will be so proud of you, and that goes double for me. Please believe me when I say how sorry I am, Lydia. Jack called me a jackass, and it appears rightfully so. I've gone about everything the wrong way. I'm sorry for jumping to conclusions. I guess I still have some growing up to do. From now on, I won't make demands or set time limits on our relationship. I know I can't offer you much, but what's mine is yours. I love you with all my heart. I'll wait, hoping you'll realize how much I care."

"Billy, I worried because I was determined to stay in town and start my business that you wanted me to fail so you could prove me wrong. I had to prove to myself I could make my dream come true.

"I'm not going home with you tomorrow, Billy. I'm not angry or trying to punish you, but I don't have everything in place here. There's a fabric order coming, and I need to stay. More importantly, I have much to think about. When you come in April to pick up the seed, I'll let you know what I've decided about us."

"My business is successful. Tell Ma and Grandma I sold eight dresses my first day open. I have most of the details worked out, so I'll be able to work from home and still keep the shop open. I trust Jillian and Mary to run the store in my absence. My plan is to make one trip a month to check on things and add new designs." Lydia drew in a deep breath. "I need to give our relationship some serious consideration. You're not acting like the person I thought you were. I loved you, Billy Henry, and now you've made me doubt that love. I need time to think things over before committing myself to you again."

Sadness enveloped the two young people; Billy for the stark realization that his dreams could possibly slip between his fingers because of his behavior, and Lydia because of the possible loss of belief in the man she thought she loved.

"We must remember to talk to each other when we're upset or disagree," Lydia said, taking Billy's hand, yearning for the comfort of his arms but wondering if his affections would be enough to reassure her. "Grandma told me once that she and Grandpa would never go to bed angry. Life is too short to stay mad at each other all the time. She said that's the key to a happy marriage."

"Please, let's agree to talk things through in the future," Billy implored. "I hope you can find it in your heart to believe in me again. I want us to be together forever. I pledge my love to making it happen. I promise I will work through this with prayer and hope and ask that you do the same. Deal?"

"Yes, deal," Lydia agreed.

Chapter Forty

The next morning, Billy met Lydia and Ezra at the back door of the shop, and they walked in together. Billy said, "I want to stay, but I can't. I need to stop at Jack's, then spend the night at my place before heading to the Hewitts." I want to make sure nobody's squatting on the farm like last year."

Billy yearned to take Lydia in his arms and embrace her to show his love but was acutely aware she had asked for time to sort out her feelings. He could no longer take her love for granted. His only hope was a fresh start, and he was determined to keep heading in the right direction.

Lydia uncovered the necklace from under the collar of her dress. If I didn't have this locket and the photo of us, I'd never have made it through the past few months. I can't wait to come home and see the family. These next few weeks will fly by." Lydia rested her head on his shoulder for a brief moment. "I think I might still love you, Billy Henry," she said, "But I still have to resolve those hesitations I have about us."

"I understand. Remember I love you, Lydia Clark. Take care of yourself, and I'll see you soon." Holding back a ragged breath, he pressed his lips to her forehead and started toward the door.

"Lydia grabbed the package of fabric scraps she had saved to give her mother, a sack of food she had put together, and a half dollar from her moneybox and ran after him. "Wait! Wait, Billy," she shouted. "Here, this is for paper, pencils, and candy for the children, and a newspaper for Ma and Pa. And give this material to Ma, please. I bet she's making a quilt for Oat, isn't she?"

Billy nodded, smiled, and mouthed the words: *I love you.*

****

On his way home, he checked to make sure the young Hewitt family had survived the winter. "Everyone at home will be happy to learn you're safe and sound. And my, how the twins have grown over this long, cold stretch. Here's more good news…I have something to share about Lydia. You know I told you how I messed up last fall? Well, I'm working on making things right. I finally came to my senses. I never told the folks about our problems, so I ask that you don't mention it. I'm proud of Lydia, and that her business is doing so well. She is planning to come home mid-April when I go to town for seed. We still have things to work out, but we agreed to always talk to each other about our thoughts and concerns."

"I know she loves you," Abby said.

Jack added, "But if you ever hurt her again, you'll have to answer to me."

"No need to worry about that. I learned my lesson," Billy admitted. "I promise I'll never hurt her again as long as I live."

"We're happy for you both," Jack said, and Abby gave Billy a reassuring hug.

"Please tell Ma and Pa we'll come visit when the weather breaks," Jack said.

"I'll let them know. Everyone is anxious to see the twins."

Arriving at his place, finding everything undisturbed, he took care of the horses and started a fire to warm the house. Savoring the hearty leftovers Lydia sent with him, he truly and completely relaxed for the first time in a long while. Tucking a quilt around himself, he slept in front of the fireplace. Awaking the next morning a little stiff but well rested, he realized that last night was the first restful sleep he'd had in months. He had slept deeply and dreamlessly, free at last from his anger and at peace with the self-growth, he had finally achieved. The relief was overwhelming. A light dusting of snow covered the ground, and the sun was out. If he left right away, he'd get to the Hewitts in time for the mid-day meal.

****

Sitting around the table with the family, Billy reported on Jack and Abby surviving the winter and how much the twins had grown. He explained he found nothing out of place when he stopped at his farm. To everyone's great delight, he announced that Lydia was planning on coming home in April. With pride, he read aloud the newspaper clipping about Lydia's Ready-Wear opening.

Mark grinned broadly, Grandma clapped with joy, and Sarah's smile brightened the room. The children hooted and hollered. "Lydia wanted me to tell you that she sold eight dresses that first day!" Billy boasted, encouraged for the first time in months that, while not everything had been settled, at least his anxiety was gone, and he dared hope for a brighter future.

****

Mark and Billy were working in the barn a week or so later when Mark drew Billy into conversation. "Your ma and I have talked this over. We feel the time has come to tell Jack and Lydia the truth about how their father Samuel really died and about your connection to him. I decided to keep Samuel's secret from Sarah when we married, and when she found out, we went through a rough time. We don't want you starting a new life with Lydia by keeping a secret from her."

"You mean you'll tell them the whole story?" Billy asked with an astounded look on his face.

"Yes. They need to know the truth, and I truly believe they will understand why we withheld this information as long as we did. The next time everyone is together, we'll talk with them. Of course, since you play such a crucial role, we'd like you there." Mark let out a sigh. This conversation with Billy released a weight that he was ready to cast off.

"I want to be there, of course, but I confess part of me is afraid that Jack and Lydia may think I'm the reason their father died." A sickening ache invaded Billy's body. His voice rose in anguish, "If Samuel hadn't stopped to help, he wouldn't have gotten involved in the first place."

"No! No! You mustn't think like that. Samuel made the decision to help with the stagecoach. Nobody blames you, Billy, nor will they ever. I felt responsible for years, and now I realize Samuel's death wasn't my fault, either. I need to tell the whole story and let the facts speak for themselves. In my opinion, Samuel died a hero. That's the way Sarah feels too. Jack and Lydia will have to make up their own minds, but I can't see them not agreeing. You have nothing to worry about. This truth needs to be told for Sarah's sake," Mark assured Billy.

"All right, if you say so," Billy said and changed the

conversation to farming. "Let's plant your fields first while Otis and Steven, and I are here. Living quarters will be a little cramped with all of us under one roof, but this way I can keep the livestock here, and the boys won't have to stay at the farm alone to take care of them. Everything will work out better."

"That's fine with me. I doubt anyone will complain about the tight living quarters. We've been doing all right so far. This way, we can start plowing as soon as the ground is ready, and with everyone helping, planting should go faster." Mark poured water into the milk cow's trough as he said, "Our seed order may not be complete when you go to pick up Lydia in April. Get what they have, and you can get the rest on the next trip."

"All right, Pa. Oh, and while I'm in town, I might consider buying five or six apple saplings to plant near that small creek that runs through my land. What do you think?"

"I think you're going to be busy this year, that's what I think," Mark said as they walked to the house, his hand on Billy's shoulder.

Chapter Forty-One

Billy returned to Dead Flats mid-April. When he walked through the door of the dress shop, Jillian smiled. "Lydia's not here at the moment, but every time someone walks through the door she looks to see if it's you. I know she's eager to see her family."

"Why, hello, you must be Billy. I'm Mary Bellows, Johnathan's mother. It's nice to finally meet you. Lydia has told us all about the farm you own and the hard work you do to keep up with the crops."

"It's nice to meet you too, Mrs. Bellows. I'm grateful to your son for saving Lydia's life, and I'm thankful for both of your friendships."

Billy noticed the clotheslines were full of frilly dresses and skirts. "You ladies have been busy. Has business picked up yet?" He asked.

"It's starting to," Jillian said, "We certainly are ready for the ladies to come to town after our long winter. Lydia created new designs, and we're going to release two styles this month and then one each month so customers will keep stopping in to see the latest."

"With three of us working the last few weeks, we've been able to get ahead on the cutting, sewing, and detail work," Mary added. "We have twenty-four dresses on display now. For someone so young, Lydia certainly has a good business head on her shoulders. I think she has done remarkably well in the short amount of time her shop has been open."

"That's Lydia," Billy agreed. "I'm happy that she's doing so well. Just look at all the lives she's touched. I'm proud of her. And I also know three youngsters who will be glad to see her home."

Lydia walked in the front door. "Billy, you're here," she exclaimed. "I have a few things to pack then I'm ready to leave. I can't wait to get home and see everyone."

She did not offer a kiss hello or even a hug, and Billy's fears grew. "Hello, Lydia," he said, following her lead and not attempting to kiss her.

Dread returned as he realized things were still strained. "Take your time," he said. "I have to go to the hardware and pick up any seeds that have come. Ma gave me her garden list as well, so I'll be gone for a while. Oh, and I have to pick up Johanna and Oat's money from the sheriff. When I return, we can load the wagon and go to Ezra's and pick up your things there. Is there anything you need at the store before we leave?"

"No, I've done all my shopping, and I have something special to give everyone," Lydia answered. "And Ma will be pleased. I have mail from back east."

Billy picked up what he could at the hardware, and as Mark predicted, not everything on the order had arrived. Sarah would be happy, though. There was a fair number of garden seeds available, so she could plant early if she wished. Paying the bill, Billy asked the sales clerk, "Will you be getting any apple saplings? I'd appreciate you setting aside five for me if you do. I'll be back next month."

"We never know what kind of fruit trees or what varieties we might receive, but if there's apple, I'll hold

309

five for you." The clerk wrote a reminder to add saplings to Billy's order.

Stopping at the dry goods store, Billy picked up supplies and headed to the sheriff's office. Sheriff Sloan wasn't in, but the deputy gave him the two-hundred dollars the four men had paid in restitution for their actions. Finished with his errands, he walked back to the dress shop, where he loaded the bed, nightstand, and a few boxes. "The wagon's loaded, Lydia. Are you ready?"

Jillian and Mary gave Lydia hugs.

"Saying good-bye is bittersweet. But you're not getting rid of me," Lydia reminded them. "I'll be back next month. We have a fabric order that should arrive in two weeks, so you'll have plenty to do. I trust you'll be fine without me, and I'm sure business will continue to prosper. I'll miss you both. Jillian, you're like a sister, and Mary, you're my second mother. I'll be back the middle of May. Meanwhile, have fun." She gave them each another hug and headed to the back of the store to say good-bye to Ezra and Johnathan.

"Well, I'm ready to go to the house and pick up my clothes and crates. I'll see you next month," Lydia said as she gave Ezra a hug.

"I'm going to miss you, young lady. You've been good company, and I'll miss your good cooking. You know if you come to town and need a place to stay, you can always stay with me. That goes for you too, Billy. I have plenty of room." Ezra shook Billy's hand.

"Sure appreciate the offer, Mr. Gray. I may oblige you from time to time," Billy said.

Stepping forward and giving Lydia a hug, Johnathan said, "Don't worry about Ezra, Lydia. Ma and I will look after him." He shook Billy's hand. "Have a good trip home. We'll see you next month."

"You've certainly acquired a lot of things in seven months. What is all this?" Billy asked as he made his seventh trip loading the wagon with items from Ezra's house.

"I have special gifts for everyone, and I have more clothes now than I started with. I want to show everyone my new designs. Another load, and we'll have everything." Lydia laid an envelope on the table before she locked the door behind her.

****

Billy had stopped at Jack and Abby's on his trip in, so they knew he and Lydia were coming for dinner and spending the night. That evening, when they arrived, Abby and Jack greeted Lydia warmly and proudly showed her the twins, pointing out how they had grown since she had last seen them. At dinner, a twin sat on each parent's lap as they were spoon fed while the adults enjoyed Abby's home cooking and talked.

"I told the family how big the twins are getting, and they'd love to see you before the planting season," Billy said. "Any chance you'll be able to visit soon?"

"First, Abby wants to go to town to see her folks before we get tied down, putting in the garden and planting. I guess we could come in a few weeks for a couple days." Abby nodded her agreement as she held a spoonful of mashed carrots to Annabelle's mouth.

"You've turned into quite the father, Jack." Lydia smiled as Jack bounced Benjamin on his knee to quiet his fussing.

"Wait until you have your own." Jack looked at Lydia with a slight smile. "Babies keep you busy, and

311

two at once is twice as much work and twice as much fun."

As Jack commented, Billy cast a look at Lydia. They had not opened the subject of their relationship on the ride to Abby and Jack's. They'd have time enough on the next leg of their journey for that discussion.

****

Setting out the next morning, Billy finally got up enough courage to say, "Lydia, no matter what you have to tell me, I want you to know that I haven't changed my mind about us or my love for you. I've given much thought to our last time together and realized that my misguided temper was the cause of so much trouble. I apologize again. I don't want to press you now, so I'll wait until you're ready to share what you've decided with me, about us."

Lydia was quiet for a few minutes while the horses plodded on, then said, "Thank you, Billy. It's encouraging to hear you say that. To be truthful, in a month, I haven't come to any decisions about us, about how I feel toward you. I was busy getting things ready to leave. That's not an excuse, but every time I start to examine my feelings, I can't move beyond a certain point. I guess I need more time and ask that you grant me that. Right now, I'm eager to return home and see the family."

Billy reached over and softly patted her hand. "Of course. I cannot ask for anything more. I'll wait for you."

Let's talk about something a little lighter. Billy. Tell me what's been going on while I've been gone."

"Well, we've all missed you, of course. The holidays were the hardest. Oat celebrated his first Christmas as a free man, and we made the time special for him. With you not there, I had my hands full helping the children make their presents this year. The boys whittled whistles for each other. Oat whittled a nice horse for Johanna, and Steven did his best to make a cat. Grandma taught Johanna how to knit, and she made scarves for the boys. The adults sure enjoyed seeing the children with their gifts.

"You won't believe how much Oat has grown. He suddenly sprouted up and is almost as tall as me. Steven and Johanna have missed their big sister something awful. They'll be so happy to have you home. I took to helping Johanna brush her hair in the evenings, but once she sees your new hairstyle, I'm sure she'll want to wear hers the same way."

There was a lull in the conversation. Lydia said, "I'm going to go in the back and take a nap. Wake me when we get close to home."

As the wagon dipped into the creek on Hewitt land, Lydia awoke, climbed over the seat, and soon the house and barn came into view.

When Billy stopped the wagon, Lydia jumped to the ground and ran to her family, arms wide and tears rolling down her cheeks. She was wearing one of her newly designed dresses, and her hair was done up. She looked sophisticated and poised, not like the farm girl that left for town more than half a year earlier.

Mark and Sarah enveloped their daughter in loving hugs. Grandma kissed Lydia on the forehead. Oat shyly allowed Lydia to kiss him on the cheek, and Johanna reclaimed her big sister with kisses of joy.

"Am I allowed to hug you?" Steven asked.

Lydia looked puzzled and said, "Of course, you are, Steven. What would give you the idea you couldn't?"

"Well, what if I get your dress dirty or something?" Steven answered.

"Then I wash it. Don't ever feel you can't hug me, and I still have clothes for farm work." Lydia reached out and embraced her brother and then paused a moment to reflect that her latest designs sported a lot of lace and frills. She also needed to create day dresses for every women's needs, for everyday wear. Steven's question made that clear, and her mind started swirling with ideas.

Inside, Sarah and Grandma immediately began peppering her with questions and commenting on her hair and latest dress designs.

Billy said, "I need help unloading the wagon. I don't know where we're going to put everything that Lydia brought home, but I do know it's more than she took with her. And, we have seed to unload too."

"Come on, boys," Mark said, "let's give Billy a hand. We can catch up with Lydia later."

Beef stew simmered on the stove, and with bread baking in the hearth, the house smelled like home to Lydia. When the men came in, the family sat down to a lively reunion celebration.

Lydia gave the meal prayer and afterward said, "It's so good to be home. I've missed you all more than you can imagine." Her words rang out with passion and enthusiasm, touching each family member's heart where they needed comfort the most.

As the family shared a wide range of topics from Christmas and birthdays to the foals and calves that would soon be born, Johanna voiced what was on everyone's mind, "Lydia, will you go back to live in town again?"

"I assure you all, I plan to design from home and

make one trip a month to check on the shop. I may have to stay overnight, but I promise I'll come home again." Then she changed the subject. "You should see the twins," she said. "I can't believe how much they've grown. They are crawling everywhere, standing, and saying a few words. They say 'Ma, Pa, Up,' and 'No.' And when they don't want to take a bite of food, they say 'No' really loud."

"Benjamin squeezed my fingers and didn't want to go to his mother when we were leaving," Billy said with pride. "Jack told us they are coming for a visit in a few weeks before he starts on his fields. He was concerned there would be too many of us for sleeping arrangements, but I told him we'd make room and to never let that stop him from coming to see his family."

"Oh boy, Benjamin and Annabelle are coming to visit!" Johanna beamed.

"It's getting warmer," Oat offered. "Maybe Steven, Billy, me, and Jack can sleep in the barn?"

"That's a thought," Grandma said. "It sure will be good to have the whole family together again."

Billy reminded everyone, "The last time we were together was at the creek for a picnic the fall before the twins were born. Maybe when Jack and Abby are here, we could go to the creek for a picnic?"

"That's a lovely idea, Billy," Sarah agreed. "Let's hope that warm weather comes soon."

****

That evening, with her bed back in the loft, Lydia began unpacking her things. Johanna was right by her side, asking question after question about living in town. Then she asked Lydia, "Would you please brush my hair in the morning and fix mine up like yours?

"Of course I will, sweetheart. We'll fix you up real pretty."

****

Next day, with the whole family present, Lydia said, "Since I missed Christmas and several birthdays, I've made something for everyone and brought store-bought surprises as well."

Lydia passed out the clothing first. She had made dresses and vests. A treat for the ladies, who couldn't wait to try them on, but not so thrilling for Steven and Oat. Lydia made the boys try on the vests and was pleased that everything fit perfectly. Steven and Oat were growing boys, and she'd had to guess on sizes.

"You look so handsome," Lydia smiled. "The girls will be sure to take notice at the next dance."

She reached in the sack for the boys' surprises first. Steven and Oat's eyes grew wide when she handed them slingshots and leather pouches that she made from scrap leather Ezra gave her. "No shooting at animals or each other," she warned. "I remember when Jack got his first slingshot. We practiced hitting a board first, and then an old frying pan set up as a target in the barn made a great sound. It's probably still out there somewhere. I'd practice a lot, though, before trying to get a rabbit for supper."

Oat pulled back on the strap, testing the elasticity. "We'll practice good."

"Yeah, and we'll start today," Steven added, eager to head to the barn.

Lydia handed a brush, comb, and mirror set decorated with painted flowers to Johanna and scented soap and stationery to Grandma and her mother.

"My own mirror and brush! Now I won't have to use

316

Ma's. When I learn how to do my own hair, I'll look beautiful every day. Thanks for my pretty dress, too. I love the colors," Johanna said.

"You're welcome, sweetheart. I'm glad your dress fits. You always look beautiful," Lydia reminded her.

"Thank you for the lovely, scented soap," Grandma said. "Such an indulgence. Maybe I'll keep the bar to perfume my clothing instead of washing with it."

Sarah added, "And we can always use pretty stationery."

To Mark and Billy, she gave leather gloves to wear for plowing. She had remembered the condition of Billy's last year and the blisters he got on his hands. "I know they are kind of an odd gift, but I don't want blisters and sores holding you back this year. I know how much getting the crops in means to a farmer and hope these will help."

"They'll help for sure," Billy said.

Mark nodded. "They are a thoughtful gift, Lydia. Thank you."

Steven asked, "Can we give Lydia her gifts now?"

"Why don't we wait until Jack and Abby come with the twins? We can exchange presents then," Lydia suggested.

"Good idea," Oat said, picking up his slingshot. "Come on, Steven, race you to the barn."

With the warmth of family around her again, Lydia drew a deep sigh of contentment. She started realizing how much stress she had been under opening the dress shop and working so hard to make the business run smoothly. *Maybe I can think about Billy with more clarity,* she thought. *Could coming home really be all I needed?*

Chapter Forty-Two

As the weeks passed waiting for Jack and Abby to arrive, the doubts Lydia had about Billy faded a little, but not enough to say she truly loved him. At least they were talking, taking walks, and feeling more comfortable with each other again While Lydia did not refuse him when he asked to hold her hand, she still kept her true feelings close. Building trust and moving forward was a slow healing process.

When Jack and Abby arrived, Jack handed Benjamin to Sarah and Annabelle to Lydia, who carried them into the house and set them on the rug for everyone to enjoy.

"Let me help you with your things," Billy offered, reaching for one of their bags in the back of the wagon.

Mark peered into the wagon. "I can help too." He held out his arms as Jack loaded them with packages.

"We'd have been here sooner, but Abby kept adding things that she thought we might need for the twins."

Billy came back for another load. "Jack, I hope you're up for sleeping in the barn with me and the boys tonight. Oat's idea. The women need room in the house."

"You're not leaving me with the ladies all by myself," Mark said. "I think I'll join you in the barn."

"The boys would love it, Pa. Do you think your back can take it?" Billy grinned.

"Well, I guess that depends on how many nights

you're staying, Jack." Mark headed toward the house.

"Only one, Pa." Jack chuckled.

"Don't worry about me. I'll make it. Now, who has a free hand to get the door for me?" Mark asked as he stumbled up the steps and onto the porch.

****

While the children played together, the adults sat around the table, catching up. The women talked about the twins celebrating their first birthdays, Lydia's dress shop, and the long winter that passed by too slowly for everyone's liking. The men talked about seed orders, apple saplings, the plans to plant the fields, and how they would help each other with these tasks.

"It's time to start supper, or we won't eat tonight," Sarah said. "And boys, we'll need the table you made for Lydia that's in the barn and extra chairs."

"We should probably head out to the barn and make preparations for sleeping," Mark said. "I call claim to the back of the covered wagon."

"There's probably plenty of room for two young boys to join you in there, Pa." Jack teased with a straight face.

"Yeah, I think that's where Steven and Oat planned on sleeping too," Billy said, not cracking a smile until Mark did, and then they all laughed.

They spread horse blankets on the wagon floor and decided that with the quilts they'd bring from the house, they could manage. They stayed and talked until Johanna called them for supper. Jack and Billy carried the table to the house, and Mark followed with the chairs his mother brought with her on her wagon train trip west and a rough barn bench. They set the table in the front room, so there was plenty of space for everyone.

Grandma Hewitt said the prayer, adding her special touch at the end. "And we are thankful for having our family together again under one roof healthy, safe, and with plenty of food from the bounty of the earth."

After a hearty supper, the family gathered to exchange belated Christmas and birthday presents. While everyone was together, Sarah also shared the good news from back east. "Aunt Matilda had a baby boy they named Robert, Uncle Mathew and Netty had a beautiful outdoor wedding as planned, and Aunt Emma had another little boy they named Richard."

****

In the afternoon, as the twins napped, Mark glanced at Sarah and said to Grandma and Abby, "Would you mind if Sarah and I have time alone with Jack, Lydia, and Billy? It's important."

Grandma reached for her shawl and said, "Abby, dear, let's get Johanna and see what the boys are doing.

Lydia poured tea for the five of them at the table and sat between Jack and Billy.

Mark stroked Sarah's hand reassuringly and addressed Lydia and Jack, "Your ma and I have something we want to share with you about your father Samuel and his death. We didn't tell you at the time, because we had said Samuel's death was an accident. It *was* an accident, but now it's time you hear the truth of what happened."

Lydia sat up straight, her mind racing. Glancing at Jack and Billy, her concern rose.

"Lydia, Jack, your father died a hero. Both your mother and I are in agreement with this conclusion. As you may remember, shortly before his death, Samuel and I went hunting. At one point, I realized I left my canteen behind at our last stop. I told your pa that I'd catch up and went back to retrieve it while he rode on. About a mile up the road, Samuel came across a stagecoach that had broken down. The wheel had come off, and he helped put it back on. But before he—"

"I'll explain, Mark," Billy said, taking Lydia's hand. "My father and I were on that stagecoach. Pa, the driver, and Samuel repaired the wheel and got the stage and horses back on the road. We were preparing to leave when two men rode right toward us, shooting."

"Why were you there?" Lydia asked, tightening her grip on Billy's hand.

"My father and I were heading west after my mother died giving birth to Steven. I didn't know that my father had given Steven up, left him behind, really. I thought the baby had died. Pa couldn't bear to look at him because his birth was the cause of my mother's death. We left the day after the funeral," Billy paused and took a deep breath. "I met your father, Lydia. He was a good man. He saved my life."

"What? How come no one mentioned this before?" Jack said, confused.

Lydia asked, "How did my pa save your life, Billy?"

"Two men on horseback started shooting at us. They were after the payroll money the stage was carrying. The first shot killed my father. That's when your father yelled for me to get inside the coach and keep down before he returned fire. When the shooting stopped, the two outlaws lay dead, and the driver was wounded in the arm. As he rode off, your father told us to load the bodies on the stage and get to town quickly in case there were more outlaws. We did as he instructed and took them to the sheriff in Marysville. It turned out that your father had been shot, but the driver and I didn't know it at the time. He never gave us his name. He told us to tell the sheriff what happened and that he'd come soon to corroborate the story."

"So you didn't know my pa's name or that he'd been hit?" Lydia asked.

"No. Not at the time," Billy said, shaken by reliving the circumstances of the events.

Mark took a sip of tea. "I heard the shots and rode hard to catch up and found Samuel on the ground where he had fallen from his horse. He knew he wasn't gonna make it. He told me what happened and made me swear not to tell Sarah that he was responsible for taking two lives even though they were outlaws. He explained that to Sarah's way of thinking, this would make him a murderer, no matter how justified. He asked me to claim any reward money for his family. He told me about the orphaned boy on the stage and mentioned the scar on his neck. I promised Samuel I would honor his wishes and held him as he slipped away."

Mark's voice broke as he struggled to hold back a sob. "Samuel was my best friend. I'll never forget him. I brought Samuel's body back here to Sarah, lied about how he died, and we buried him up on the hill."

"I remember that day," Lydia said with a note of sadness in her voice.

Jack commented, "I'll never forget it. I remember Ma taking the little body of Baby Walter from the small casket and putting him in with Pa. We buried them together in the same wooden box."

"A week or so later," Mark said, "I rode to Marysville and pretended to be Samuel. I told the Marysville sheriff everything Samuel had told me. He accepted my story and gave me the reward for killing the two outlaws. While I was there, I asked about the boy on the stage. He told me the boy was gone but didn't say where.

"A year later, I met Billy in Dead Flats. I recognized him by the scar on his neck. He wasn't in a good situation. He was with a peddler selling elixir. I lied and told the man I knew the boy and that I'd make sure he was returned to his family. The man didn't want to let Billy go, but I said I'd go to Sheriff Sloan if he didn't let me take him. Finally, he released Billy to me. When I brought Billy here, I admitted to him I lied to get him away from the peddler."

Mark glanced toward Billy and smiled. "He wasn't happy with me that day, but had no other real choice. I told your ma he needed a good home, and we took him into our family."

"Your father is a hero," Billy said. "I know you were told that he fell and hit his head and died, but the truth is, he saved my life, and he took a bullet while helping me."

Jack stood and started pacing the floor, visibly upset at the years of deception. "You still haven't told us why you waited so long to tell us. You've known the truth for years, Ma!"

"Mark didn't tell me the whole story at first," Sarah said, fighting back tears. "He made a deathbed promise to Samuel that he wouldn't break. When I finally put most of the pieces of the puzzle together, he still wouldn't speak until I forced him to do so. Then, I didn't want you to know we had lied to you. I know I should have told you as soon as I learned the truth, but I wanted to protect your father." Sarah's voice choked with unrepressed agony.

"Don't blame your ma," Mark said. "If you need to blame someone, blame me." He hung his head. "I kept the truth from your ma because Samuel made me promise not to tell her about him killing two men. He needed me to collect the reward for his family. I kept my promise even when we married. Starting a marriage carrying a lie is difficult. Damned near tore me apart, but I still wouldn't go back on my word to Samuel. Your ma and I didn't want Billy to have to keep a secret any longer. That's why we're telling you now."

"I'd say Mark keeping his promise to your pa was him being a true friend, plain and simple," Billy stated. "Mark didn't want me to have to keep a secret from Lydia, so he asked what I thought about telling you the truth. I was sure you'd understand. Please don't be mad at Ma and Pa.

Lydia looked at Billy and said, "So, all this time, you knew my pa was the one who saved your life."

"No," Billy said. "I didn't figure anything out until Mark and I were in Marysville, and I stopped to see my pa's grave. I read the date on my father's tombstone, and the date seemed familiar. Later I realized the date on your father's grave was the same. I asked Mark, and he confessed. Don't blame your ma and pa. If you want to blame someone, I guess you should blame me. Your pa was helping me when he got killed."

Jack shook his head, returned to his chair, and said, "We can't undo or change anything now. My father died a hero, and that's the way I want to remember him. I miss him a lot. There are days I wish I could talk to him and ask him for his advice. But Mark, you've been a great father to us and a loving husband to Ma."

"Yes," Lydia said. "I agree with Jack. You've been

good to us, Mark, and made Ma happy. Pa died a hero in my eyes, too. And I'm glad to hear that you met my father, Billy. He was a good man and loved us very much."

"I'll never forget what Samuel did for me," Billy said. "I wouldn't be here today if it weren't for your father and Mark." He looked earnestly at Lydia and Jack.

"There's no reason not to tell the rest of the family if you want, but your ma and I wanted you to hear the truth from us first," Mark said, and he stood and put his hands on Sarah's shoulders. "I pray there are no hard feelings. The whole truth is out now."

"I'm not sure how I feel that you kept this from us all these years, but I understand why Ma may have wanted to hide the real story. You could never abide killing, could you, Ma?" Jack said.

Shaking her head, Sarah released the burden of carrying the secret with a soul-cleansing breath.

"It's good to know pa died a hero and saved Billy's life," Lydia said. "No more secrets, please. I don't want our family to keep any more secrets." Lydia turned to Jack and said sadly, "I think I'll go visit Pa's grave for a bit. You want to come along?"

"I'd like to join you," Jack said. On the way up the hill, he said, "Don't blame Billy, little sister. The secret wasn't his to tell."

****

The following morning the sun shone brightly, and the day promised to be warm. Billy asked Sarah as she was scrambling a pan of eggs, "Can we have the picnic at the creek today?"

Sarah replied, "Yes, Billy, today is a perfect day. The picnic is on."

Billy offered, "If you need any help with anything, I'll be glad to lend a hand."

Arriving at the creek in plenty of time for the boys to drop a line, the women spread quilts and began chatting and putting out dishes of food.

Returning from downstream, Steven exclaimed, "I caught one, Oat caught one, Pa caught one, and Jack caught two! Billy didn't catch any."

"We decided since Jack caught the most, he should take all of them home. But we'll help him gut and skin 'em," Oat said, and the boys set to work.

"Wash your hands good when you've finished. The meal is ready to eat when you are," Sarah called to them.

"We'll hurry, Ma. I'm hungry," Steven yelled back.

The picnic repast was a feast set out before them. By the time everyone had eaten their fill, there were few leftovers. Sarah packed what remained for Abby to take home. Feeling content and relaxed, the family stretched out for an afternoon rest before heading home.

Taking Lydia by the hand, Billy whispered, "Come, let's get away and go for a little walk."

Following the flowing stream, they enjoyed being in the warmth of nature. Billy's hopes had risen little by little since bringing Lydia home. They had talked often and explored the beginnings of a renewed connection. Hearing the truth about her father, Lydia had turned more to Billy for support last night. He hoped with all his heart that there was still a chance for their future together.

When they reached the downed log, Billy stopped. "Do you remember? This is the spot we claimed as our special place. I loved sitting here and talking, laying on the grass with you that day, and watching the clouds pass."

"I remember," Lydia said, reaching down and trailing her fingers over the bark of the log.

Gazing deeply into her eyes, Billy took her hands and dropped to one knee. Looking up at her innocent face, the love now evident, Billy smiled.

"Lydia," he said, "We've had our ups and downs. I've learned from my mistakes. I promise I'll never keep any secrets from you ever again. I am truly proud of you. Starting your own business took bravery. I know now that your success isn't a threat to our relationship. It's a blessing."

Smiling, Lydia squeezed his hands in encouragement and gratitude.

"I pray you know how much I love you and how much I want you to be happy. I pray that you can be happy with me by your side. When you're ready, we can be together as we dreamed, welcoming children and watching them grow as we make a forever life on our farm. I want to grow old with you, sweetheart."

Taking a deep breath before continuing and realizing this moment would decide everything, Billy asked, "Will you marry me, Lydia?"

A word about the author...

Judy's series is inspired by her passion for history and the simpler life of settlers. Writing is her second career after more than 30 years in education. She writes daily in the northwestern mountains of Pennsylvania, appreciating the outdoors, the changing of the seasons, and a good cup of coffee in the morning. She loves to bake. Pies, cakes, and breads are her favorites.

To learn more about Judy, her next book releases, or to sign up for her newsletter, please visit her website:

https://judysharer.com

If you enjoyed this novel series, please leave a review at your favorite book retailer or reader website. Your comments are much appreciated. Thank you.

Thank you for purchasing
this publication of The Wild Rose Press, Inc.

For questions or more information
contact us at
info@thewildrosepress.com.

The Wild Rose Press, Inc.
www.thewildrosepress.com